THE MURDER OF PATIENCE BROOKE

Charles Dickens Investigations
Book One

J C Briggs

SAPERE
BOOKS

THE MURDER OF PATIENCE BROOKE

Published by Sapere Books.

20 Windermere Drive, Leeds, England, LS17 7UZ,
United Kingdom

saperebooks.com

ISBN: 978-1-912786-83-1

Take her up tenderly,
Lift her with care;
Fashion'd so slenderly
Young, and so fair!
Loop up her tresses
Escaped from the comb,
Her fair auburn tresses;
Whilst wonderment guesses
Where was her home?
Who was her father?
Who was her mother?
Had she a sister?
Had she a brother?
Or was there a dearer one
Still, and a nearer one
Yet, than all other?

The Bridge of Sighs by Thomas Hood (1799–1845)

1: The Singer

Thrown on the wide world, doom'd to wander and roam,
Bereft of my parents, bereft of my home.
The singer's voice was a high, horrible, falsetto, mocking and caressing at the same time.

The woman leaning against the railing on the steps seemed to sway. Her head fell forward; suddenly, shockingly, blood gushed from her throat, soaking her dress, dropping in fat red gouts onto the step.

The singer vanished into the curling loops of fog, the voice fading, the last note dying away then lost in the dark.

Fog. Fog in the kitchen, creeping like an inquisitive guest, fog tip-toeing around the cupboards and the chairs, bending into the copper in its brick setting, folding itself under the table and peering out of the window, looking at itself trying to get in. Mrs Georgiana Morson, resident matron of Urania Cottage, Charles Dickens's home for fallen women, aware of the pinching cold of the flagstones, standing amazed with her candle in her hand, wondered how it had got in when she had shut the door at ten o'clock. In the light of one candle, the fog looked sinister, an uninvited visitor. Mrs Morson felt somehow afraid of its yellowish ghostly presence. But she was not too afraid to go forward across the large, square, stone-floored apartment where she saw that the door was open and that more fog was swirling in. Her practical thought was to close the door and shut it out.

It was as she was shutting the door that she saw that there was someone outside on the steps which led up to the garden.

It was the figure of a woman — an unusually tall one; she appeared to be standing against the railings, her head bowed, her hair falling about her shoulders and her dress open, revealing naked shoulders and the full white bosom upon which there appeared to be some ruby-coloured jewels. Mrs Morson speculated that she might be someone looking for sanctuary — there was something about the figure which suggested exhaustion, as though she had reached the end of her endurance. Young women came to the Home recommended, but once or twice one would turn up unannounced, hoping for help, having, perhaps, run away from some bully of a man.

Mrs Morson held up her candle. In the flickering light, she saw how one of the red jewels seemed to tremble, and slide down the white skin. Then another and another so that they formed a scarlet pool gathered in the V of the dress. She went up the first step to look more closely; then she saw that the woman was not simply standing against the railings but that she was tied to them. She lifted up the chestnut hair which tumbled about the shoulders, and realised that the red was not jewels but blood; and that the metallic smell was blood; and that the blood had soaked into the woman's dress; and that it was a great apron of blood, clinging to the limbs, and staining the white lace of the underskirt. And her eyes travelled down to the sticky pool of it next to her own foot, and she saw the naked feet of the woman shod in red. She looked up again at the white throat encircled by a slash of scarlet, up again at the white face. It was one she knew. It was the face of Patience Brooke.

Mrs Morson stepped back; she saw now that the woman was not unusually tall, she was hanging from the railings and had only seemed to be standing upon the third step up. Mrs

Morson had seen death — her doctor husband had died early and she had nursed him, but he had died in his bed, she holding his hands. A child had died at a few months old — a terrible time, but an explicable death from scarlet fever. She had delivered the dead child of a servant girl. She had once seen a man die in the street. Passing a crowd one afternoon, she had seen through a gap a policeman supporting a man whose legs were mangled and whose head was a mass of blood. Nearby was the wagon that had run him down. But she had never seen a murder, and Patience Brooke had been murdered.

Mrs Morson stood, still as stone, unable to tear her horrified eyes from the brutal gash in the white throat. Her heart seemed to have ceased its beating; the silence gathered round her like a cloak, stifling her so that she could hardly breathe. Time itself stopped as she stared at the figure. There was a sudden, terrible movement when the head nodded and the chin knocked against the chest, and was still again. The silence broke when time restarted; Mrs Morson heard the distant chimes of the clock of St Mark's. She listened as each stroke sounded through the foggy air. It was eleven o'clock now. She must act quickly. Her horror at what she had seen was superseded by her natural practical resolution and her quick understanding that this could not be known until she had sent for Mr Dickens. No one must see. The girls were in their beds and had been since nine o'clock — not likely to come down until morning. Davey was in his cot in the little room off the kitchen, fast asleep she hoped, but she must wake him and he must take the message. Mr Bagster, the gardener whom she would normally have sent for, was away at his daughter's at Kensal Green. But first, she must cover Patience. Time later to think what it all might mean. She went back through the kitchen and into the passage that lead to the front of the house. There was kept an assortment of cloaks; she took one which she draped over the hanging woman.

Now paper and pencil. These were kept on the table for lists and notes. She wrote her message:

Mr Dickens, you must come immediately. Patience Brooke is dead this night. Bring our friend, Superintendent Jones, if you can. G. Morson.

Now she must wake Davey. Opening the door to the little room off the kitchen, she saw that he was huddled under his blankets, his head buried in his pillow. There was something about the hunched form that suggested fear. What might he have heard — or, worse, seen? Mr Dickens could ask him later. Now, he must take the horse and trap and go. She approached the cot and touched his shoulder. The boy remained still. He was not asleep.

She whispered to him, 'Davey, you must help me. I do not know what has happened but I need your help, however afraid you are. You must go to Mr Dickens and bring him.' The name of Mr Dickens roused him as she knew it would. He stared at her with those transparent hazel eyes. He was afraid. 'Get dressed. I will wait in the kitchen — but be quick, I beg you.'

In a minute or two, he was ready.

'Take the note. Go to Wellington Street first. We must hope he is there — if not, go to Bow Street, send in the note for Superintendent Jones.'

She opened the door onto the fog and onto the shrouded form by the railings. Davey hurried up the steps, keeping his head averted, and then he was dissolved into the fog. He would go out of the side gate into the private lane and then to the stable. She waited in the stillness, straining to hear the sound of the stable door opening and the clink of the harness which must be followed by the sound of the trap and its horse.

It must. Davey would not run away, would he? She did not know what had frightened him but he could have nothing to do with the figure at the railings. He could not. Of that she was sure. He would go for Mr Dickens whom he revered — the man who had rescued him. He was intelligent, sensible — if he had to go to Bow Street, surely someone would send the note in for the superintendent. She did not dare think that Davey would come back alone. The silence seemed to congeal around her. The stillness was solid. She realised she was holding her breath, waiting.

Then she heard it. The stable door creaked. Mrs Morson let out a ragged breath. The faint metallic clink meant that Davey was harnessing the horse and putting it into the traces. She held her breath again, heard the sound of wheels, and then the clip-clop of the horse's hooves as he walked down the lane. She imagined Davey squinting through the fog, hunched over the reins, making his way to the road where he would turn right and on to London. He was turning now; the clip-clop sounds were faster, then fainter. She waited still until the sound faded away and she was left in the misty darkness with dead Patience on the steps where the blood pooled into a sticky, black wetness.

She went back into the kitchen, not wanting to close the door on the dead one outside, but if she left it open she knew that she could not stop her gaze from turning on the shrouded thing. She closed the door. The candle was nearly burnt down now, but there was a faint glow from the great black range. She lifted the iron lid and put on more coal from the scuttle bedside the range. In the darkness she sat thinking of Patience Brooke and her terrible death and mysterious life.

Patience Brooke had come from nowhere. And Mrs Morson had employed her. Mr Dickens had met her and had agreed. It was unusual, for most girls came through recommendation. George Chesterton, Governor of Coldbath Fields Prison, had given some of his female prisoners a letter written by Dickens which offered the chance of a new kind of life, a quiet home, a means of being useful, peace of mind, self-respect and the possibility of being restored to society, albeit in another country; some came from the workhouse and others from ragged schools or orphanages. But Mrs Morson knew — or thought she knew until this moment — that Patience Brooke was not a girl from the streets for whom the Home, so named by Mr Dickens, was a chance of redeeming a wrecked life. She was not a fallen woman. She had stood on the doorstep one day in her neat, shabby grey dress and black bonnet under which the chestnut hair was tidily coiled. Mrs Morson wondered at the significance of that hair tumbling over naked shoulders. Patience Brooke had brought nothing with her — nothing at all, not even a handkerchief. With her thin pale face and her quiet manner, she reminded Mrs Morson of the governess, Jane Eyre, in the novel she had read. It was clear that she was educated and Mrs Morson employed her to help her teach the girls in the mornings. Patience Brooke told not a thing about her past; in that she was like Davey though for a different reason — Davey simply could not speak; Patience would not.

It was unusual for Mrs Morson to act without consulting Mr Dickens first, but she knew that Patience would elicit his sympathy and curiosity and so she did. Mr Dickens seemed fascinated by her. He told Mrs Morson how intense his anxiety was to know her secret, but Patience resisted, which testified to her strength of character, for she revealed nothing to Mr Dickens; she even avoided him, as if fearful that one day he would prevail, such was his power.

That Patience had a secret, Mrs Morson did not doubt, and that it was a terrible one, the cloaked figure on the steps outside confirmed. Mrs Morson sat on in the darkened kitchen. She heard the clock of St Mark's strike twelve, every chime echoing through the stillness. The house was silent. She wondered where Davey was now. He had been gone for just over an hour; he ought to be there soon. Mr Dickens must be there, he must. Then they would go for Superintendent Jones. Restless now, she went to the door and opened it as if to check that Patience was there — she was. Mrs Morson regarded the dark shape. How long must she wait? Another hour or two, or more? The thought was almost unendurable but she had endured before. She remembered the long hours of darkness when her husband was dying and the long days of anguish that followed his death.

She turned back to the kitchen and again fed the dying fire, but she did not light a candle. Feeling a chill, she looked again at the door. This time it was open and that dreadful fog, more of a misty vapour now, drifted in, turning back on itself as if beckoning someone outside to come in. Mrs Morson felt terror. It was the worst moment, worse even than finding the body, for Mrs Morson who had loved Patience Brooke experienced only horror at the thought of her coming in. She strode to the door and shut it, restraining herself only just in time to stop it slamming. She stood motionless, her breath suspended, her heart knocking at her ribs until the stillness and silence settled again and she sat once more, waiting.

2: Dickens and Jones

Charles Dickens was looking out at the fog. It seemed to be lifting now though there were greenish wreaths of it still twining round the gas lamps so that the long line of street lamps was blurred as if seen through tears, and wisps of vapour lingered in the air like fading ghosts. The street was empty. Dickens had watched until his friend Forster had disappeared across the road on his way to his lodgings at Lincoln's Inn Fields, along the Strand to Chancery. He was restless and unsettled — it was a Friday, a day of portent.

Dickens and Forster were old friends — friends from 1837. They shared a similar history, both born in the same year, 1812, into poor circumstances, Forster the son of a Newcastle butcher who had worked his way up to being literary editor of *The Examiner* and editor of *The Daily News*. When Forster told him that Charles Dilke had once seen Dickens as a boy working in a warehouse near the Strand, Dickens felt it as a blow, as if Dilke had exposed him as a fraud, a man who was not as he had presented himself. It was as if a disguise had fallen from him to reveal to the world a shabby boy, grubbing for a living in a factory which was exactly as it had been — while his family had lived in the Marshalsea where John Dickens was imprisoned for debt. It was as if the velvet jackets, the flamboyant waistcoats, the plaid trousers had been stripped from him to show the rags beneath yet he had been impelled by some desire he could not restrain to tell more whilst at the same time he found it unbearable. He had given Forster a manuscript detailing the first part of his life, a part he had never revealed — the story of his time as a boy at the blacking factory, a time of humiliation and misery. He felt like the haunted man of his Christmas story for 1848.

Now, in this bitter cold spring — more like winter — he had started his new novel, *David Copperfield*. The starting of a new novel was a kind of agony. He was irritable and wanted to be solitary yet he desired the streets, walking about at night into the strangest places, seeking rest and finding none.

He ought to be at home; there was a new baby, Henry, to look to and Catherine to care for but he was dissatisfied and disquieted. He looked at himself in the glass as if to check that he was still there. He saw the self he gave the world. If someone had been at his shoulder, looking at the reflection in the mirror, they would have seen a face looking back, characterised by a broad forehead with rich brown curled hair brushed to the side. The eyes, large and brilliant, could light up a room, shining with good humour and tenderness. But, looking into those eyes they might see there two deeper, darker points of melancholy, and their lustre spoke often of restlessness as tonight. There was, he thought, a kind of sickness in him, such a sense of loss sometimes that he felt he was foundering. He turned back to his desk and took up his goose-quill, but wrote nothing.

The knocking woke him. It was loud and insistent. His heart misgave. A message from home? The child ill? He looked out of the window to where a horse and trap stood in the street under the gas lamp. Recognising it, he took his candle, hurried downstairs to open the door and find Davey holding out a piece of paper. The boy's face expressed fear and agitation. Having read Mrs Morson's message, Dickens told Davey to wait while he went inside for his coat. He came out again to find Davey already with the reins in his hands. It was no use asking the boy for more information. Davey could not reply. He was mute but not deaf so Dickens reassured him.

'We will go for Superintendent Jones as quickly as we can — we must go to Bow Street. Then we will get to Mrs Morson. She is a good, sensible woman, Davey. There is nothing to fear.'

Was there not? Dickens thought. Patience Brooke dead, the urgency and brevity of Mrs Morson's message, her sending Davey, all pointed to something dreadfully wrong. And, he had to hope that Superintendent Jones was at Bow Street and not further north at his home in Norfolk Street.

They travelled along the dark street not speaking. Dickens could feel the weight of the boy's fear as if it were something actually leaning against him. Davey knew something though it might only be that the girl was dead. He had responded to her quiet gentleness and she had taught him to read and write. Dickens looked at the white face — poor Davey of whom he had become fond. Dickens had found him curled up in a doorway like a lost dog, a child of the streets who seemed to have no name nor anyone to whom he belonged. There were hundreds like him and Dickens could not rescue them all. He had done what he could, finding employment for a crippled boy at his publisher's, placing a shoe-black boy in a ragged school. All these boys were his other self, the one who would have slaved on in the blacking factory had he not been rescued. This boy who could not speak, and whose transparent hazel eyes had gazed at him in wonder from the doorway, stirred his immediate compassion. Here was a boy who needed not just a place in a school or an office; here was a boy who needed safety and the care of a mother. Mrs Morson needed a boy to do the odd jobs, to chop the wood, bring in the coals, to look after the horse and the stables. Dickens would take him to her.

Dickens had much liking and respect for the matron of the Home who mothered the fallen girls and referred to them as the family. Most of those girls loved her too and wept when they left. She, a mother of three children, would care for the boy; he would not be a slave.

Davey had flourished under the care of Mrs Morson and of Patience Brooke. Dickens had given him his name, oddly prescient of the name he was to give to David Copperfield, the boy who lost his loving mother and was turned out to work in the bottle factory. Davey had flourished, but he had not spoken. Whatever his memories were, they were locked in, too terrible, perhaps, ever to be told. And now, this death had come which might wreck them all.

So they travelled on, the silent boy and the silent man, through the dark streets. The fog had fled; there was a moon now to light their way to Bow Street, and then to Shepherd's Bush and Lime Grove where Mrs Morson and dead Patience waited for them.

'Not far now, Davey.'

Bow Street Police Station loomed ahead. A policeman keeping watch let Dickens in. He hurried down the long passage to the bare room like a guard house — without the drums and muskets, Dickens always thought. In the right-hand corner of the room was a window at which an inspector presided to hear charges. By the window stood Police Constable Rogers, in his strong, leather pot hat and his brass-buttoned, stiff-collared coat, a red-faced, cheerful young man whose good temper seemed at odds with his calling amongst the confined, intolerable rooms burrowed out in the gloomy courts and narrow alleys like the holes of rats where hide the coiners, and smashers, and thieves and rogues. He greeted Dickens as an old acquaintance. The superintendent was in and

Rogers would take a message. He vanished down an ill-lit corridor.

Soon, Dickens saw Superintendent Sam Jones coming along the corridor, a tall and commanding man whose swift walk suggested the authority and decisiveness which made him so successful as a policeman. Burly, greying and imperturbable, he evinced no surprise at seeing his old friend Dickens. A being of acute intelligence, he knew that whatever business brought Dickens to Bow Street at such an hour must be urgent. Silently, Dickens offered him Mrs Morson's note which he read and understood the import of at once. Dickens saw in his keen, grey eye that the superintendent thought what he had also thought — such a message told that it was death by suicide or murder.

'Davey is waiting,' said Dickens and out they went.

'I need not tell you what I think of this,' said the superintendent indicating the message. 'You have guessed what it might mean and what the implications might be for the Home.'

'I fear,' replied Dickens, 'what it could signify. There are those who do not like us, who do not believe that kindness can be a cure; they would like to see these girls shaven-headed, punished, and confined in a silent regime. They don't believe that it is possible for fallen women to be rescued and to lead better lives.'

'Aye, they'd rather leave them in the streets to become more depraved and diseased, and to commit more crime.'

'If — and we do not know all yet — if a crime —' Dickens glanced at Davey and then back to the superintendent to indicate his caution. The superintendent nodded. Dickens continued — 'If a crime has been committed it will surely justify those who believe that a criminal is always such.

Suspicion will fall on our girls, on Patience herself and about her we know nothing. I regret now that I did not insist on knowing something.'

'She may have said more to Mrs Morson than you know — some confidence she was asked not to break — even to you. Now it can be broken, and if there is something then it may help us in investigating this death. I will keep it as quiet as I can. Mrs Morson, admirable woman, has seen to it that, as yet, no one knows but we two.'

'And Davey — he knows. Look at him.'

'Aye, but he can't tell,' the superintendent remarked, 'but you are right, he is afraid of something and you, Charles, will have to be the means of finding it out. He trusts you.'

'I don't think he would be involved,' said Dickens quickly, afraid suddenly that he had placed Davey under suspicion.

'Nor do I. He is a good lad and an honest one. He'll tell you the truth if you can get it from him, by some means. Meanwhile, let us be quiet and think. If we talk more, he will be all the more frightened. Stop a minute, Davey. Let me take the reins and you get by Mr Dickens here.'

They drove on under the impassive moon, and Dickens slept while the solid bulk of Superintendent Jones warmed Davey who slept, too. Superintendent Jones looked into the night, at the dark road ahead, revolving many thoughts which centred on one word — murder.

3: The Man with the Crooked Face

Mrs Morson slept without knowing that she did so, and in her dream, Patience Brooke — with her red hair streaming and red jewels on a black velvet band round her neck — danced in a room lit by a hundred candles, her partner a man with a crooked face whose hard eyes were hot with lust, who changed into young Davey who looked at her with love. The dance went on, but when she stopped, the jewels round Patience's neck dissolved into scarlet liquid which poured down her white throat and bosom, until she seemed to be covered with what seemed to be a cascade of blood, the ripples created by the folds of her white dress where the scarlet flowed unchecked. Then she was gone, and Mrs Morson murmured in her sleep. The kitchen door stayed shut; the fog dispersed, its vapours disappearing beneath the wet fields. Patience Brooke slept on, never to wake again, never to dance again — if she ever had, for no one knew.

The clock of St Mark's struck two. Mrs Morson woke, shuddering at the dream and remembering that Patience Brooke was still outside with blood on her grey dress. Strange that it was white in the dream. The fire had almost gone out and the kitchen was cold now. Mrs Morson felt the coldness of the floor, shivered, and was aware that she was still in her nightdress. The dream had shaken her; she felt vulnerable, exposed, and a sense of something like shame sent her to the passage where old cloaks were kept. And her feet were bare. Somehow she wanted to be covered when Mr Dickens came — soon surely. Nearly three hours had passed. Wrapped in the cloak and an ancient pair of boots that she had found with the cloak, she put coal on the nearly dead range, stirring it into reluctant life with the poker. Thirsty, she took a cup of water and stood by the window, noting the moonlight which now shone over the gardens, creating shadows of trees and bushes in which there were things hidden. The silence seemed palpable as if it were crushing her. 'Come, come, please,' she found herself whispering, 'come, soon.' She tried to comfort herself, focusing on the side gate. Soon, surely, she would see them come this way, across the garden, the superintendent's strength dispersing the shadows. Davey would bring them to the kitchen door not to the front. They would not knock for the message, brief as it was, would be a warning not to wake the house.

The half hour struck. And in the silent distance she heard the sound of hooves. It must be them. A desire to rush out and fling herself into the safety of Mr Dickens's arms almost overmastered her. She almost smiled at the incongruity of the picture. A foolish thought. Mrs Morson knew what Mr Dickens would want of her — common sense and calm. She could hear the wheels of a trap. It was turning into the lane, rolling towards the stable. It stopped. They were coming across the garden and she could make out the reassuring figure of the superintendent next to the slighter Mr Dickens in his greatcoat. Davey would stable the horse before he came in. The shadows fled; there was warmth in the light which the superintendent carried.

She opened the door. They stood at the top looking down at the figure on the steps.

'Let the boy come in first — before we see her.' Jones looked down at Mrs Morson's face, white and strained in the light of his lamp. 'He hasn't seen?'

'I don't think so.' They came down the steps and into the room. 'Some tea?'

Mrs Morson put the kettle on the range — how odd that she had not thought of making herself anything. She arranged cups, milk and sugar while Mr Dickens and Superintendent Jones stood before the range to warm themselves. Putting the cups on the table, she spoke. 'I am very glad to see you both — I hoped...'

Dickens responded, 'I was where you hoped I would be and so, thankfully, was Superintendent Jones. I was very glad to see him. The boy did well. We will wait until he has had his tea and then we'll send him to bed. How long do we have?'

Mrs Morson understood. 'There should be no one down until six at least. If I do not call them we may have longer.'

'Four hours should give us time to take her away after I've looked at the evidence. We might have to send Davey for a constable —' The superintendent broke off as Davey came in. The kettle boiled and Mrs Morson made the tea, giving Davey his first. He looked exhausted and cold. Dickens and Jones took theirs and drank.

'Now to bed, Davey,' said Mrs Morson as he drained his cup. 'We will come for you when we need you. Thank you, my dear. You cannot know how much I depended on you tonight.' The boy attempted a smile and she took him away.

'Take your time,' said Jones.

Mrs Morson nodded in understanding and shepherded the boy into the little room.

Jones put down his cup. 'Best have a look.' Dickens nodded. He was, as always, torn. His pity for the dead girl was matched by his writer's desire to see what was under the cloak. He had written about death; he had written about violent death. He had shuddered himself at the murder of Nancy; he had imagined the terrible death of Carker in *Dombey and Son*, but he had not seen murder at first hand nor had he known the victim. Jones was careful. Dickens almost expected, even wanted him to remove the cloak with the flourish of a magician, but the superintendent took the cloak in two hands from the top and gently pulled it away from the figure and stepped back to see what Mrs Morson had seen, Patience Brooke with her hair about her face and shoulders and the white bosom stained with red. Dickens, holding the lamp, saw, too, and could hardly understand the transformation from the modest girl he had known. She looked curiously voluptuous, even in death.

'Look there,' said Jones, 'someone has rouged her cheeks.'

Dickens saw the crude colouring, a horrible parody of beauty, ghastly against the white face. Pity twisted in him.

'And the dress has been torn open,' Jones observed.

Superintendent Jones stepped back and lowered his head, crossing himself. Dickens saw how his lips moved in silent prayer and bent his head, too. He was, as always, impressed by the superintendent's sensitivity. The burly man at his side could frighten the toughs and rogues with whom he came into contact; he could be ruthless, sure of hand and eye in pursuit of criminals. Dickens had once seen him in a den of thieves, Sultan of the place, every thief cowering before him like a schoolboy before his schoolmaster, all watching him and answering when addressed. That night the cellar company alone had been strong enough to murder them all, Dickens and the constables included, and willing enough to do it, yet if Sam Jones had been of a mind to pick out one thief in the cellar, if he had produced that ghastly truncheon and said, with his business air, 'My lad, I want you!', all Rats' Castle would have been stricken with paralysis, not a finger moved against him as he fitted the handcuffs on. Yet, here, before the death of this one girl, he prayed for her before taking her down and beginning the grisly search for evidence. Dickens felt, not for the first time, a little humbled and a little ashamed of his failure to think of a prayer. He knew the large, solid man by his side to be an admirable man and felt his own smallness.

Jones indicated to Dickens to lift the lamp, and as he did, lifted the hair to see the gash encircling the slender throat. Dickens's hand shook and the light shuddered, casting shadows on the face of the hanging girl, and the blood seemed to ripple as if it were still flowing.

'Murder,' said Jones. 'You see that the knife went in here on the left side of the neck, and the direction of the wound is from left to right — a right-handed killer. Not that it helps much since most folk are right-handed. But it is murder.'

Dickens saw what he meant. He imagined only too vividly the knife cutting deeply into the white flesh and its swift, wicked progress to the other side. Seconds it would have taken and then the waterfall of blood.

'Now, you know, Charles, what must be done. Here is, we believe, if we are to trust our instincts and we do, an innocent girl done to death in this cruel way, and no one to stand for her except us. And yet, if we pursue this, we do not know into what danger we put her nor, indeed, into what danger we put Mrs Morson, Davey, and this good home of yours and all in it. Yet, we must act, must we not?'

Dickens had thought already of the significance of a violent death to the Home. He knew it would be possible to allow the murder of Patience Brooke to be investigated in a cursory way. Who would miss her? She was a mystery; she came out of nowhere. They did not even know if her name were her true one. She would be forgotten, an unsolved case. He looked again at the blackening wound and the violation of her modesty.

'We must, Sam, we must.'

Sam Jones nodded. 'Now,' he said, 'this must all be done properly. If it comes, in the end, to a trial, we must have our evidence documented. Before we take her down, you must sketch what you see here and you must sign your drawing. I must fetch the constable who must take down our and Mrs Morson's evidence. We'll not trouble him with Davey — what the boy knows is for us alone. Mrs Morson must go for the doctor and he will write his evidence. Now, to work. There's pencil and paper in the kitchen. When you have done we will take her into the kitchen — I don't want her hanging here. Mrs Morson will make her right again, and we'll have your sketch and our testimony to prove what we have seen out here. While you sketch, I'll go in and speak to Mrs Morson.'

They went down the steps, Dickens to get his pencil and paper and the superintendent to knock gently on Davey's door to bring Mrs Morson. Dickens went back outside. It was a grim task. Dickens, who had sketched meadows and trees and essayed the odd likeness, knew his limited skill but, as Jones had assured him, what was needed was the position of the body, the rope that held her, an indication of the bloodied dress. There was no need to look again at the wound — the doctor would give evidence on that. Dickens set the lamp on the step, forced himself to look and not to shudder, and made a beginning. Imagine you are writing it, he told himself. You have written of horrors — now you must draw what you see for the girl's sake. It did not take long and when he was done, he took it inside to Jones.

'That'll do well enough. Now, we'll bring her in. She will be put in her own room next to Mrs Morson's.'

25

In the superintendent's arms, Patience Brooke was light as a bird. Dickens watched as he came in. Suddenly, he said, 'Stop — look there.'

He had seen what had been hidden before: the matted hair at the base of the skull and the blood congealed there. Jones carried her easily up the stairs and laid her gently on the bed. Then he looked carefully at the wound.

'He must have hit her. She was stunned, which is how he managed to tie her up. Then he drew his knife. You did not see anything left there?' he asked Mrs Morson. She shook her head. 'He'd be too clever, I daresay. Still we'll have a look in the light tomorrow.'

'What terror she must have felt,' said Dickens. He had written it. He remembered how he had imagined the terror of poor Nancy as she saw the pistol descend and felt the first horrible blow, and the second as Bill Sikes killed her.

Mrs Morson covered Patience with the cloak. They locked the door. It was agreed that Mrs Morson should go for the doctor.

'I'll hunt up that constable and you, Mr Dickens, must keep watch. Listen for any sound above. If anyone comes down, you may say that Mrs Morson has gone to fetch the doctor, that Patience is unwell and she is sleeping — there is no need to disturb her. Send whoever it is back to bed. They will know soon enough about Patience and we will question them about her later.'

Mrs Morson went out followed by the superintendent with his lamp. Dickens felt suddenly alone. Restless, he prowled round the kitchen, opening cupboard doors and peering at the shelves. He shovelled coal into the range and lit the candles — the darkness and cold was beginning to oppress him. He looked out of the window at the night and, driven by an impulse he could not control, he looked out again at the place on the steps where the body had hung. *The sleeping and the dead are as but pictures*, he told himself, but he still pictured that crimson gash and the blood-soaked, torn dress.

He thought about Patience Brooke and what he would have to tell Miss Coutts who had financed the Home and to whom he reported about the girls and their conduct. She had disapproved of Mrs Morson's engagement of Patience Brooke on the grounds that nothing was known of her, but Dickens, as he most often did, prevailed, expressing his confidence that he would be able to probe her secrets. The rules of the Home were that only Dickens should know the backgrounds of the girls who came there. It was to him that they told their stories and these he wrote up in his casebook — the details were never shared with the matron nor with Miss Coutts, though she dealt regularly with the matron, knew each of the girls by name and, from time to time, visited the Home. Dickens was proud of his skill in questioning the girls; he eschewed leading questions and any kind of persuasion, believing that the interviewee would be driven on to the truth and in most cases would tell it. Most cases, he thought, but not the case of Patience Brooke. For all her gentleness, there was a steely core to her, and he had wondered what experience had forged that toughness. She assured him that she had no criminal history, that she was not nor ever had been a prostitute, and that her secret history was hers alone — and now she was dead, and Dickens felt that her secret had killed her.

There could, of course, he admitted to himself, be some other cause. It might be that the murderer's intention was to discredit the Home; it might be that the murderer wanted to discredit him, or even Miss Coutts. He thought about the boy in the blacking factory — the secrets he had thought buried

27

until Forster had told him of what Charles Dilke had said. But, then, what was Patience Brooke doing on the steps late at night? The only conclusion was that she was meeting someone, yet Mrs Morson had told him that Patience Brooke had no letters, no contact with anyone outside the Home. But she did accompany the girls to church and on shopping expeditions. Someone could have given her a message, someone, perhaps, from her past — if only he could have penetrated that past, they might now be able to find some clue to her murder. But she was a mystery. His thoughts went round in a coil.

Do something useful, he thought. He found bread and cheese. Food and drink for the superintendent and Mrs Morson when they came back. Putting the kettle on the range, he was startled to hear a door opening. For a moment he felt terror but, on turning, saw that it was Davey's door and the boy was coming out.

'Are you hungry, Davey, thirsty?' he asked gently. 'Sit here where it is warmer.'

Dickens gave him bread and cheese which he ate though, Dickens thought, more to please than for hunger. Davey looked at him with what Dickens thought of as his speaking eyes; the intensity of his gaze showed that Davey wanted to tell him something. Dickens silently offered him paper and pencil. His own eyes could be speaking, too, and the boy seeing the question in them, nodded.

'Did you see something, Davey?'

A nod.

'Did you see Patience going out?'

A nod.

'Did she have anything with her?'

A shake of the head.

'Did you see anyone else?'

A shake of the head.

Where to go now? What Davey seemed to know was not more than they knew themselves, yet his eyes told that there was more. What to ask now?

'Did you hear anything?'

A nod.

Keep that perfectly imperturbable face you are so proud of using with the girls.

'Write down what you heard, Davey, please.'

A song.

Baffled, Dickens asked again, 'You heard someone singing?'

A nod.

'Was it Patience?'

A shake of the head and then the words written in the childish hand: *A man.*

'Do you remember the words? Can you write any down?'

More words written on the paper: *wide, rome, home, joy, boy.*

Dickens shivered. It was uncanny and horrible in a way for the words were familiar to him. By *rome*, he was sure that Davey meant *roam*. The words came back to him from down the years, and he saw not Davey but, for a moment, his ten-year-old self at Ordnance Terrace, singing with his sister, Fanny. Unwittingly, he sang the plaintive words from his happy childhood days in Chatham:

'Thrown on the wide world, doom'd to wander and roam
Bereft of my parents, bereft of my home,
A stranger to pleasure, and to comfort and joy,
Behold little Edmund, the poor peasant boy.'

As his voice faded, he looked at Davey. There was terror in his eyes. Guiltily, Dickens reassured him, 'Never mind, Davey. It was only a poor man passing, I'm sure. Nothing to do with Patience.'

The boy shook his head in agitation and wrote again: *Man selling. Sang about poor boy.*

'A pedlar?'

A nod.

'He sang the song?'

A nod.

'Tonight?'

A nod.

'You saw him here before?'

A nod.

'Selling things here?' Dickens wanted to be sure.

A nod. The hazel eyes frightened.

'A frightening man?'

A twisting of the head. Two hands pulling the face round.

'A man with a crooked face?'

4: To London

The clock of St Mark's struck four. Davey was in his bed. The doctor and the constable were gone. The death certificate was signed, and the constable had written his report, all subject to the authority of the superintendent who had assured both that the case was now in his hands. In exceptional circumstances, which these were, a policeman had the authority to remove dead bodies from private houses at the request of the householder who, Superintendent Jones had explained, was, in this case, Mrs Morson who would be glad that the matter could be taken care of.

'What now?' Dickens asked.

'We take her to London. We have five days before the death need be registered and we can keep her safe until we find out more.'

'But —' Mrs Morson interrupted, her face strained with pity.

'I know. It's hard but if you don't want those girls to know, if you don't want a rabble of newspapermen here, if you don't want Mr Dickens's name in the headlines, as if he were the murderer, then this is what must be done.' Jones's tone was harsh but they had to see what might ensue. 'Do it for the girls,' he said. 'Protect them.'

Mrs Morson saw his logic. Dickens was a few moments behind them, his imagination conjuring the sensation of his being accused of murder. In a moment, he had seen himself dangling on the hangman's noose. Sam Jones gave him an appraising glance which almost had a smile in it. Dickens recognised his own weakness for self-dramatization and half-smiled, too.

'When we get to London?' he asked.

'I will summon the aid of my faithful, and discreet Constable Rogers, and we will take her into the police mortuary. I must see the Commissioner at Scotland Yard, and I must give him the facts and ask him to keep this matter quiet. He will agree when I tell him that the case involves the reputation of Charles Dickens — he is a great reader — and possibly, the reputation of Miss Coutts, the greatest heiress in England. I shall mention your supporters, Mr Tracey of Tothill Prison and Mr Chesterton of Coldbath Fields Prison. The Commissioner, in turn, will speak to the Home Secretary, Sir George Grey. The same names will be mentioned and you and I, Charles Dickens, with the help of Mrs Morson, and Constable Rogers, will be left to pursue the case as we think fit and we have already decided what is fitting. We should like justice for Patience Brooke. Are we all agreed?'

'We are,' asserted Dickens and Mrs Morson.

'Then we must bring her down. Mrs Morson, we will leave you to deal with the girls tomorrow, or today, rather. It will be enough to tell them that Patience has disappeared, and if anyone here is involved, he or she will be much disturbed by our false story which may lead to the guilty party being panicked into some kind of action. We shall see. We'll rely on your discretion — see what you can find out. It would be best to leave Davey alone. Let me see, it is now Saturday. We'll try to come back on Sunday with news and some ideas to pursue. Mr Dickens can question the girls. They'll be suspicious and defensive if a policeman is brought into it.'

They went up to the room. Mrs Morson had done her work well. Patience was dressed in an old grey gown of Mrs Morson's, a white band covered the hideous scarlet gash, her hair was smoothed back under a white linen cap and the

32

cheeks were as pale as they had been in life, all trace of the crude red gone.

'*After life's fitful fever she sleeps well. Nothing can touch her further,*' murmured Dickens.

'Aye, she looks peaceful now, thank you, Mrs Morson.'

'You have given her back herself,' said Dickens, 'a self that someone tried to take away.'

'And who we will find, Charles. Now let us be on our way. Time goes on. It'll be nearly light when we get to London. I should like the dark to hide us when we get there. Mrs Morson, is there cart or wagonette there instead of the trap?' Mrs Morson nodded. 'Then I'll harness the horse to it whilst you and Mr Dickens wait below. Think on any questions we need to ask. I will come back soon.'

Dickens felt relief that the superintendent would take charge of the practical necessities to do with the horse. He had always been a rider, taking the beasts rather for granted until one bit him and nearly tore off his arm — an event which had left him more ill than he had ever admitted. There had been something almost cruel in the horse's rolling eye, and Dickens had felt the injustice of it. What had he done that he should be attacked so viciously? Any exposure of his vulnerability seemed to create in him acute distress.

They looked at Patience once again, tranquil in her white cap — she looked nun-like in her death. Dickens wondered if that was what she had sought at Urania Cottage, the seclusion of the nunnery and the peace of celibacy. And that meant that somewhere in her past, perhaps, there was someone who threatened that peace. They descended the stairs and the superintendent went out to the stable.

Mrs Morson and Dickens were somehow bereft. They felt his absence as a loss of comfort, as if they were children left in the dark. Mrs Morson began to clear the bread and cheese and tea cups; Dickens put more coal on the range. He felt a kind of intimacy in the situation as if they were married and tidying their house together. Mrs Morson stood at the sink, her back to him, and he watched her slight figure and wondered at her strength.

This was a young woman whose husband had died in Brazil and left her with a child on the way, and two little girls in a wild land with no resource. She had travelled hundreds of miles by mule to find a ship which would take her home. Arriving in England, she found that her brother-in-law had embezzled the money left by James Morson, and yet she had mustered her courage to find a job, to make a living for herself and three children who were now living with their grandparents. He could not forbear from comparing her with Catherine, his wife, who was nervous and unwell so often, and who, he thought, was temperamentally unsuited to him, and who had lost her girlish delicacy. Mrs Morson turned to him and he admired the fineness of her features, and how, when she smiled, her face still looked girlish. He could not stop himself. Taking a step towards her, he grasped her hands.

'Mrs Morson... What a terrible night you have had, we have had. I must tell you how much I have admired your courage and the delicacy of your treatment of Patience.'

Mrs Morson thanked him gravely but allowed him to keep her hands, which were warmed by his. And there they stood, she looking at his tender face with a gaze of her own. Something settled between them. And then the superintendent came. They did not jump apart. Why should they? What had passed between them was nothing about which to feel embarrassment. Jones took both their hands in his.

'We must be away; it is time to take Patience Brooke on her last journey.'

5: Bow Street

It was still dark when they laid Patience Brooke on the floor of the wagonette. She was covered in Mrs Morson's thickest and best cloak with a pillow to rest her head. The crescent moon, pale as silver sand, cast its weak light on the empty road and the darkened fields on either side. He turned and saw Mrs Morson go back into the house, the little light from the kitchen suddenly extinguished, and he thought of her tired face looking at his in the candlelight, and how tenderly he had thought of her — a good woman. Ahead was London and the sickly corridors of the morgue where they must leave the body, though, Dickens hoped, her spirit was elsewhere, free of whatever had wounded her in that secret, mysterious life that they must examine whether she wanted it now or not. Nothing, he thought, could harm her now, and he almost felt that they should leave it, be done with it, bury her deep under winter snow. He would remember her fragile beauty which sometimes looked like plainness, her paradoxical strength and her gentleness. Davey would not forget her patient kindness nor would Mrs Morson, but her murderer would remember, perhaps with satisfaction in the killing. He would recall with savage pleasure what he had done and how he had left her for the world to think she was a harlot. No, they could not leave it. They would find him, and he must live to be afraid of the crime he had committed.

His thoughts were interrupted by Jones, who had been equally lost in his own thoughts. 'Well, Charles, what did Davey tell you?'

'He saw Patience go out of the kitchen and up the steps. She carried no bag so she was not about to leave with whoever came in the night. But she must have been going to meet someone. He saw no one but he heard something strange — a man singing, singing an old song, the words of which I recognised, words about Edmund, the poor peasant boy, all alone in the world. And, he wrote about a man selling things, a man with a crooked face who came to the home sometime before. But I hadn't time to ask more for that was when the doctor came and you brought the constable, and Mrs Morson put Davey to bed. I should have —'

'No matter. He'll have gone now, vanished, but we can ask Mrs Morson about him — a pedlar I assume, when he came — and if Patience saw him. What about those girls? We are sure, aren't we, that one of them could not be involved?'

'They are often foolish, sometimes intractable, sometimes given to outbursts of passion and jealousy of each other, and they have led hazardous and forbidden lives; some have seen violence, some have been at the receiving end of brutish treatment, some cannot conform to the quietness of our regime, but I do not think that any of the present group would murder.'

'No,' said Jones, 'I think this was a man's crime. It would have taken some strength to tie her to the railings. This was not a crime of passion in the sense that the killer was provoked into murder — let us say, the kind of killing where a knife is plunged into a heart at the height of rage or jealousy or fear. It seems to me to have about it the desire to shame the victim. He took time to disarrange her hair, to tear the dress, and to rouge her face.'

'And I do not think any of our girls would have motive to degrade Patience,' Dickens offered.

'No, I was more wondering about one acting as a go-between.'

'I see,' said Dickens, 'though I do not like to see. There is one fairly new girl, Isabella Gordon, who is something of a troublemaker. She is impudent and can be sly — she might think it a joke to get Patience into trouble by setting up a meeting with a man. She is easily bored, often restless. Once she told me she wished she could go to the races. I don't know — I do not want to think that she — in any case, Augustus Tracey, Governor of Tothill Fields Prison, remembered her fondly from her prison days. I don't think she is vicious —'

'But, as you say, she might think it a joke to get someone she thought was an authority figure into trouble — she might enjoy the irony of plain, in her view at any rate, modest Patience Brooke meeting a man. Well, we'll see. Mrs Morson might find out something. Now, if we think that this is a man's killing, we must consider, apart from our mysterious pedlar who else might have had contact, however slight on the surface, with Patience. Who else can you tell me about? Never mind how far-fetched.'

'There are only the gardener and Davey at the Home. And the gardener, Mr Bagster, is away at his daughter's in Kensal Green — his son-in-law gardens at the cemetery.'

'When did he leave?'

'Mrs Morson said he went away on Friday afternoon — but you cannot think — he hasn't a crooked face — his face is as straight as his garden hoe.'

'We cannot assume that it was our crooked man who was singing last night — it is the kind of song anyone might sing. You know it yourself.'

'But I wasn't singing it last night!' Dickens exclaimed.

'No, I'm sure you were not, but my point holds — it could be a coincidence. Or simply that someone had the tune in his head. It might have been someone other than the murderer, someone passing by.'

'But Davey seemed to be certain that the singer was the man with the crooked face. I suggested the passer-by notion and that's when he became so upset — if you had seen him then —'

'I don't doubt that Davey linked the two, but he was afraid, as you said yourself. He is imaginative, young, and he was bewildered by the fact that Patience had gone out — it's not surprising that he believed that the singer must be the man with the crooked face. Think how the man's appearance affected him — think of that face from a child's viewpoint. To you or me or even to the girls, he might have seemed a bit unusual, unfortunate in his looks perhaps, but to Davey he must have been a figure from a nightmare, and who knows what nightmare figures inhabit Davey's memory — and he can't tell us.'

Dickens was much struck by the Sam Jones's perception. It was exactly what he had experienced himself. He recalled a poor idiot man from his boyhood days in Chatham, how his ten-year-old self had been horrified by the face all awry and the dreadful hands.

'It is true,' he said. 'I have often thought what secrecy there is in the young, under terror. I suppose I was like Davey then, ready to believe in the bogeyman come in the dark, singing his song whilst wielding the knife.'

'To get back to Bagster, the gardener, all I am saying is that we must question him. And he has to be a suspect until we eliminate him. We need to know about his relationship with

Patience. Who else can you think of who might have had contact with her?'

'She went to church with the girls so there is the Reverend Mr Goodchild and his curate, Mr Fidge. They may know something of the pedlar, even something about Patience. Mrs Morson could tell us if she ever went to church other than on Sunday.'

'Earlier, when you came for me, we both thought about the implications for the Home and that the Home Secretary is to be told that the reputations of Mr Dickens and Miss Coutts may be involved in the matter. So we need to think about anyone who might have disapproved of your work, who might have wished to damage the reputation of the Home.'

'I have tried to keep the purpose of the Home secret. Our near neighbours were not to be told and I thought that the girls' neat dresses would disguise them in a way. There would be no shades of the prison house about them, but things get out. There is the dissenting chapel — the Reverend Obadiah Godsmark does not like us. He is a believer in punishment — the mortification of the flesh. I think he would rather they were whipped and pilloried because, of course, they cannot be saved. There is, naturally, a place in Heaven for him and the other elect. He stopped Patience in the street to warn her that he knew she was living in a house of sin. He wrote to me, a ranting, canting epistle foretelling my doom and the surety of hell's pains for the harlots — his word, not mine — I was harbouring. He clearly believes that I'm keeping a seraglio there. And at the end, he had the nerve to suggest that if I were in need of a spiritual guide in the house, he would be willing to come here to teach them their sin and their punishment.'

'Well, we shall have to see this true disciple — though my gorge rises at the thought.'

They drove on, each with his troubled thoughts. Dickens, in a state between sleep and waking, saw in his mind's eye the man with the crooked face, saturnine and menacing, with no eyes or mouth, just a twisted yellowness, dressed in Godsmark's black cassock then with Godsmark's face, white and raging, spittle on the thin lips, shouting silently at a woman in a grey dress.

Superintendent Jones thought also of the man with the crooked face and how to find him. He thought of Isabella Gordon whom he had yet to meet, and if there was a connection between them. He was inclined to think that Isabella might know something.

The city was near now. From somewhere at a distance came the shrill note of a far-off railway whistle. They were going past Kensington Gardens, shadowed and silent under the moonlight, past the deeper dark of St George's burial ground from which Laurence Sterne's body vanished, to turn up later in Cambridge — the body snatchers at work. There was traffic now ahead, the lumbering waggons and carts making their way to the markets from the nurseries and gardens of the suburbs and villages. They reached Oxford Street, waking up to the cold early morning and turned into Endell Street.

The wagonette stopped in the yard behind Bow Street Station. Superintendent Jones got out and went to fetch Constable Rogers. He glanced worriedly at Dickens's white, strained face.

'I'll be back in a few moments.'

Watching his companion disappear through a stained wooden door, Dickens felt suddenly alone, not knowing what he should do next. He ought to go home to see Catherine and his children yet they seemed distant, hardly real compared to the lurid events of the past hours. And it wasn't just that; he felt that he belonged more to the superintendent, to Patience — and Mrs Morson. Houseless Dick, he thought. That was how he saw himself, belonging nowhere, essentially alone — what an irony. A man so well known that people stopped him in the street to tell him how they loved Mr Pickwick and his faithful Sam Weller, how they had trembled at the death of Nancy, how they had wept at the death of Little Nell, and he had a wife and eight children. Sometimes it seemed to him that he cared more intensely for his fictional children — how he had hated to kill off Paul Dombey; how he had felt pursued by Little Nell, and that he was a kind of murderer. Perhaps it was because he knew them to their very souls and he could not know his own children so deeply.

Superintendent Jones came back with the rosy-faced Constable Rogers.

'We'll take care of her, Mr Dickens,' Rogers said, his natural cheerfulness moderated by his understanding of the meaning of Dickens's white face.

Dickens got down from the wagonette and Constable Rogers drove it in through the wooden door.

'Time to go home, Charles,' said Jones.

Dickens glanced at the concerned face. Sam Jones cared about him. Fatherless Dick, he thought, was nearer the mark; here was the man who was as good as a father to him — solid, dependable, straight and simply just good where his actual father was everything else — unreliable, dishonest, and not always very good at all.

'Thank you, Sam, I'll be off then.'

'Take a cab.'

'No, I'll walk, I'd like the air, and it will give me some time to think. When shall we meet again?'

'I must get moving. I shall go to the Commissioner's house. He'll see me — he'll know it's a matter of urgency. I'll make arrangements for Patience's body.'

'What will you do?'

'Well, as I said, we have five days before the death should be registered, probably longer when the Commissioner has seen the Home Secretary, so we need to find a safe place for her. The hospital, I thought. We will need to keep her on ice until she can be buried. I must do that today. I'll go home tonight, and tomorrow morning we should go back to the Home. You must question the girls whilst I see the local constable and get him to make enquiries about the pedlar. Then, since it is Sunday, we might go to church.' Jones smiled.

'Not to chapel?' Dickens smiled back.

'I don't think I could face him on a Sunday.'

'It might be a good time to catch him — at the height of his ranting — then you'll see what kind of a creature he is.'

'A good idea. We'll try to make time for him.'

'What about the constable at Shepherd's Bush? Can he be trusted?'

'Oh, I think so — two things: first, he is young and ambitious and will be told how discreet work in this case might lead to promotion. Second, you remember that Mrs Morson told us the story of his escapade with one of the girls — drinking tea in the kitchen when he should have been on patrol — he knows I haven't forgotten that.'

'Will I meet you at Bow Street? Might I suggest we take breakfast before we go?'

'A capital idea. Shall we say ten o'clock? In the meantime, go home and take some rest.'

'I shall. Goodbye, Sam — until tomorrow.'

'Take the lamp — it's still dark. If you meet any ruffians, they may take you for a policeman. You can invoke the authority of Bow Street and they'll scatter. No need to arrest anyone.'

'A pity. I should rather like to chase down a ruffian — if you'll lend me your handcuffs.'

Dickens took the bull's eye lantern and turned out into the street to make his way towards Covent Garden where the market was stirring. All night long, the wagons laden with their mountains of fruit and vegetables had been rumbling along suburban roads and through the main streets. Numbers of men and women who carried on their heads heavy baskets of fruit, winter pears, apples of every colour, the brown russet, the golden bob, and Ribston pippins, made their way in a long straggling line to the market. It would soon be day, and the young seamstresses, milliners' girls, barmaids and shop women would come to market to buy what flowers there were to be had on a cold winter morning — in winter, pots of snowdrops and crocuses and bouquets of real grasses were to be had, tinted to unreal colours; there were dried weeds and, marvellously, flowers carved from turnips and beetroot all in brilliant contrast to the dark green pine boughs.

Beyond the market, across Long Acre, his way took him to Seven Dials, at the entrance of seven obscure passages, a place he had described in *Sketches by Boz* as a place inhabited by unwholesome vapours and smells so vile it was hard to breathe. He traversed a street of dirty straggling houses and dingy little shops with unidentifiable objects in their grimy windows; surely nothing was ever sold from these dark caves. He was aware of the presence of various huddled forms in shop doorways. Once, one of these shapes rose before him from the gutter itself. It could hardly be human; it seemed to have no face and what might have been its head was swathed in some kind of ragged turban. A dark arm stretched towards him, ending in a bandaged stump rather than a hand. Dickens wondered how it could beg with no hand, and as he hesitated, feeling in his pocket, the shadowy thing vanished like a ghost down a hole in the pavement which seemed to Dickens to be the entrance to some underworld. And such a foetid stench came up from these foul openings that he hurried on, sickened. He saw a thin cat slithering through a broken window. It turned, giving him a haughty stare like some ragged aristocrat still holding on to his nobility in the face of starvation. He saw a boy, another Davey, curled up by a broken wall, dressed in a coarse, torn canvas jacket which would not fetch a penny at the ragshop; Dickens shivered at the sight of the bruised and filthy feet, naked in the bitter night.

He came out of one of the vaporous lanes and turned into Crown Street. Here was some respectability and at least some signs of prosperity. He passed a stationer's doorway where a little dog was sitting gazing out into the street with a comical air of proprietorship, its little black eyes appraising the stranger and one ear cocked interrogatively. Beware the dog-nappers, thought Dickens, unaware that he had spoken aloud. The little dog nodded and pulled back into the doorway where it lay down upon a few rags which made up its bed.

Dickens turned into the wider thoroughfare of Oxford Street; here were gas lamps so he put out his lamp. He passed the all-night coffee stand, a large brightly painted truck on four wheels with polished tin cans. Dickens was tempted by the thought of hot coffee and a sandwich, but there was a crowd. He noted the flash men and their bold girls, some good-looking, others like bedraggled hens, their feathers damp and ragged in the night air. Now there were some cabs about and men going to their work. He turned right into Cavendish Square and on to Portland Street, the grand houses such a contrast to what he had seen in Seven Dials. At last he came to Devonshire Terrace — home.

Superintendent Jones went about his business at Bow Street. Apparently, it had been a busy night, so the inspector on night duty informed him, yawning the while as he reeled off the list of beggars, brawlers and drunks and children swept in and swept out again. One or two were lying contentedly snoring in the women's cells to be released to their gin and porter when daylight came. Jones had work to do, and summoned Constable Rogers to go to the hospital to see a doctor of his acquaintance who, he hoped, would take care of Patience after he had walked to Scotland Yard to see the Commissioner. In the meantime, he would go out to Wills, a nearby coffee shop, to take his breakfast — coffee at threepence a cup, eggs, bacon and kidneys and bread and butter.

6: Dickens at Home

Number 1, Devonshire Terrace was a very good house, leased by Dickens in 1839. It was on the Marylebone Road, last in a terrace of three — a house of thirteen rooms. Dickens's progress from his tiny attic room at Bayham Street, a shabby, dingy, mean, yellowish house in Camden Town, where his parents had landed from Chatham in 1822, to this near mansion in fashionable York Gate, was a story of rags to riches and Dickens was proud of his rise, of his own efforts.

Yet, he stood before the bright green door, seeing the house as a passer-by might, wondering who would live there. Sometimes Dickens could stand outside himself, a stranger in his own life. He could hardly imagine himself as husband and father to eight children; he was still often in his own mind the solitary forlorn boy who felt himself set apart, and who had to walk three miles to the dreary wharf where the blacking factory seemed to rot into the brown river. Devonshire Terrace was still shuttered, and like a stranger, he did not dare go up to the front door. He went round the back to the kitchen door. He knew that by now, the little kitchen maid, Amy, would be feeding the range. He knocked and waited. Then he heard the bolt being drawn back with a teeth-grinding creak. He made a note to see that it should be oiled. Such domestic details were never beyond him. The door opened. The little maid with her pale, almost white eyes with no lashes, looked out, puzzled to see her master standing at the back door.

'Do let me in, Amy,' he said and stepped into the kitchen. 'No need to disturb anyone. I shall go upstairs directly.'

He put his fingers to his lips and was rewarded with a smile from the child, who was delighted to share a secret.

In his library, Dickens took off his heavy coat, lay down on his velvet sofa, promptly fell asleep, and did not dream. At nearly nine he woke, refreshed, the terrors of the night dispersed. He was himself again, filled with energy and purpose, ready, he thought, for the chase — and hungry for breakfast. There was a knock at the door; his sister-in-law, Georgina Hogarth, came in with the two girls, Mamie and Katey, or Lucifer Box, as Dickens called her, she being known for her fiery temper.

'Papa, breakfast time — time to get up,' cried Katey, coming in and standing over Dickens. Dickens, in a deep voice, intoned solemnly, '"'Tis the voice of the sluggard; I heard him complain. You have waked me too soon, I must slumber again."'

Katey and Mamie took up the poem, shouting in delight, '"As the door on its hinges, so he in his bed, turns on his sides and his shoulders, and his heavy head." Sluggard, sluggard!' they cried as Dickens stood up.

'I'll come soon. Now go to Mama, and we will have more poems afterwards.' They skipped away. 'Georgina, I must change my clothes and bathe before I come down. How is Catherine this morning?'

'She is well enough, Charles — a bit tearful over the baby, but she will cheer up if you spend a little time with her after breakfast.'

'I will.' He would spend time with Catherine, but he would not tell her of Patience Brooke. He had not told her much about the Home, assuming, as he always did, that she would not be interested, and, after all, Catherine had lived a protected life. What could she know of the lives of these fallen girls? He was not aware of the contradiction in his own nature. It was all right for the spinster Miss Coutts to know, for the well-born Mrs Morson to know, but not his wife. The truth was that he had begun to believe that they were not made for each other. He recognised her good nature; she deferred to him and was always agreeable, but often tearful and unwell, especially after each pregnancy. And, he felt, as many husbands do, that she did not understand him, forgetting, of course, that often he did not understand himself.

After a little time with Catherine and the older children whom Dickens entertained with more poems and some magic tricks, he returned to his desk where everything was precisely ordered, including a vase of fresh flowers. There were goose-quill pens, blue ink and the blue-grey slips of paper on which he wrote. Today on the desk lay the beginnings of *David Copperfield*. He forgot Patience Brooke and Sam Jones as he re-entered the house at Blunderstone with its latticed bedroom windows and sweet-smelling air, to which David returns to find Mr Murdstone of the ill-omened black eyes as his new father.

Not many streets away, at number 20, Norfolk Street, Superintendent Jones was home at last, having completed his arrangements with the Commissioner. It had not been difficult, especially when he had the sudden stroke of brilliance to mention Miss Coutts's friendship with the Princess Adelaide — the reference to a member of the Royal Family concentrated the Commissioner's mind wonderfully and Jones was given rein to investigate the case as he thought best — with the 'utmost discretion', of course.

He entered his own home at last and the young girl, Posy, who served as parlour maid, kitchen maid and all round help, took his coat. An absurdly small girl, even at fourteen, she had come via Charles Dickens, another orphan from the street for whom a home had to be found, and here she was, looking like a sprite, yet welcoming him to his own home as if it were one of the great houses in nearby Fitzroy Square. She opened the parlour door to announce him — to the only other occupant of the house, his own wife, Elizabeth. He managed to repress a smile and to take seriously her pronouncement, 'Superintendent Jones, ma'am.' She got her ideas, no doubt, from reading the newspaper reports of the doings of society. In the two years she had lived with them, Elizabeth had taught her to read and write — attention to this child filling the aching space where their own daughter should have been. Posy, the name given to her by Elizabeth who had said that a pretty name might make up for the plain face, scuttled back to the kitchen to make the tea.

'All night, Sam? A serious case?'

Elizabeth had expected him sooner, but experience told her that when he had not come in the morning, it must be something important. He often told her of the cases he investigated, trusting her shrewdness and kindness to judge fairly, and often trusting her intelligence to unravel knotty pieces of evidence. Now, he told of the terrible murder of Patience Brooke, his journey through the night with Charles Dickens, Mrs Morson, Davey and the man with the crooked face, the disposal of the body to be packed in ice, his meeting with the Commissioner, his inspiration regarding Princess Adelaide and finally, his and Charles's determination to find the murderer.

'And this murderer who is to be brought to justice, who are the suspects?' asked Elizabeth.

The door opened and Posy came in balancing the tray with the brown pot of tea, the cups and saucers with their pattern of roses, and the plate of neatly made sandwiches without their crusts — another invention got from the society pages. Posy's progress was somewhat irregular, but she made it safely to the table where she placed the tray, beaming at her success.

'Shall I pour, ma'am?'

'No, thank you, Posy, the superintendent and I have matters to discuss. Go back to the kitchen for a while and play with the kitten.' The former instruction was received with grave recognition of the superintendent's importance, the latter with a grimace which indicated that a person of such importance in the house had better things to do than play with a kitten. Posy departed with dignity.

'Why have I taken to referring to my husband as "the superintendent"?' asked Elizabeth, laughing. 'If that child reads any more society papers, I'll have to refer to you as the master. "La, sir, will you take a dish of tea?" She seems determined to improve us whether we will or no. We'll be having evening parties next.'

'She is a delight,' said Sam. 'Consider the scrap of rags she was when she came. You have done wonders.'

'I am fond of her, and she is good company.'

Yes, thought Sam, looking at his wife with love, Posy fills the vacancy in those lonely hours when they remembered Edith, their dead daughter.

'Suspects,' he said, resuming their earlier discussion to banish the dark thoughts which crept into their minds when they remembered Edith. 'Well, there is the man with the crooked face who appeals to Dickens's imagination, and who is certainly worth following up, if he has not vanished without trace, which is more than likely. There is the gardener, Bagster, who left Urania Cottage on Friday to visit his daughter in Kensal Green — we'll need to question him — at least he might have seen something or someone. And there is the Reverend Godsmark who fulminated against the girls, condemning them as sinners who cannot be saved, and the Vicar of St Mark's and his curate — not suspects, as such, but men who had contact with Patience Brooke.'

'It is important that they are men? You don't think that the girls at the Home might be involved?'

'Yes, to the first — you can tell me why in a moment, and unlikely to the second, at least according to Charles. I'm inclined to agree with his analysis of them — often restless, sometimes quarrelsome, sometimes maudlin, but not, he thinks, murderous.'

'You think it is a man because...' She hesitated.

'Go on.'

'Well, apart from the obvious physical strength needed to tie her to the railings — though two girls could have done it —'

'And they might have given some story which would have tempted Patience to meet them outside,' interposed Sam.

'True, but what would their motive be unless they knew something about Patience — she was a mystery woman, as you said, or —' she was warming to the theme now — 'she knew something about them.'

'But their histories are known to Charles, and, to some extent, to Mrs Morson. However, we'll bear them in mind. We are going back to Urania Cottage tomorrow to interview them. Go back to the masculine theme.'

'I think that there is something deeply personal about the way in which Patience was treated — her dress was torn to expose her, her hair was taken down, and then there is the rouge daubed on her face. It is as if the murderer wanted to tell something about her — that she was not what she seemed, that there was a different Patience under the demure grey governess dress.'

'That's the puzzle. Charles said that Mrs Morson had given Patience herself back after she had tidied her up, but we do not know who the real Patience was. Was she really the quiet, modest assistant to Mrs Morson or was she really a woman with a past? We need to investigate Patience.'

'She came from nowhere, you said, but how or why did she come to the Home? Who told her about it?'

'The answer may lie in the Home. One of the girls may know something, a stray remark from Patience, a tiny clue that was not important at the time. Tomorrow may give us an answer. My dear, as always, our discussions bring clarity to my thoughts and point me in new directions.'

They talked on about other things as the evening drew on. Then it was time for the lighting of the lamps and the drawing of the curtains against the bitter night, and for a comfortable supper for two in front of the fire — though Posy might have preferred an elegant dinner in the dining room — if they had possessed one.

Night fell and the silent stars looked down on Devonshire Terrace where Dickens slept, dreaming of Little Em'ly, David Copperfield's boyhood companion in Yarmouth and Patience Brooke who became one in his dream; and they looked down on Norfolk Street where Sam Jones dreamt of his lost girl, Edith.

7: At Shepherd's Bush

If the dark had a lowering effect on his spirits, Dickens always felt energetic and hopeful in the mornings. He rose at eight, took a cup of coffee, worked on his manuscript for an hour, writing about Miss Murdstone, that metallic lady whose heavy-browed countenance he sketched on a scrap of paper, giving her a beard to match. Then, taking his thick coat to guard against the cold, he walked with his characteristic briskness to meet the superintendent for breakfast at a favourite haunt, the Piazza Coffee House in Covent Garden.

Making his way down Crown Street, he had a sudden fancy to check on his canine friend from the night before. He found the stationer's shop — no dog in the doorway. In he went — to buy a pen would be a sufficient pretext. Behind the counter were the head and shoulders of a girl who gazed at him as if he were descended from some lofty planet.

The head spoke, 'You're Charles Dickens.'

'Am I?' The head looked at him pityingly. 'I mean I am.'

'I am Eleanor Brim, and this,' another head appeared without shoulders this time, 'is my brother, Tom.' Tom stared, too, but said nothing, his mouth being full of something round and large. 'And this,' a pair of white and brown ears popped up, 'is Polly. And we are all looking after the shop, and we all know about Oliver Twist, and we did not like that dog, Poll especially.'

'I am very sorry, but was he not what Bill Sikes had made him? He was loyal in his way, and he knew no tenderness — unlike Poll here who knows what it is to be loved.'

The three pairs of eyes looked consideringly, and the three heads nodded. 'Poor dog,' said Tom, and Poll gave a small yap in agreement.

'In any case, there is to be a nice dog in my next story — Jip, he will be.' Where did that come from? he thought. 'Look out for him.'

'We will. Is there anything we can get for you? You might need paper, or a pen, or ink, black or blue, or we can recommend a pen-wiper — you ought to have one if you use ink. It can be messy.'

In the face of such choice, Dickens was unable to decide. The three pairs of eyes gazed at him, two blue and one black.

'A pen, and yes, of course, you are right — a pen-wiper, please.'

'Poll, a pen-wiper, if you please, and Tom, a pen.'

Poll jumped onto the counter. Rooting about in a box, she came out with a pen-wiper in her mouth and offered it to Dickens.

'Thank you, kindly, Miss Poll,' he said.

Tom handed him the pen. The purchase complete, Dickens bade them farewell.

'If you should need anything again, Mr Dickens, we would be happy to supply you,' said the little entrepreneur.

'I shall certainly call again.' Dickens resolved to change his stationer immediately, and he went out with a lighter step to make his way to the coffee house.

Substantial quantities of toast, two eggs apiece and a dish of kidneys for the superintendent filled them enough for the journey. They took a fly to the Home, Constable Rogers having set off earlier with the wagonette and Punch, the horse.

'I have thought,' said Sam.

'I have not,' said Dickens. 'I have been away in Suffolk with my Davey Copperfield. My new book,' he added in explanation to Jones's puzzled look. 'But I am here now to listen to your thoughts, so —'

'I have thought,' repeated Jones, 'about how Patience Brooke came to Urania Cottage, who told her about it. That is something you must try to discover when you talk to the girls. Someone may know something. You never discovered it? Nor Mrs Morson?'

'No, indeed, Patience was, in that matter, most unforthcoming. But, I see your point. If we can find out about that then this might lead us to some information about Patience.'

'I have thought, too, or rather my wife —'

'Ah, the perceptive Elizabeth — what she has thought must be worth hearing. Tell me.'

'I told her the details of the murder. The point which I think was perceptive was that Elizabeth thought that the murderer might have been sending a message, as it were, about his victim — was he trying to tell us that Patience was not what she seemed on the surface, and to me that is an important consideration: who was Patience Brooke?'

'I see it exactly — you, and Elizabeth, are saying that she wanted us to see her as a particular kind of woman, the kind of woman whom Mrs Morson and I would believe a fitting addition to Urania Cottage, but that it is possible that she was very different, and that the murderer, for whatever reason, wanted to expose her... You think that we may have been deceived.' Dickens said the last words with some reluctance — he thought of himself as having a particular gift for reading character, and to have been deceived was something of a blow to his pride.

'It is something that we must consider,' Jones said.

Dickens thought for a few moments, turning over the idea of Patience as a fraud, then he said eagerly, 'Wait — if we believe the murderer to be a man, let us imagine a man whom she rejected, and who then took his revenge in the basest way. She was virtuous and this is what he hated.'

'So, we need to find out if any of the men she had any contact with harboured sexual feelings for her.'

'One of the girls may have noticed something — they are shrewd, and experienced enough with men to notice what Mrs Morson, or Patience herself might have missed.'

Their talk took them to the Home. Jones went off to seek out the constable to ask about the pedlar, and to find out if the pedlar and the man with the crooked face were one and the same. He would come back to look about for a weapon that might have been used to hit Patience Brooke, and he would talk to James Bagster. Dickens went to the front door. A little girl called Jenny Ding, one of the youngest girls in the Home at thirteen, let him in and Mrs Morson came from the parlour to meet him. Dickens wanted a word with her so they went to her little, private sitting room.

They spoke at once, 'Is Patience —?' and 'Have you any —?'

'You first,' Dickens said.

'I just wanted to know. Is Patience safe? Has Superintendent Jones achieved all he set out to do?'

'You may trust him for that. I am sure he was very persuasive with the Commissioner. He did say he had mentioned Miss Coutts's friendship with Princess Adelaide, and that seemed to clinch it.' He smiled at her. 'And you, have you discovered anything of interest?'

'They know that Patience is missing. I have told them you have come today to ask if anyone saw or heard anything, or if they have seen any strangers nearby. I was purposely vague, thinking it best not to alarm them or, worse, to give any impression that someone was under suspicion. You know how fiery they can be — they may have committed crimes in the past, but to be wrongfully accused provokes almost laughable indignation.'

'Yes,' said Dickens drily, 'they are very sensitive. Any signs, though, of anyone unusually quiet?'

'Lizzie Dagg is tearful — it might be that she is upset at Patience's vanishing, but I'm not sure — she may be hiding something. The others are curious, of course, and will have gossiped — it's natural. Their lives are quiet and this, for some, at any rate, is a diversion.'

'Did they like her?' Dickens asked suddenly.

'Patience? Well, yes, and no. You know that Patience was unlike them. I don't think they knew that she had come without recommendation — I presented her as a new assistant which gave her a position apart. She did her work, she took an interest in them, and was kind, but there was always a distance. I assumed it was her natural character but I have thought much about her in the last hours, and now I think —'

'That she held herself in check?'

'Yes, that is it. It was deliberate. She did not wish for closeness. We are so busy — the girls take up my time so I took her as she was, a naturally reserved person. Now I think of it, when we were alone, she never volunteered any information about herself. I didn't ask — I suppose I sensed that questions would be an intrusion, and I liked her. I thought she might unbend in time. After all, it is only six months since she came. Have I failed somewhere? If I had asked, could she have been —'

'Saved? I doubt it. The solution to this murder lies in the relationship between Patience and her killer. Of that, I am sure.'

Dickens was surprised to find that he was sure. 'And I am beginning to believe that the cause of the crime lies in her past, not here, though the superintendent is right to search for clues here — we are right to trust his policeman's experience. Where is Davey?'

'He is in the stable, having been reunited with Punch who is his special charge, as you know. Mr Bagster is with him. He came back earlier this morning. They are firm friends.'

'The superintendent will wish to question James Bagster. It is part of his method. I know you won't believe that he has anything to do with Patience's death. Nor do I, but, as Mr Jones says, he may have seen something or someone.'

'Well, let us go into the parlour and find out what these girls know.'

They went into the room where the girls were waiting. Talk stopped immediately. Dickens noted the various groupings. Bold, red-haired Isabella Gordon and her acolytes, Hannah Myers and Anna-Maria Sisini — Sesina as she liked to be called — were giggling together. Isabella flashed him an impudent look as much as to say we know what we know. The quieter girls were sewing and had obviously been talking, too. Only Lizzie Dagg sat apart.

Mrs Morson began. 'You know that Patience is missing —'

'Gone off with her fancy man, 'as she? I knew she was a dark 'orse. You wanter watch them quiet ones.' This was Isabella interrupting. Again, she flashed her knowing glance at Dickens. He could not be sure if she was just being provocative. He would come back to her later. He indicated to Mrs Morson that she should carry on.

'Mr Dickens would like to find her and he is here to ask if there is anything you know or can remember which may help him.' Dickens noticed her careful choice of words, her appeal to them to help him.

He continued, 'I am sure that you will want to help. You may, for example, have heard or seen something unusual in the last few days. Has anyone been here?'

Sesina, not to be outdone by Isabella, wanting to claim her share of attention, said, 'There was that old pedlar wot came a week or two ago. He was unusual, wasn't he, Izzy?'

'Yer, 'e was a man — we don't see many of those, 'ceptin' you, of course, Mr D —' both girls laughed. They were enjoying themselves — ''E 'ad all sorts for sale — an' we woz buyin' — not sellin' — this time.' Isabella rolled her eyes at Dickens. This was a performance for his benefit, but it was time to take the limelight for himself.

'Apart from his attractions as a man —'

'O, we didn't see no attractions of that sort,' Sesina said with mock primness. 'Wot are you thinkin' of, Mr D?'

'Apart from his manly virtues, Sesina, which I will not describe —' she laughed, good-humoured now — 'what else can you tell us about him?'

''E was an ugly old critter wiv a face all twisted up —'

Dickens heard Mrs Morson take a sharp breath. Had she remembered something?

''E wore an old canvas jacket and a scarf — reddy colour it woz an' — yer, 'e 'ad trousers! Told yer we didn't see his manly virtues.' She and Isabella giggled at her wit.

Dickens wanted to turn the attention from Isabella and Sesina, and to test out Lizzie Dagg. 'Did any of you buy anything? Lizzie?'

She turned her pink eyes upon him. 'No, sir — I don't remember.'

Mary-Ann Hyde, one of the quieter girls, offered, 'Most of us did. It was a nice change. He had some ribbon, and a few pincushions. I bought one for Esther — it was for her birthday.'

Now for the important question. 'Did Patience buy anything? Can anyone remember?'

Mary-Ann said, 'She was there for a bit. She said she liked the black velvet ribbon and I said, "Treat yerself, Miss," and I think she did, but we was all gathered round so I didn't see.'

Isabella shot Mary-Ann a sharp look — it was time for her to be the centre of things again.

'Wot about 'er fancy man? Bet she's gone off wiv 'im.'

'What are you talking about, Isabella? Patience had no follower.' Mrs Morson was impatient. This was just silly.

'O, yes, she did, ma'am. That funny little feller at church. He was sweet on her — followed her — I saw.'

'Don't be stupid, Isabella Gordon. Mr Fidge didn't follow Patience.' Lizzie Dagg sounded angry suddenly.

'O, 'e was followin' you, was 'e? Beg pardon, I'm sure.' Isabella's words were mocking, and the sudden flush in Lizzie's cheeks seemed to suggest that the jibe had gone home.

'That's all then, I think,' said Dickens. 'I don't think the pedlar can have anything to do with Patience's going nor, Miss Gordon, do I think much of your "fancy man" theory, but if you have anything you wish to add, then come and see me in Mrs Morson's sitting room.'

'It is time for you do your chores; there is lunch to prepare, the laundry to be sorted, and the gardens to tend. No one need be idle. You know your duties.' Mrs Morson was brisk. They needed to be busy not to be gossiping about Patience. The girls departed obediently enough though Isabella Gordon could not resist whispering something to Lizzie Dagg as they went out.

Mrs Morson went back to her sitting room. 'I forgot about the pedlar. It was over a week ago, a week last Friday. But, oddly, I remembered him in a dream — the man with the crooked face. He was in my dream, dancing with Patience who was dressed in white with a black velvet ribbon round her neck — how strange. And, I — oh, I remember — in the dream — the way he looked at her — as though,' she hesitated, as if recalling something dreadful, 'he desired her. What does it mean?'

'I think it means that he made an impression on you that surfaced in your dream — unconsciously, you linked him with Patience's death although at the time of his visit you did not think him more than just an unfortunate itinerant. Which is true? The dream or the reality? Mrs Morson, I believe in the power of dreams. They interpret what has occurred, they tell us what might be, and, I firmly believe, that they uncover our deepest fears. That is why he is important, though I don't know if the superintendent would agree. He'll want the proof of the living, breathing man. Davey mentioned him, too — he was frightened by him. A child would be, and Davey cannot articulate his fears. He must live alone with them, poor boy. He said he heard the pedlar singing when he came here, and then he heard the same song on the night Patience went out of the kitchen. That was what he was so afraid of. I didn't have time to tell you when you came back with the doctor.'

'I don't remember the singing, but what the girls told you is right. I did let them buy a few things. He seemed harmless enough though odd-looking.'

'Can you say exactly how? Davey tried to show me by twisting his own face up.'

'His mouth was turned up to one side so one side of his face seemed higher than the other — lop-sided, you know, and his nose was twisted, too. He did look odd. I suppose I felt sorry for him. But, could he have known Patience, given her a message, perhaps when she was paying for her velvet ribbon?'

'He could. It would be quite easy, but you discerned no difference in her in the days after his visit?

'No, but then she was so self-controlled. Where did she learn that, I wonder?'

'Very interesting — it takes us back again to her past. What about her "fancy man", as Isabella so eloquently puts it? Do you believe any of that? And what about Lizzie Dagg? That jibe of Isabella's about being followed seemed to hurt.'

At that moment there was a knock on the door. Isabella sailed in without waiting for permission. Not one for circumlocution, she got straight to the point.

'It's true Mr D, swear ter God. If 'e wasn't exactly 'er fancy man, 'e wanted ter be. Saw 'im, didn't I — nothing much else to do in church is there but watch wot's goin' on.'

'So, what did you see Miss G?' He paid her back for the new appellation, but, of course, she liked it. She sparkled.

'That'd be tellin'.'

'I'm serious, Isabella. I don't want to think that Patience has come to any harm so if you do know anything, now's the time.'

'I get yer, Mr D —' she was serious now — 'Francis Fidge, 'e's called. You know 'im, Mrs Morson, the curate, they calls 'im. 'E's a little runt, one leg shorter than the other. Pale as a corpse but burnin' eyes, yer know, when he looked at 'er, Miss Brooke, that is. Fat chance, I thought. It made me laugh to see 'im tryin' to catch up with 'er after church.'

'Did you see him catch up with her at any time?'

For all the lurid description, he sensed she was telling the truth. He could imagine her watching and laughing. Those bright amber eyes would not miss much.

'She used ter walk sometimes, through the graveyard, yer know, lookin' at the graves — morbid, she was — well, yer know what I mean. He followed 'er once and they woz talkin'. I didn't see no more cos they went off through the trees. I bet he was tellin' 'er of his undying passion — sorry, Mr D.' She saw him frown. 'I'm tellin' the truth, yer know.'

'I'm sure you are. Did you tell anyone what you had seen?'

'Only Ses and Hannah, we 'ad a good laugh about it.'

'Well, don't discuss it any more. It might not be anything to do with Miss Brooke's disappearance. Let's not cause trouble for poor Mr Fidge. Promise, Isabella?'

'Cross me 'eart, Mr D. I won't say nothin' more.'

'Thank you. Off you go now.'

She went, reluctantly. He wondered what would become of her. She was impudent, and there was a spark of life and colour about her that he couldn't help liking, but could they change her into a neat little servant? He doubted it.

'Well, Mrs Morson, what do you think?'

'It's probably true. Like you, I think she would be amused by it all — an entertaining story to gossip over with her allies. But I can't see Mr Fidge as a murderer — he is a poor, weak thing — you'll see for yourself, no doubt. What do we do about Lizzie Dagg?'

'Let us have her in. A few direct questions are in order — no use waiting for her to come to us.'

Mrs Morson went to fetch her. Dickens thought about the pedlar and Mr Fidge. The pedlar could have given a message to Patience, some request for a late-night meeting which ended in murder or, he reasoned, a message from someone else, a someone whose summons she felt she must answer. Perhaps that someone was the murderer. And Fidge must be seen and questioned.

The door opened and a frightened-looking Lizzie Dagg was ushered in. Her pink eyes gazed at Dickens. She had something to tell, he was sure. He would be straight to the point.

'Lizzie, if you know anything, you must tell us. Patience might be in danger. All we want is to help her, if we can. Do you know anything about Mr Fidge, for example?'

The girl burst into tears. 'I didn't do anything. It wozn't my fault.'

'Just tell us, Lizzie. You will not be in trouble, I assure you.'

The girl's sobs became more of a hiccupping; she blew her nose with the handkerchief offered by Mrs Morson.

'Mr Fidge liked 'er. I know he did — Isabella and Sesina laughed about it, but 'e's a good man. 'E was kind to me — sometimes spoke to me after church. 'E said he was sure I was a good girl — 'e don't know, though, do 'e? Don't know nothin' about girls like me. 'E don't know wot's wrong with me — if 'e did, 'e'd 'ate me.'

She cried again for the girl she could never be. There was something so hopeless in her sorrow that Dickens was stirred to pity. She was not one of his favourites; she was often sullen and listless, and the lessons bored her, but he could see that she had no faith in herself.

'You must be hopeful, Lizzie. That is why you are here. The Home is here to help you start again, a new life, in a new land. Think about Julia Mosley, Martha Goldsmith and Jane Westaway on board *The Calcutta* now, sailing for Australia and a new life — you can do that too, Lizzie.'

'I ain't never seen the sea,' she sniffed, 'an' I 'ates that river.'

Dickens could have laughed. She was a child, really for all her rotten experience. He thought of Eleanor Brim, half her age and twice as sensible.

'We believe in you, Lizzie, and we know that you have not done wrong on purpose.'

'But I 'ave!' she cried. 'You don't know wot I done.'

'Not unless you tell us,' said Mrs Morson, patiently.

Dickens was alarmed. What had she done? What did she know? Did she know that Patience was dead? He made himself be calm. 'Tell us, Lizzie, and you will feel better.'

''E gave me a note — Mr Fidge — for Patience — we met 'im — Mary-Ann and me when we were at the shops with Mrs Morson last Thursday. 'E said to give it 'er.'

'Did you?' Dickens sensed Mrs Morson holding her breath as he was doing. The answer was crucial.

'No.' Dickens heard Mrs Morson breathe out as he did.

Gently, he asked, 'What did you do with it?'

'I tore it up, an' I let it float away.'

'Why?'

'Why should 'e write to 'er?' Lizzie was passionate now in her anger against Patience Brooke. 'She was stuck-up. She didn't like 'im; she thought she was too good for 'im. I like 'im — 'e ain't much to look at but I like 'im but he don't see me.' The words tumbled out of her. 'I didn't like 'er — it was like she was pretendin' to like us when she didn't, really. She thought she was better than us. Well she's gone now an' I bet she don't come back.' Now she was sobbing again.

'Did you read it?' Dickens had to be sure. Had Francis Fidge wanted a meeting?

'No, I just tore it up and threw it away — in the gutter — in the water.'

Dickens looked at Mrs Morson. She would know what to say.

'Well, Lizzie, it doesn't seem so bad to me. If Miss Brooke did not like him, then perhaps you did her a good turn. You must not think of it again. See, Mr Dickens is not angry.'

Lizzie gave Dickens a weak smile. 'I'm sorry, sir. It was temper, I know.'

'Good. Now, cheer up Lizzie and think on the better things to come.'

'I'll try, sir.'

'Go upstairs, Lizzie and wash your face. Then go in to your lunch.' Mrs Morson stood up to open the door.

Lizzie went out, turning as she went to say, 'Thank you, sir.'

'Phew!' Dickens said. 'I was terrified for a moment. I really thought she had done something terrible. Just jealousy and frustration. She is usually so dull and quiet, but underneath that there is the same anger and restlessness that they all have.'

'Yes, I do feel sorry for her — it is hard for her to believe that there will be a future. It's as if most of the time she is too depressed to care and then something triggers a break-out of emotion, as it were.'

'It is interesting what she said about Patience. She was jealous, I think, that Patience was a lady, that she seemed self-assured, even contented. And the business with Fidge was the trigger which provoked such anger against Patience. We need to find out what was in that note.'

'You don't think she read it?'

'No, I don't. I can see her tearing it up in temper. It didn't matter to her what it said. What is interesting is that Lizzie said that Patience was pretending. That annoyed her. What we do not know is what or who Patience really was. We thought we knew her, but now I wonder who was hiding under that demure exterior.'

There was a knock at the door and Davey was there, looking considerably more cheerful than he had on Friday. He had enjoyed the company of the jovial Constable Rogers whom the superintendent had enjoined to make friends with the boy, and he had welcomed Punch back to his stable, and Mr Bagster. Davey gave Dickens a note. It was from the superintendent who was presently in the stable, ready to listen to what Mr Bagster had to say about Patience Brooke. Dickens was asked to join them while Davey had his lunch in the kitchen. He told Mrs Morson that he and the superintendent would go to St Mark's, and then to Godsmark's chapel, and that he would probably return to the Home on the following day.

'You will manage?' he asked.

'I will do my best to keep them occupied. The making of bread and soup for the poor will keep them busy.'

'I see how tired you are. I will try to find someone to assist you. I'll ask Miss Coutts — which reminds me, I shall have to tell her about Patience. Fortunately, the superintendent has done his work well in keeping the matter quiet. That will please her, and she will be sorry about Patience, even if she disapproved of our manner of employing her.' He sighed. 'I hope that this doesn't put her off our work. We can't do without her money.'

'I hope so, too. I hope it is not my employing Patience that brings ruin here.'

'We both did it, and we both had faith in Patience, but I can't help wishing that we had known more about her. Still, what's done is done. I must go now.' He took her hand. 'Mrs Morson — take good care. Lock the doors carefully at night.'

'I will.' She smiled at him. 'Until tomorrow then. Goodbye, and you must take care, too, Mr Dickens. Don't forget that you are in pursuit of a murderer.'

'I have the redoubtable Sam Jones to protect me. He'll make sure that Constable Jenkins keeps an eye on the house, and you have James Bagster.' I hope, he thought.

Dickens went out through the kitchen door and up the steps past the railings where Patience had hung. He quickened his pace, the memory urging him on to see whether it was possible that Mr Bagster had anything to tell them. Entering the stable, he saw Jones seated comfortably on a bale of hay with Bagster opposite. He saw a strong-looking, thickset man about the same age as Jones. He had large, capable hands, and large feet in workman's boots and wore a canvas waistcoat and faded corduroy trousers. His eyes were bright blue in a weathered brick-red face and his hair was a faded straw colour. He looked what Mrs Morson said he was — a solid, good-natured, dependable man. He did not look like a murderer.

Bagster greeted Dickens as an old friend, turning his frank but troubled gaze on him. 'I can't hardly believe what the superintendent has told me.' He shook his head. Dickens gave a surprised glance at Jones.

'I have told Mr Bagster of Patience's death,' said Jones calmly. 'And I have explained why it must be kept secret. He understands and has given me his word.' James Bagster nodded in affirmation. 'He understands, too, why I must send Constable Rogers to Kensal Green to ask James's daughter to confirm his arrival at her cottage on Friday and that he stayed until this morning. He knows that I must have evidence about anyone who had contact with Patience in case we are able to bring a suspect to trial. We need now to know if James, here, can shed any light on the matter. We'll begin with the pedlar.'

Dickens was glad that Sam Jones had decided to trust James Bagster whom he knew to be a good, honest man — he was like Sam in that.

Bagster thought awhile, and then in his slow, deliberate way, began, 'I remember him coming. I saw him at the garden gate. He was a strange-looking man, with a crooked face —'

There it was again — the man with the crooked face who had disturbed Davey, and who had played a curious role in Mrs Morson's dream. Haunting the story, the twisted face of the man appeared, vanished, and reappeared like some spectral presence.

'Had you seen him before, perhaps calling at other houses, in the village, perhaps?' Jones wanted facts, not a ghost.

'Never. He just appeared. There are some regular street men and women. I know them — we don't have too many hereabouts — there's the cat's meat man. He passes by sometimes, but there's not much call for it here — mostly farm cats, and our Nell.' Jones raised his eyebrows as much as to say 'I haven't heard of her before.'

'The stable cat,' grinned Bagster, 'not my wife, nor fancy woman. Nell has to do with scraps and what she gets herself — a mighty hunter, she is. There she is —' Nell, no doubt having heard her name, came to investigate the superintendent, and finding him wanting, strolled out of the stable, her tortoiseshell coat shining momentarily in the sun. Dickens, she ignored. He preferred Poll who had won his heart.

James Bagster went on to give an account of some of the regulars. There was, occasionally, a muffin man though it was a bit far out; the florist's cart came in all weathers and Jopp, the clothes-pole man with his fresh-cut poles, new ropes for drying, and his wife with her basket of clothes pins, all items manufactured by themselves. James knew these as an honest couple, and repeated his statement that the pedlar was new, and had never been seen again.

Jones considered this. 'That's interesting. You might think that having found some customers, he might have come back to try his luck again. Constable Jenkins is making enquiries — we might have him in our sights yet.' He glanced at Dickens, indicating that he should ask his questions.

'James, what about Patience? What did you think of her?'

'I liked her though she was mortal quiet — she came in the garden often. She liked the peacefulness when the girls were not in here. They're a cackling lot sometimes. She was good to Davey, teaching him and that, patient — like her name — cos he can't speak, of course, but he's a quick learner.'

'Did she tell you anything about her past — before she came here?' Dickens asked.

'No, and I didn't ask. No more than I did the other girls. But there is one thing I thought about her.'

Dickens looked at Jones — this might be something.

'Last year, in September, when she'd not long been here, my Annie's husband brought their little girl to spend a day and night here while she was confined for her coming child. It was warm and she played in the garden. Patience came in and it was pleasant to see her teaching the child the names of the flowers and feeding her a plum from the tree, and when the little maid fell and grazed her knees, Patience took her on her lap and dried her tears. She sang a little song, too, a nursery song. Anyways, I thought —'

'That she'd be a good mother,' interrupted Dickens.

'No, sir —' looking straight at him — 'that she *was* a mother.'

Jones asked, 'You thought she'd had a child?'

'That's just it. Course, I've no proof, but I've watched my Annie with that little maid, and Patience was exactly like her, exactly, sir. I can't describe how. It just was — you'd have to see it. And I saw something in her face when Barnaby came to fetch her and said the new child was well, and it was a girl. Something longing, sir, something lost. You may think it's my fancy, sir, but —'

'Not I,' said Jones. 'We know nothing about her, and I believe you saw what you saw — and it makes her more mysterious than ever.'

Dickens and Jones got up to go. They shook hands with James Bagster and thanked him. As they walked away, Jones observed, 'Much to think about, Charles. But not now. Time for church.'

8: Francis Fidge

They walked the half-mile or so to the church. On the way, Dickens apprised the superintendent of his interviews with Isabella Gordon and Lizzie Dagg, making plain their conviction that Francis Fidge had been in love with Patience Brooke.

The old church of St Mark to the south of Lime Grove dated from 1631 when it had been established as a chapel of ease. It was built of brick, now attractively mellowed to a faded terracotta. It had a bell tower and was surrounded by a quiet burial ground shaded by elm trees, now bare black lines against the winter sky. Snowdrops, like crystallised snow, white with delicate green veins, and a few tiny yellow suns of crocuses pushed up through the dark soil, a promise of something warmer to come, though the bright sun of earlier had faded to a hazy whiteness. The chill air was very still and no birds sang, but it was peaceful.

'*And all the air a solemn stillness holds,*' Dickens murmured the lines from Gray's *Elegy in a Country Churchyard* as they looked down at the heaps of turf and tombstones, some upright and other, more ancient ones, leaning towards each other as if in solemn conversation. The Reverend Octavius Goodchild was the incumbent and Francis Fidge, his curate.

'I want you to observe him, Charles. If they are both there, I'll ask some nondescript questions, nothing more than a polite inquiry as to their knowledge of Patience. You know Goodchild and you consider him a worthy man?'

'I do — he has said nothing against the Home, and he is a benevolent man who believes, as we do, that these girls can be restored to a better life, and he welcomes them to his church. They don't all come at once for we don't wish the congregation to speculate overmuch as to the nature of the Home. He has visited us, and given instruction to some of them, but he is a gentle man and not young, so I protect him from some of the more outspoken ones. Our Isabella would devour him, and that piece of tattered finery, Sesina, might well offer herself to him for sixpence, so they are brought by Mrs Morson with two of the younger, quieter ones, sometimes to matins, and sometimes to evensong. Mrs Morson says her heart is in her mouth, and she prays only for a speedy deliverance from the pew before riot breaks out!'

Jones laughed — he had heard enough from Dickens about Isabella and her cohorts. 'I take it that young Mr Fidge has not been left to their tender mercies!'

'Heavens, no! If you'd heard them this morning, you'd keep them locked up and throw away the key. But he has come to the Home with Goodchild, and no doubt that's where he made the acquaintance of Patience about which we want to know.'

They went into the church where they saw to their satisfaction that Francis Fidge was alone there, kneeling before the altar in prayer. They went out again and waited in the shelter of the lychgate.

'Let us watch and wait,' said Sam. 'I should like to observe him when he thinks he is unobserved.'

'We'll tell him she is missing, not dead?'

'We have to lie. If he is the murderer, our lie will confuse him, for if he knows she's dead he'll have his story right and we want to surprise him. You can cross your fingers if you don't like lying to a man of God.'

'I shan't care if he is the murderer, and if he's not, then the lie will spare him — for the time being. Lizzie Dagg and the other girls were convinced that he had feelings for her so we must find out whether those feelings provoked murder.'

It was ten minutes at least before Francis Fidge emerged. 'A long time a-praying,' Dickens murmured, 'guilty conscience?'

'Let us hope his sins are small ones. See, here he comes.'

Francis Fidge looked up at the white sky as he came out. He was small, and as Lizzie Dagg had so pertinently observed, he was not much to look at. He was not much above five feet, noted Dickens, and he was thin to the point of emaciation in his black suit, and he did limp, dragging his left leg a little behind him. He wandered to the graves nearest the church, and stood contemplating the inscriptions, his lips moving, though whether in prayer, they could not tell. Then he turned as if to go towards a little side gate.

Jones moved swiftly. 'Mr Fidge,' he called.

Francis Fidge looked towards them. He came nearer, and Dickens could see his thin, white face and feverish eyes. He looked ill. He was clearly startled but recovered himself. 'How may I help you?'

'I am Superintendent Jones of the police, and you know Mr Charles Dickens who has charge of the Home in Lime Grove. The girls come to church here.'

'Mr Dickens, I am very glad to meet you again. I have read your books. Of all of them, I love your story of Nicholas Nickleby and Smike, that poor neglected soul, and Superintendent Jones, I am glad to meet you, too, though I do not know what brings you here to our churchyard on a winter's afternoon.'

It was quite a long speech; perhaps he was giving himself time to steady himself. It was difficult to tell, thought Dickens.

'Patience Brooke is missing,' said Jones briskly. 'We wondered if you could tell us anything about her.'

It was painful to see how his white face with two burning spots like fever was suddenly suffused with ugly red, and how his eyes filled with sudden tears. Dickens saw how his face betrayed him. But what was written there — guilt, grief, horror?

'You knew her well.' Jones was making a statement not asking a question.

The hectic colour faded briefly from Fidge's cheeks and then came back. 'You think that my attentions were so repugnant to her that she has run away.' He was not mocking nor was this the arrogance of a man who could not believe a woman might reject him — he spoke the truth. He believed what he said, that she might find him repugnant. Dickens wondered whether she had shown it. And pitied him.

'I cannot say until you tell me what those attentions were.' Jones was merciless. Dickens, who knew his kindness, marvelled here at his sternness.

'I am not afraid to tell you. I loved her, and she knew it. When we talked, about books and poetry — we shared a love of Mr Tennyson — I thought that there might be a chance for even one such as I. I know what I am, Superintendent. I am not a man with whom a beautiful girl would fall in love. Your girls' laughter tells me that, Mr Dickens. But I hoped. How could I not? When she was so good, so gentle; so —' He broke off, the tears pooling in his eyes. 'We must all have hope, and I am ashamed to say that my love for my Lord was not enough. In any case, He has deserted me, or, rather, I have deserted Him.'

Dickens wondered. Had this slight, intense young man committed some terrible act when his hope was gone, and his faith, too?

'There came a time when I knew that I could hope no more. Patience told me that she could not love me. She was gentle, but there was a firmness in her which I knew to be unmoveable. She said that she could not love again. And I accepted it. I did not pursue her, superintendent. I did not want to distress her.'

'But you sent her a note. Why?'

'For the reason I have given. I knew she would not want to see me, but, I wanted to give her something. I sent her a note to tell her that I had left a copy of Tennyson's poems for her in the porch. I did not want to keep it, and I thought she would, at least, remember me with kindness not pain. I am sorry, Mr Dickens, I should not have involved Lizzie Dagg. And if Patience has left, I hope it is not because of me.'

Dickens, who had listened intently, asked a question. 'You said she used the word "again". Did she tell you about a former love?'

'No, I am afraid I thought only of myself and my own misery. Are all lovers so selfish, Mr Dickens? I did not think of her enough, of what hurt lay behind her quietness.'

'You know nothing, then, of her former life?' This was Jones, kinder now.

'Nothing. We knew nothing of each other, only that there was refuge in our reading. We walked sometimes, here, in the churchyard, and beyond, into the lanes. She would come to meet me on Sunday afternoon when she had some free time. For only an hour or so.'

'I am sorry to have distressed you, Mr Fidge, but we are concerned about her, and I wanted to be sure —'

'You thought I might have driven her away?'

'Something like that.'

'What will you do now?' asked Dickens. 'Will you stay here?'

'I will not. I am no use here. I am no use to your girls, Mr Dickens. I applaud your work, and I wanted to help, but they do not like me. Perhaps a young man is not suitable. Lizzie Dagg, I think, mistook my intentions. And I hate Isabella Gordon and Sesina —' The hectic burned in his face again then subsided. 'I am sorry; they are too much for me. I must go elsewhere.'

'Perhaps I can help,' said Dickens. 'I am acquainted with men of the Church who might do something.'

'That is most kind, Mr Dickens, but, as I told you, I have deserted my Lord, and I must make my own way. May I go now? Reverend Goodchild will be waiting for me.'

'Yes, and may God protect you,' said Jones.

'I hope he may.' Francis Fidge walked away, a forlorn figure, to whatever future he might fashion for himself.

'There is death on that man,' said Dickens. 'He will not live to beyond the summer.'

'You are right. I do believe that one may die of a broken heart,' said Jones gravely.

'And of tuberculosis. The hectic in his cheeks was not just his emotion.'

They watched for a moment in the quiet churchyard where, as Dickens foretold, Francis Fidge would lie in his cold grave under the summer sun, mourned only by the Reverend Goodchild who was coming through the little gate and who, they saw, placed a comforting arm on the little man's shoulder. Francis Fidge would not die alone nor forsaken by his Lord.

They stood for a while gazing down at the silent graves, each preoccupied by what they had heard and seen. Dickens looked upon one greenish-stained tablet where most of the inscriptions had been worn away by time, but he could make out *and Georgiana, wife of the above*. Who, he thought, was *the above* and when had she joined him in that eternal marriage, and was that all she was, wife of? He thought of Georgiana, widow of James Morson dead in a remote land. His wife would not lie with him again. He looked at his friend and saw in that countenance an unwonted sorrow, and he thought about the lost girl, Edith, and of another, Mary Hogarth, his sister-in-law, dead these twelve years and whose ring he still wore. She was only seventeen at her death, but she had died in his arms, not in terror at the hands of a murderer. As if reading his thoughts, Jones spoke.

'Is Francis Fidge a murderer?'

'I am not sure now,' said Dickens. 'Part way through our interview, I wondered — when he said he had deserted his Lord — whether he had killed her and that was why, but then I felt the truth of his love for her — his words were so simple when he said that he accepted it, and when he talked of their few hours together. But —'

'Yes?'

'There was that remark he made about Isabella and Sesina — the word "hate" was unexpected but he meant it. I had not thought he was a man who could hate, and his face at that moment revealed it — the blood gave him away. But men are made of many parts, and still I pitied him.'

'I, too. I don't think he murdered her, but we cannot dismiss him entirely. For now, we'll leave him with a question mark. If we find out more — perhaps you can question the Reverend Goodchild — find out if Francis Fidge was out on Friday night. He may not know, of course. If Fidge vanishes in the next few days, then we'll know. If he stays, then I think we can believe that he is not our man. Now, we must visit your friend, Mr Godsmark, in his chapel.'

9: Godsmark

They left the churchyard and walked back towards the Home and north to the village of Shepherd's Bush, and in a little alley, dank and narrow as a tomb, appropriately named Sepulchre Lane, they came upon the Primitive Methodist Chapel. It was a gloomy little building with a stern, blackened wall in which there was a door partly opened. It could hardly hold more than fifty. They went in to find a plain whitewashed interior with pitch-pine pews facing a pulpit where the Reverend Obadiah Godsmark stood contemplating the ceiling. A haggard-looking woman in black was distributing hymnals on the pews. They waited at the door. Godsmark saw them, but he began to speak from his pulpit, looking at them directly.

'For the time is come that judgement must begin at the house of God: and if it first begin at us, what shall the end be of them that obey not the gospel of God? And if the righteous scarcely be saved, where shall the ungodly and the sinner appear?

'My Brethren, hark unto the word of the Lord. Some of ye are the righteous. Yet shall ye be saved? Only by doing His works. Ye must be sober, subject to your masters, and ye wives, be in subjection to your husbands, ye must be patient, and above all, abstain from the lusts of the flesh. The sinners and the ungodly, they shall be damned for they are unrighteous; the sinner does evil and the ungodly thinks evil. None of these can be saved. For they shall burn in the pit of hell.'

The voice was high and grating like a hinge needing oil, the words 'damned', and 'pit' and 'hell' flew up into the beams and swooped down again, no doubt intended to fall upon the sinners' heads like live coals. Godsmark came down from his pulpit and waited. They were, it seemed, to creep as supplicants to him. He was, in every way, the opposite of the skeletal Francis Fidge; he had a rosy face, puffed up with good eating, and round from the same cause.

'The lusts of the flesh?' murmured Dickens as they approached him.

Jones kept a straight face, whispering back mischievously, 'Stolen waters are sweet, and bread eaten in secret is pleasant.'

'I am Godsmark, you are welcome to my church — if ye seek salvation, this is the place. I am marked by God. I was his chosen at birth — witness my name.' His plump, pink mouth seemed to give a welcome but his little eyes in their folds of flesh were calculating. He made a steeple of his smooth white hands as if to pray for them already.

'We seek information not salvation,' said Jones with some asperity.

'We must all seek salvation whatever our business.'

'I am Superintendent Jones of —'

'My son, forget not my law; but let thine heart keep my commandments.'

'Of Bow Street.' Jones articulated the words clearly and firmly. 'I am here to investigate —'

'Aye the path of the just is as a shining light.'

'We are hoping you might shed some light,' Jones said, then wished he hadn't.

'For the commandment is a lamp and the law is light.'

It was like trying to catch an eel which kept slipping out of the hands, twisting and turning its own way. Dickens suppressed a smile as he saw Jones's lips tighten in irritation.

'Mr Godsmark, I appreciate your sentiments. They do you credit but I should be glad if you would listen for a moment. This is my colleague, Mr Charles Dickens.'

'The words of a talebearer are as wounds, and they go down into the innermost parts of the belly.'

A hit, thought Dickens, again suppressing the urge to laugh, a very palpable hit.

The superintendent tried again to catch his eel. 'Mr Dickens is concerned about a young woman.'

'I beheld a young man, void of understanding. Passing through the street, and he went the way to her house. In the twilight, in the evening, in the black and dark night, there met him a woman with the attire of an harlot.' The last word brought spittle to the plump lips, and Dickens remembered his dream. Desperate, he thought of seizing one of the black bibles to beat the man round his fat head to shut him up. Sam Jones took a deep breath and spoke loudly and slowly as if to a deaf man, which, indeed, Godsmark was.

'Mr Godsmark, we are here to ask if you know anything about a young woman, Patience Brooke, who is missing from Mr Dickens's Home. You knew her, I believe.'

'Oh, yea, I had met the unfortunate woman. I bade her to leave her sinful ways though she be damned as they all are. I have seen them. That is a house of sin, Mr Dickens, and all are damned that inhabit therein. If she has left that house, having heeded my words, then I praise the Lord in His holiness. The years of the wicked shall be shortened —'

'You would like to see them dead, Mr Godsmark,' Jones interrupted.

'To everything there is a season — a time to be born, and a time to die. God shall bring everything to judgement — not I.'

'Perhaps that lady could tell us something?' Jones knew that she would not, but it was something to stop the man's mouth.

Godsmark beckoned to the woman in black who had stood silent but watching Godsmark with obvious admiration. She came forward, a gaunt, jagged woman, in her rusty black, thin as an iron railing, and as hard, thought Dickens. All her features, hair, eyebrows, nose, mouth, lean cheeks were one hue — the colour of damp yeast.

'This is Mrs Tender of my congregation. She looketh well to the ways of her household and eateth not the bread of idleness.'

Nor any bread at all, thought Dickens, looking at the starved frame. As tender-hearted as the kitchen poker. She inclined her narrow head, but said nothing, the lipless mouth a long thin crease in the colourless face. Jones, knowing it was all hopeless, made one last valiant attempt.

'You have not seen the girl?' he asked Mrs Tender.

'Her house is the way to hell, going down to the chambers of death.' The voice was a hoarse whisper, and on the word 'death' the long mouth clamped shut.

They heard the door open; a pretty young woman of about fifteen or sixteen years came in; she was dressed in black and wearing a close-fitting white cap. She looked at the strangers, puzzled, and a faint blush coloured her cheeks.

'My child,' said Godsmark, predictably. 'Alice Brown, my niece.'

'Uncle, our meal will be prepared soon.' She looked at Godsmark warily, twisting her red, chapped hands. Dickens wondered what she was afraid of.

The calculating lizard eyes flicked a glance at the superintendent. 'If that is all?'

'Yes, thank you, sir. We will leave you in peace.'

'Go thy ways, and walk in the paths of righteousness.' Godsmark followed the girl to the door, and Mrs Tender, whose long mouth seemed designed more for the posting of letters than eating, turned back to her hymnals.

Dickens gave in to temptation. 'He that winketh with the eye causeth sorrow: but a prating fool shall fall.'

The door closed with a smart rap. Dickens and Jones hurried out just in time to hear the squeaky hinge declaiming once more: 'Job Grime, the eye of God sees all. Be not among winebibbers, among the riotous eaters of flesh.'

Whoever the unfortunate Job Grime was, he hurried by, his face averted from wrath. The door to the house opposite opened and Godsmark went in to his meal. They leaned on the black wall, giving in to laughter.

'Oh, Charles, I'd have given a thousand pounds to have remembered "a prating fool" — a stroke of genius.'

'Pity we couldn't see his face. I take it you don't think he's our man.'

'I wish he were. I'd march him to the scaffold myself. But, no, on balance — despite his relish in the short days of the wicked. But here is Alice Brown — we could ask a few questions.'

The superintendent stopped her. 'Miss Brown, may we have a word with you?'

'I am going to the pie shop. I must not be long.' She looked back anxiously at the house.

'This will not take much time. Does your uncle speak of the girls from the house in Lime Grove?'

'He says they are wicked, sir, and a warning to young women. He says that those who fall from the paths of virtue are damned.'

'Have you heard him speak of Patience Brooke?'

'No, sir.'

'Does you uncle go out much at night?'

She was puzzled at the turn of the questions, but answered willingly enough. 'Yes, sir, he visits the poor of our congregation to give them instruction if they have not come to chapel.'

'What time does he come home?'

'I don't know, sir. I am sent to bed early.'

'Last Friday night,' Jones trod carefully, 'was your uncle out of the house at his visiting?'

'Yes, sir, but I had to send the boy to find him. My aunt, she has lost her wits, fell out of her bed. I heard the bump. I was frightened. I had not strength enough to lift her so I sent for Uncle and he came.'

'At what time?'

'It was near ten o'clock, sir, for after he came, I heard the church clock strike the hour.'

'Are you happy at your uncle's?' asked Dickens.

The anxious look shadowed her face again, and he noticed the faint red on her neck rising to her cheeks. 'They gave me a home, sir, and I must be grateful. My aunt is bedridden, and I have much to do to care for her. My uncle can be stern, but I am sometimes deserving of correction. I must go now — he will be angry if I am too long.' She was impatient to be gone, shifting from one foot to the other.

'Thank you, Alice. You may go now.'

'Thank you, sir.' She scampered away into the darkness.

'I wonder what form his anger takes,' said Jones. 'A beating, I shouldn't wonder — deserving of correction, indeed.'

'I expect he enjoys it. It is interesting that the aunt has lost her wits, as the girl said. It leaves her very much in his power.'

'And he is a man of appetite, I think.'

85

'Yes, there was something about his mouth that repelled me, plump and voluptuous. And his hands — that thick whiteness was somehow horrible.' Dickens shuddered.

'And the girl's hands were red and work-worn, and the nails bitten down — signs of too much drudgery and anxiety. Poor girl, I wonder whether she will escape his clutches.'

'Clutches is the word. He is a lascivious knave, a fool, a canting hypocrite but not a murderer, I think,' said Dickens.

'No, indeed. I am not sorry, in a way. I do not think I could stomach him again.'

'I've thought of something,' said Dickens.

'What?'

'The name Alice Brown made me remember someone. You said we must try to find out how Patience came to the Home. I was thinking whether she had met someone who had once been with us. The name Alice Brown reminded me of Alice Drown, a girl who left us. She vanished over the garden wall, dressed in her Sunday cloak and bonnet. She was not troublesome like Isabella. She was too good-natured for that — a big, laughing, blowsy girl. I knew in my heart that the place was too small for her — too confined. When I mentioned the races at Goodwood to her, she said she wished she could go, too. She had a fancy for cold chicken and champagne, if you please. She'd been in prison for theft of a hat — with red feathers, she said, as if she regretted the feathers more than the sentence. But, before that she'd been on the stage. Patience must have met someone from the home — Alice is one possibility; there are few others whose fate we do not know.'

'But could we find her?'

'She had a brother —' Dickens paused as if he were about to produce a rabbit out of a top hat — which he was — 'Edward

Drown — I remember because of the singularity of the name, and the contiguous singularity of his calling — he is or was — a longshoreman.'

Jones laughed, 'Are you sure you didn't make him up? He sounds like a character in one of your books.'

'No, I am sure I did not, though I rather wish I had. I remember writing the name in the casebook I keep about the girls — Edward Drown or Drown-Ed, as I thought of him. And, I remember where he lived — Jacob's Island — he was a longshoreman down there. Surely we can find him?'

'We will look. We can engage the services of the river police — it's not a place we should go unaccompanied. We should go towards the end of the day, when he might be at home. It's a grim place and dangerous — apart from the risks of cholera — ' he gave an ironical smile — 'there are the prigs, the fences, the cracksmen, the murderers and the laggers who infest the place. But, you know it, of course.'

'Research, of course; I wasn't fencing the family silver! I went with the river police — and you're right, it's a sinister place — just the place for Bill Sikes. But, I don't think Drown is a criminal. As far as I recall, Alice Drown said he was a respectable man who earned an honest living.'

'That'll make him easier to find then. Now, I will tell you what I was thinking. First, I would like you, when you can, to talk to the Reverend Goodchild. I want to know the truth about Francis Fidge. I feel him on my conscience. He's an unhappy man, and I'd like to leave him alone to find whatever peace he can. Secondly, as I am a man and not a spirit, I am hungry and my mind dwells on that pie shop Alice Brown spoke of.'

They walked away from Sepulchre Lane to a street with a few shops. They saw Alice Brown buying her pies, and waited across the road until she came out. As they approached the door, Dickens said, 'I used to sing the song of the cat's meat man when I was a boy — it was one of my most successful turns; the words are engraved on my memory — *Fango, dango, with his barrow and his can!*' He grinned at Jones, 'Not that I was suggesting —'

'Yes, you were, but this looks a respectable place. You will join me?'

Jones handed over a penny apiece, 'My treat,' he said with a grin. They ate the eel and mutton pies when they reached the precise temperature at which they were delicious to swallow, and they were good with tender chunks of meat and golden crisp pastry. They went back into the cold air to find the omnibus which would take them back to London.

'I dine out tonight,' said Dickens. 'When shall we begin our search for Drown-Ed?'

'Tomorrow, I think. Are you able to go down to the Home then?'

'I've work to do in the morning. I'll go down in the afternoon to see the Reverend Goodchild. Then I can go and consult my book at the Home, and check that Mrs Morson is managing. She looked very tired when I left. I said I would see about getting some help for her. I must go home then, but I will send you a report if I find out anything about Francis Fidge which is urgent. You and I might dine together on Monday in the early evening before we visit the river.'

'Come to my house at five o'clock. We can talk more easily over supper there — if you do not object to Elizabeth hearing what we say.'

'I do not.'

'Remember Posy — she is — er — ambitious.'

'Oh, court dress, is it? I have not enough faith in my legs for white stockings!'

'I think she will accept a bright waistcoat — perhaps brass buttons — and the diamond pin might pass muster.'

Dickens laughed, 'It shall be done.'

The green omnibus was waiting with the conductor standing on a step next to the door, steadying himself by holding onto a leather strap fixed high on the back of the bus. Inside, the bus was narrow and cramped; there was a layer of straw on the floor, damp and dirty now from the feet of the many travellers who had passed to and from town. They stepped in to join the company of passengers. There were not many at this time, a girl, perhaps the maid in a grand house, returning from a Sunday visit home with a basket of fruit; a portly man in a well-worn greatcoat; a young woman with a scrap of a baby in a dingy shawl and a pale clerkly looking young man reading a pamphlet. With a jolt, the omnibus started. It would take them from Shepherd's Bush along the Bayswater Road through Notting Hill to Oxford Street where Dickens and Jones would go their separate ways, Sam Jones to Bow Street then home to his Elizabeth, and Dickens to dine with Mark Lemon, editor of *Punch* magazine and John Forster at Forster's lodgings at number 58, Lincoln's Inn Fields.

10: A Face in a Crowd

Dickens, having furnished Miss Murdstone with her hard steel purse and jail of a bag on its heavy chain, and condemned Clara Copperfield and her son to a life of subjection to the Murdstone tyranny, tidied his papers and laid down his pen after cleaning it with Poll's pen-wiper. He was satisfied with his morning's work on his novel and he had written a tactful letter to Miss Coutts, whom he must find time to see. Now he was ready to go in search of the Reverend Goodchild. He usually walked in the afternoons alone or with John Forster on whom he intended to call before taking a fly to Shepherd's Bush.

He walked down Devonshire Place towards Margaret Street, turning left into Oxford Street, along to High Holborn, and into Gate Street. At Whetstone Place, he stopped to listen to a group of handcart organists who had stationed themselves on the corner. The organ was a curiously convoluted piece of machinery with its pipes and metal reeds supplemented by bells, drums, triangles, gongs and symbols emitting a cacophony of sound not exactly pleasing to the ear. What attracted Dickens was the drama on the puppet stage where figures about fourteen inches high were clothed in exotic purples and gold, tinsel and spangles. There was Daniel in the lion's den, a Grand Turk with his scimitar, and Nebuchadnezzar wearing a golden crown. Dickens, who loved the theatre, was entranced, though how, he wondered, had Napoleon got himself among this Eastern tribe?

Laughter and applause followed each amazing feat, especially when Queen Victoria drew her sword to lay about the enemy. How she came there, Dickens could not imagine, but he dipped into his pocket like everyone else. Looking through the dispersing crowd, he saw a face. It was a man with a crooked face. He had a fleeting impression of a pale face, dark, brushed back hair and of furtiveness. That was all. The face vanished then reappeared, its body with it, walking down Whetstone Place towards Lincoln's Inn Fields. Dickens was sure — he started off in pursuit but the crowd was stupidly wandering in all directions, and he found himself entangled in a woman's skirt and then almost tripped up by a dog on a piece of rope.

'Gerrout of it!' a rough voice cried out.

'By all means,' said Dickens, stepping back to avoid the snapping jaws of the man. The dog looked apologetic. He found himself eye to wall eye with a skewbald horse attached to a cart carrying an assortment of pecking hens. God, he thought, it's like being in a malignant Noah's Ark. Freeing himself, he pushed his way through that portion of people going along Whetstone Place. He dashed to the end of the street and looked quickly right, down to where Searle Street joined Carey Street and left towards High Holborn, but his quarry had vanished. He stood catching his breath. There was no way of knowing which way he had gone. But what Dickens did know was that his man with a crooked face was not a pedlar — he was a man in the black suit and white collar of a clerk, and it was possible that he was going to Lincoln's Inn. Perhaps it was not Davey's twisted face, but it would be worth investigating, a job for Constable Rogers, perhaps. He had not time now to visit John — that would keep.

Going into Crown Street, he passed the stationer's shop. He couldn't resist the temptation and went in to find the three shop assistants waiting for custom. He couldn't help wondering if anyone had been in since Sunday, and, he thought, surely there must be some adult in charge sometimes.

But the shopkeepers looked cheerful enough, and Miss Eleanor Brim greeted him with the words, 'May we help you, Mr Dickens? You know our stock.'

Indeed he did, and found himself asking for a quire of paper which he didn't need. Having paid for it, he enquired whether he could leave it for collection. Miss Brim was gracious and lamented that they did not have a delivery service as Tom was far too young to have such a responsibility. The door opened, and in shot a piece of boyhood, or girlhood — it was difficult to tell since there were only a long, thatch of straggling black hair and a pair of ragged boots to be seen as the person slid along the wooden floor to land in a heap by the counter.

'Our friend, Scrap,' offered Eleanor. Poll barked a greeting and Tom nodded.

'Obliged to meet you,' said Dickens.

'Same 'ere.' Scrap was a boy, a thing of shreds and patches with an engaging grin.

'Why were you rushing, Scrap?' asked Eleanor.

'Chased,' replied the laconic Scrap. 'Lost 'em down the gate.'

'Who?' enquired Dickens.

'Pa — wants me 'ome, 'e sez, but I ain't goin' — not yet anyways. I'm visitin' today.'

'Where do you live?'

'Dials. Stay 'ere sometimes — on guard like.'

'On guard?'

'Scrap protects us when our father isn't here, when he goes on business — or something. We met him when he saved Poll's life. Poll was nearly taken by a man, but Scrap grabbed her. Brave boy.'

'Nasty prig, he woz, wiv his light 'ooks. Thort they woz mugs and he'd play a quiff on 'em but Scrap knew 'is chivvy. We does a scoot an' leaves 'im way behind.'

'Didn't go for the slop then?' enquired Dickens who enjoyed street language, and had got the gist of Scrap's speech.

Scrap looked at this newcomer with respect. 'Nah. Niver seen 'im agin. Lagged most like.'

'Do you know your way about the streets here?'

'Course. I knows all the alleys, the topers, the back streets.'

'Might I offer you sixpence for some watching? Do you know Whetstone Place and Lincoln's Inn Fields?'

'Course I does. Who'm I lookin' for?'

'A man with a crooked face, dressed in black, or he might be dressed as a pedlar. Pale face and black hair brushed back. Something not right about him.'

'Blimey. Wot's he done?'

'I don't know yet, but he might be dangerous. Don't let him see you if you find him. Just leave a message here, if that is all right, Miss Brim.'

'Certainly, as long as Scrap isn't in any danger.'

''E won't catch me, Miss Nell, I got me lamps everywhere. I ain't no mug.'

'Be careful, Scrap. Here's the sixpence, and another if you find him. I'll come back here tomorrow, or the next day. Goodbye to you all.'

Dickens made his way to catch the fly, hoping that he would not be putting Scrap in danger. He seemed to be a smart lad who knew his way about, preferring to run rather than turn and face danger — he'd be all right. And what about the other three? Who was looking after them apart from Scrap? Observant, Dickens had noted Eleanor Brim's hesitation over the words 'or something'. And why should they need protecting?

Dickens took the fast fly carriage to St Mark's where he found the Reverend Goodchild in the church. There was no sign of Francis Fidge.

'Mr Dickens, I am glad to see you as always. I am sorry I missed you the other day.' The old man's shrewd eyes twinkled. He knew they had been there and, perhaps, what had passed between the superintendent, Dickens and Francis Fidge.

'I am sorry that I did not pay you the courtesy of a visit but —'

'You and the superintendent had questions to ask.'

'About Patience Brooke — she is missing.'

'He has confessed all.'

Dickens's heart jumped. He had been convinced that Francis Fidge was guilty of nothing — only a hopeless love for a woman who had rejected him.

'All?' he asked, dreading the answer.

'His love for a girl who could not return his feelings, his loss of faith, his loathing of his work, and his desire to go from here.'

'I must tell you the truth — which the superintendent could not disclose to Mr Fidge. Patience Brooke is dead — murdered.'

'That is terrible news, dreadful. That poor girl. I shall pray for her — a sad young woman, I thought. But, Mr Dickens, I can assure you, and the superintendent, that Francis Fidge is not a murderer. He would have confessed it. You know that he is dying.'

'I do. I saw his face and the red that burns in it.' Dickens felt that the old man was right, but he needed proof for Sam. That was why he had come.

'You need proof.' Goodchild was a mind-reader. 'When did she die?'

'On Friday night at about ten o'clock.'

'Then you need not fear. I was with him. He was very ill that night with a fever. I did not leave him.'

'I am glad, so glad. He has suffered so. I did not want him to be a murderer — nor did Superintendent Jones, but we had to know for the sake of Patience. We can look elsewhere now. What will he do?'

'He will stay here. He is too sick to go anywhere. My housekeeper, Mrs Wilkes, will nurse him, and I will try to bring him back to the love of God who loves him, and he will die in peace.'

'Thank you for your kindness, Mr Goodchild. I know that you will keep him safe. I must go now to the Home to see Mrs Morson.'

'Farewell then. I hope you will find whoever did this and bring him to justice.'

That reminded Dickens. 'I need to ask one more thing if I may.' Goodchild nodded. 'Have you seen any strangers in the last week or so — a pedlar, perhaps?'

'Yes. I noticed a man with his pedlar's tray, sitting here in the churchyard — a couple of weeks ago — let me think. It was a Friday, yes, about two weeks ago.'

'You're sure?' asked Dickens, remembering that the pedlar had sold his ribbons and pins at the Home a week before Patience had been killed.

'Yes, I remember because there was snow on the ground, though it's supposed to be spring. But it was a bright day. He looked a poor wretch. I felt for him travelling about in the bitter cold. He was sitting on that tombstone just looking about him. I would have offered him something, but I was going out to visit a sick parishioner.'

'Was anyone else about?'

'Francis Fidge and Patience had walked through the churchyard into the lane beyond.'

'Did he see them?'

'I do not know. Would that be important?'

'It might be — I don't know — I'm just trying to put things together.'

'There was one thing — that is if you are trying to find him.' Dickens knew what Goodchild was going to say. 'He had a crooked face.'

Bidding farewell to Reverend Goodchild, Dickens turned and went through the churchyard to go to the Home. He walked slowly, thinking about the significance of what he had heard. The crooked-faced pedlar who might — just might — be a clerk in Whetstone Place, Patience Brooke and Francis Fidge were linked, but how? Francis Fidge was not the murderer — that was not in doubt now — but if the pedlar had seen Patience and Francis and thought they were lovers then that suggested some motive. Was the man with the twisted face the lover of Patience Brooke, the one because of whom she would never love again? If he were that clerk then Dickens thought he would hardly be the former lover of Patience Brooke — not that quiet girl he had known. The man in the suit had looked so — unwholesome. That was the word. But people made the oddest pairings, he reflected. Or was he, as Dickens had thought before, just the agent of another as yet unknown? Whichever, he must be found. Dickens hoped that Scrap might find out a man with a crooked face round about Lincoln's Inn. Such a man would not be difficult to spot. He would go to Crown Street tomorrow. In the meantime, he should see Mrs Morson.

Little Jenny Ding, once of Clerkenwell Workhouse, let him in. She would be a success, he thought. She was pretty and enjoyed her responsibility as chief door-keeper, taking his hat and coat and placing it carefully on the hall table. She was quick at her lessons too, according to Mrs Morson. The house was quiet. Mrs Morson was in her little sitting-room poring over her account books. Some of the girls were in the garden tending to their plots under the supervision of James Bagster; some were sewing or reading according to their preference.

'All quiet?' he asked as he came into the room.

'Yes, thank heaven, though these accounts are disturbing my peace. I've added up the bills for January and the total is,' she looked at her paper and bills, 'forty-three pounds and sixteen shillings. That seems right, does it not?' She looked at him anxiously. 'That includes James's salary and the fire insurance.'

'It is in line with other months. If you give me the bills, I will enter them in my book and pay them. Have you enough petty cash? Would another five pounds be useful?'

'It would, thank you.' She took the proffered note and put it in her desk.

'How is Lizzie Dagg now?'

'She is quiet and getting on with her work, but she is often tearful still. I wonder —'

'What? There is something else?'

Mrs Morson looked at him with her frank, grey eyes. 'I was a doctor's wife,' she began, 'I have learned things that you may think a lady ought not to know, but our circumstances were unusual. Out in Cuyaba, out there in the wilderness, it was not possible to — be — too fastidious — birth and death — disease were our daily companions. What I am saying is that my husband told me many things. I think that what is troubling Lizzie is physical. You heard her say that something was wrong with her and that Francis Fidge would hate her if he knew. I suspect that she is suffering from a disease contracted in her past life. She needs to be frank with Doctor Brown so that he can treat her.'

Dickens understood. 'I'll write to him and explain what you think, and ask him for a private appointment.'

'Thank you. She may improve in spirits if her health improves.'

'And Isabella, and Sesina, they have quietened down?'

Mrs Morson looked troubled. She didn't like to burden him with more difficulties, but she was wary of secrets now and what they might lead to. She would tell him her thoughts, however disturbed he might be. What she had to tell him was something she had only ever discussed with her husband and that because she had wondered about two of the European wives whose husbands were employed at the Cuyaba Silver Mine.

'I have said that my husband was a doctor and that abroad our lives were unusual. We came into contact with strange people, people who were lonely, exiled from their families, women especially — those whose husbands ill-treated them, who formed close relationships with other women ...' She paused to organise her thoughts. This was difficult. What would Dickens think of her?

'You are telling me that you think there may be an unhealthy relationship between Isabella and Sesina?' he said, his tone perfectly calm.

'I don't know. I even think that they may be pretending, trying to shock me into saying something so that they, in turn, can be shocked and offended, and have cause for complaint to you — about me. They are flirtatious with each other; Isabella behaves like a lover to Sesina, and she responds. It is hard to describe — you have to see them, and they won't do it in front of you. Isabella is too clever for that. And, at the moment, they have a room to themselves. I wonder. It is not so uncommon, and they are both of high animal spirits, Isabella especially. Sesina enjoys the petting, being the favourite, receiving the kisses — which might seem innocent, but —'

Dickens sensed her discomfort, her fear of his reaction. Of course, he knew of these things, but he had never spoken to a woman of them. He did not doubt that Isabella would love to shock, and he was angry that she might pretend such a thing to upset Mrs Morson and disturb the house. As for its being real, that was also a problem he had not foreseen. He determined to be practical.

'It is clear that you can't say anything; that you can't challenge them for the eminently sensible reasons you have given. At the same time, this is a serious disturbance for the Home. It is far more problematic than Jemima Hiscock's drunkenness and we had to expel her. Isabella Gordon will have to go.'

'Upon what grounds?'

'We'll have to wait. But, from what you say, Isabella is becoming more daring, and she will, I think, cause more trouble yet and give us the grounds we need. In the meantime, I counsel you to ignore the flirting, and she'll find something else to challenge you with. I'm glad you told me — I know it was difficult,' he said, smiling at her with sympathy.

'Thank you. I knew I must speak for we know now the danger of secrets.'

'We do. I've been to see the Reverend Goodchild who has given me proof that Francis Fidge is not our murderer. The reverend was with him all Friday night. Fidge is a sick man. He is dying of consumption. I knew it when the superintendent and I spoke with him.'

'Poor man. I guessed it, too. I knew from the hollow cough and the fever in his eyes and cheeks, and from how thin he was. I am glad that he is not guilty of killing her. What are you to do next?'

'We have discounted Obadiah Godsmark — we have proof that he was at home that Friday. We have wondered how Patience Brooke came here, and I thought she might have heard of us from a girl who had left us. I know it is a remote possibility. I thought of Alice Drown — you remember her?'

She smiled, 'How could I forget? Good-hearted, though, despite her taste for gin.'

'The superintendent and I are going to try to find her brother who worked as a longshoreman at Jacob's Island. He might know where she is.'

'And the pedlar?'

'I think I saw him — in London. At least I saw a man with a crooked face in a crowd. However, he was not dressed as a pedlar. He was wearing a black suit. I'm not sure whether it is the same man but it's an odd coincidence. It troubles me so I have someone looking out for him — a smart lad. I find out tomorrow if he has had any success.'

'When will you come back?'

'I don't know but I will write to you telling of our progress, and you must write to me if you have any more trouble with Miss Gordon. If you do, I'll come at once. I have written to Miss Coutts and I will have to see her and try to get some help.'

'I was going to ask about that. James has a sister, Ellen, who would come to help with the girls. I need someone to take charge when I am absent, and I must take some of the girls out — being cooped up here will only increase their fractiousness. I am afraid they will quarrel if they do not have some freedom.'

'Perhaps, James and his sister could take a group out to start with — perhaps Isabella — not with Sesina — and three of the other girls — then, another day you could take another group. It does concern me that we're taking on another person without proper procedure.'

'We do know James, and I have met his sister who is a sensible widow — like me —' she laughed — 'and I am certain we could trust her. She is willing to sleep in. It would help me greatly.'

'Very well. I shall tell all to Miss Coutts — no secrets, and I will explain how restless the girls are. I will not, however, tell her too much about Isabella and Sesina. She might be too shocked.'

They laughed together, ease restored between them. They parted still friends despite what she had had to tell him or perhaps because of the intimacy they had shared. Dickens could not imagine such a conversation with Catherine. A surprising and interesting woman, Mrs Georgiana Morson.

Dickens walked to the village where he hoped to find a cab to take him back to London. He thought of Georgiana's disturbing revelations. He was shocked, more at Isabella's malice, if it be so, than the possibility of a love affair between the two women. He could not understand such love, but he would not condemn it. He was a novelist, fascinated by all aspects of human passion. It was difficult to write about sex in the society in which he lived, impossible, in fact, yet sexual corruption and prostitution were rife. That was the paradox, he thought, sexual desire was hidden yet it was powerful enough to drive men to prostitutes, to adultery, and women, too, both even to murder. He wondered again about Isabella Gordon. Had she approached Patience in that way? Had Patience rejected her and had that led to murder? No, for all her faults, he still did not see Isabella as a murderer. She was corrupt, no doubt, and though he hated to think it, vicious, but that was the result of the life she had led, and, he thought regretfully, she was probably not saveable.

He hurried on. He wanted to get home. Ought he to go to Bow Street to tell Sam about Francis Fidge? He would want to know. No, send a note. Topping, the coachman, could take it.

11: Constable Rogers Has an Idea

Dickens was glad to be home. There had been no cab at Shepherd's Bush, so he had been forced to return on the green omnibus, and there were no seats inside. He had been obliged to climb onto the roof of the carriage and take an uncomfortable ride on the 'knife-board', that narrow, uncomfortable seat on top. It had come on to rain, too, and he had endured a jolting ride next to a thin, gloomy-looking carpenter who seemed to be made of pieces of wood which poked him in the side at every bump. And sneaking drops of rain managed to insinuate themselves down his upturned collar to trickle coldly down his neck.

He took off his sodden coat and ruined hat, and went upstairs to the drawing-room. The fire-dappled room looked snug. Catherine, her eyes closed, lay on the sofa with the baby in its bassinette beside her and there was little Alfred, aged three and a few months, sitting at the end of the sofa staring solemnly at the fire. Francis, aged five, was sitting on the carpet playing with a wooden horse. Dickens went over to his wife, lifted Alfred up to sit him on his knee. He took Catherine's hand, feeling a surge of tenderness for her soft prettiness in the peaceful scene. She looked plump and fresh-coloured in the firelight; he still admired her small retroussé nose and little red mouth. She opened her blue eyes and saw him there.

'Charles, you are here.'

'I am, my dear, here, in the flesh which is something fish-like in consistency. I have just had a bumpy ride in an omnibus from Shepherd's Bush. My bones still rattle.'

'Would you like tea? I can send for some fresh.'

'Not yet, let me sit awhile.'

He shifted the child on his knee so that he could see him better. The boy gazed at his father, and touched a raindrop on his chin. 'Wet,' he said, puzzled.

Dickens laughed. Alfred D'Orsay Tennyson Dickens, not much like the poet who was his godfather, he thought, grinning at his own folly in naming this plump infant with a butter smear on his cheek after the immensely tall, grave, bushy-haired man who resembled a stork which had found its nest unaccountably round its neck. Poets should look like Keats, he mused, remembering Severn's portrait of the young poet gazing into the distance with his bright, dreaming eyes.

'And novelists,' he said laughing out loud, 'should look like Mr Dickens, the Inimitable.'

Alfred D'Orsay Tennyson laughed too and Francis, desiring attention also, brought his horse. 'Charger,' he said, proudly showing off the new word.

'*Ride a cock horse to Banbury Cross,*' Dickens sang, '*to buy Alley and Frankey a galloping horse.*'

'*To buy Alley and Frankey a galloping horse,*' the boys repeated, delighted that Papa had put in their names, instead of Johnny's.

Dickens stood up with a boy under each arm, singing, '*And they shall both ride till they can ride no more.*' Round and round they went. Catherine looked on as he whirled them about. Dickens put them down. 'Papa can gallop no more. You big boys are too much for him.'

Catherine said, 'Both of you play with the horses.' Happily, they went back to the rug to play their complicated games with horses and riders.

'You are tired, my dear.'

'I am,' agreed Dickens, closing his eyes. They sat on in the comfortable firelight. Let time stand still, thought Dickens, grant me this peace just for a while. But Time would rush on like a hurrying pedestrian, poking and jolting through the crowd, heedless of the blows he gave, marching sternly onward, grim-faced through eternity.

At the same time at Bow Street, Superintendent Jones and Constable Rogers were piecing together what information they had. Jones had Dickens's note on his desk. He had been glad to know that Francis Fidge was not the murderer.

'Since we now know that Francis Fidge, the curate of St Mark's, is not our man, and we know that Godsmark is not, then we are left with the mysterious singing pedlar with the crooked face — distinctive, and yet, according to Constable Jenkins who has sent me his report, though he was seen on the Friday before the murder, he was not seen at any time after, which is odd, since you would think that he might have been about if he had found customers at the Home. I wonder,' he paused, getting his ideas into order, 'if he came that Friday, two weeks ago, deliberately to give a message to Patience Brooke for a meeting with him —'

'Or someone else,' said Rogers, interrupting eagerly. 'He mighta been set on by someone else, someone from her past.'

'That might well be the case. I was going to say that he might have been proposing a meeting the following Friday — it makes sense. A week hence — it would be easy to remember.'

'But, then, it mighta given Patience a chance to run away.'

'So, we are assuming that the message would have been from someone she did not want to see which rather negates the idea of an appointment in a week's time. Unless, it was someone she felt she had to see — something so important that she waited. If only we had found a note! Still, we cannot do anything about that. We have to find him — but where to look? We'll just have to keep Jenkins on it. God knows, he hasn't much else to do out there. I have asked him to keep an eye on the Home — let's hope he has the wits to cope with that.'

'I had an idea, sir. It came to me as I was readin' the paper. You know those notices that ask about missin' persons — I've got one here. Look, it says: *Missing. — Young man. Aged twenty years, of pale complexion with dark hair. Last seen leaving his place of employment in Chancery Lane.* I wonder if anyone advertised that Patience was missin'. The murderer found her at the Home, didn't he?'

'Sound thought, Rogers. Someone found out where she was and that's as good a way as any.' Rogers's eager face was suffused with red right up to his large ears. 'I think it's worth following up. She arrived at the Home about six months ago — that would be September so it would be sensible for you to go to the newspaper office and check their earlier numbers, to see if you can find any reference to her in the personal columns. We should be able to find out who placed the notice, and that —'

'Might lead us to her — or to her family, if she had one, or fiancée, or even husband —' Rogers's words tumbled out in his enthusiasm. Jones's face stopped him — 'What?' exclaimed Rogers, startled.

It was as if a light had shone a beam in a dark corner. Jones said, 'You said husband. We hadn't thought of that, and I've remembered two things that were said about her that might be explained if she had a husband which are: first, James Bagster thought she had had a child, and, second, Francis Fidge told us that Patience had said she could never love again. Mr Dickens picked up on that. Well, Rogers, you are a genius. Two brilliant ideas in one half hour.'

Rogers beamed, his red face shining. To please the superintendent was his daily goal, and now, to be called 'genius', it was like getting a medal. 'What now?'

'Tomorrow, you go to the newspaper — but which? You might as well start with the one you have there. Remember, discretion. Tell no one — you are on a special investigation for me, if anyone asks. Tomorrow evening, we meet the river police at Wapping Stairs. You'll come with me and Mr Dickens. We search for Edward Drown — let's hope we find him. I will ask that a lookout is kept for our man with a crooked face — just on the grounds that he's wanted on suspicion of theft. If he is spotted, you and I, and Mr Dickens, will bring him in. Now I'm going home to my wife. I'll see you in the morning.'

Jones whistled as he went on his way; the tune of the old song of Edmund, poor peasant boy wafted on the air as he walked up Drury Lane to the junction with Queen Street.

A dark shape hurrying down an alleyway in the direction of Whetstone Place heard. The figure stopped under the sickly light of a gas lamp. The crooked face grinned and then walked on, whistling the same tune.

12: At Norfolk Street

On Tuesday, Dickens stood at the window gazing at a morning of lowering cloud and slanting rain. He was thinking about *Macbeth*. As a boy in Chatham, he had seen the play at the Theatre Royal. It had been the witches that had impressed his imagination most, their terrifying incantations in the flaring footlights, and the impossible fact to him, as a boy, that they bore an awful resemblance to the thanes of Scotland. Later, he had seen William Macready in the role; this time it was the murderer who had harrowed him with fear and wonder. It was the wearing away of the man by his guilt, the terrible suffering had held Dickens spellbound. And his wife, driven to madness and suicide. He thought of Sikes fleeing from Nancy's bloodied face — even Sikes knew guilt as he wandered like Cain, pursued by the glassy, blind eyes of his victim. Dickens had written that the murderer does not escape justice in the agony of his fear, but he wondered about the man who had sung as he crept away into the darkness from Patience Brooke. He saw in his imagination the crooked face twisted into a smile and he shuddered, glad now that he had not caught up with him in some dingy alley. He hoped too that the boy Scrap had not come near him.

Work first — David Copperfield was to go to school, Mr Creakle's establishment, where he would wear as his introduction to the institution a placard announcing that "he bites". Next he would write his report on Francis Fidge and the pedlar, and his sighting of a man with a crooked face in Whetstone Place. He would finish his article on the orphanage at Tooting Fields. He would then go to see Miss Coutts, and ask about employing James Bagster's sister — Dickens would have to persuade her for Mrs Morson's sake; that done, he would make his way to the stationer's shop to see if Scrap had any news. Then he could take his finished article to John Forster at the offices of *The Examiner*.

There was a customer in the stationery shop — a portly man with a white waistcoat embellished with a heavy gold chain. He looked prosperous and ill-tempered. Dickens listened.

'I am afraid Father is not here,' Eleanor was saying politely. Tom and Poll obviously had their heads down under the counter.

'When will he be here?' barked the man impatiently.

'Tomorrow, perhaps; may I help you?'

The man did not answer, but walked swiftly to the door, banging it as he went out. Dickens felt the silence left by the jangling bell and looked at Eleanor, whose little face wore an anxious frown. Before he had time to speak, the door burst open and Scrap flew in. Tom and Poll popped up from behind the counter.

'Chased,' said Dickens, sympathetically.

'Nah — jest in a rush. 'Oo's that cove wot went out, Miss Nell? Bad-tempered, 'e looked.'

'Just someone wanting Father,' she said.

'Oh — y'awright, then?'

'Yes, Scrap, don't worry.' An understanding seemed to pass between them, Dickens thought, but exactly what he could not fathom. He would keep his eye on them when he could.

Eleanor filled the gap. 'Here is Mr Dickens, Scrap.'

'Have you seen him?' he asked Scrap.

'Nah — watched the street like you sed, watched at Lincoln's Inn and the fields, but nuffink. I can keep watchin' if yer wants.' Scrap looked at him hopefully. Dickens knew that another few sixpences would be more than welcome.

'Yes, if you will, Scrap. I would be very pleased to employ you until you spot him — would sixpence a day be sufficient — and a bonus when you have found him?'

The boy's eyes gleamed, 'Yes, sir. Trust me — I'll find 'im for yer.'

Dickens thought of the cold-blooded singer with his twisted face, 'Mind Scrap, do not go near him — just watch.' He had an idea suddenly. 'Try Gray's Inn, up Chancery Lane, across High Holborn.'

'I will, sir. When yer coming back?'

'I'm not sure, perhaps tomorrow. Leave a message with Miss Eleanor. If that is acceptable?' he enquired of the girl.

'Yes, we shall be glad to see you at any time, Mr Dickens.'

'Goodbye, then.'

'Goodbye, Mr Dickens, and thank you.'

Dickens left the shop. He had time to go to the offices of *The Examiner* and see John Forster on whom he had neglected to call the previous day. As he walked, he wondered. Perhaps his crooked man and Davey's were not the same at all — there were plenty of odd-looking people about. Yet, there had been something about the face, something darting, something which suggested a man with something to hide — an impression, certainly, but a powerful one. It was worth Scrap looking at Gray's Inn. He had assumed that his crooked man was going to Lincoln's Inn, but he could be a clerk at Gray's Inn where Dickens had started his career as a lawyer's clerk. He thought, too, about Eleanor and Tom and the bad-tempered man in the shop, and Eleanor's wordless communication with Scrap. Something was not quite right there. He would have to find an opportunity to ask about the absent father. After seeing John, he would go home and change for the early supper with Sam and his wife. He remembered Sam's words about Posy — it was time to put on the coat with the brass buttons, the bright waistcoat — and the diamond pin.

Dickens knocked at the door of number 20, Norfolk Street. It opened suddenly as if someone had been waiting just inside, which Posy had. She took Dickens's greatcoat and his hat, laying them reverently on the hall table. She looked at him approvingly. Here was company indeed. Opening the parlour door, she announced, 'Mr Charles Dickens.' Elizabeth came forward to meet him, smiling at the child's gravity.

'Good evening, Mr Dickens,' she said with the right amount of formality, 'and thank you, Posy.' Posy bobbed a curtsey to both and went out.

The room was small and neat in the firelight which glowed on the glasses and silverware arranged on a small table. It was obviously a quiet and well-loved home. There were candles on the mantel over which a gilt mirror shone reflecting the dark-haired Elizabeth in her deep red dress, and Dickens whose diamond pin caught the light. She smiled again at him.

'How do you like our parlour maid? She is changed is she not?'

'She is. You have looked after her well. When I think what she was. She is a credit to you.'

'And to herself. She looks forward, she is eager to learn and has much potential, I think.'

'Indeed. What she might have been does not bear thinking about. I have written about that shocking place at Tooting where she started out. It was brutally conducted and vilely kept, a hateful pace and a stain on a civilised land.' Dickens was fierce. He had fulminated in *The Examiner* against the orphanage run by Benjamin Drouet who had been brought to trial for manslaughter then acquitted in the teeth of the evidence that the cholera victims in his care had been left starving and without medical care. Posy, who had no idea of her age or birthday, had started life at the orphanage after which she had been apprenticed to an artificial flower maker whose business had collapsed. Posy's discoloured teeth had been created by the poison used to dye the artificial leaves, arsenite of copper, probably. Posy had lived on the streets until Dickens found her, like Davey, hunched in a doorway where she was offering a pitiful bunch of dilapidated flowers for sale.

Elizabeth saw how the passion of his indignation glowed in his luminous eyes. She had read his articles in *The Examiner* and she had read his books. He was extraordinary, yet oddly vulnerable in his slightness. She was nearly as tall as he. She could understand Sam's liking for him and the almost protectiveness of her husband towards Charles Dickens, a man whose fame should give him all the confidence in the world, and yet who looked at Sam sometimes as if he envied him.

'I am sorry, Mrs Jones, to go on so but this is a matter close to my heart.'

'Elizabeth, please.' She smiled at him and he admired her rich, glossy brown hair, dark eyes and dark rose complexion. Sam Jones was a fortunate man in having this lovely, bright woman as his wife. 'I share your feelings,' she said, 'and so does Sam who sees so much misery in his work.'

'He's a good man,' said Dickens. 'I admire him for his good heart and his toughness. He has been so careful in this matter we are investigating.'

'Yes, he has told me of Patience Brooke and your determination to find out who killed her.'

Sam Jones came in. 'I'm sorry, my love, to be so late. I've been delayed at Bow Street. Charles, I am glad to see you here. Let's eat now.'

Elizabeth went out to return with Posy and the food: almond soup followed by beef a la mode, and then baked apple dumplings. They talked of Patience Brooke, and Dickens told of the disappointment that Scrap had not yet found the man he had seen in Whetstone Place, of Dickens's suspicion that the man he had seen was Davey's man with the crooked face, and of his idea for Scrap to extend his search to Gray's Inn. He told them about Eleanor Brim, Tom and Poll, and his anxieties about who was looking after them. Elizabeth thought she might visit the shop — she might befriend them and find out more. Sam told them of Rogers's idea about the missing persons notice, and he reported their discussion of Patience having perhaps been married and had a child.

'Then it might be as you thought, Sam; that our man with the crooked face is not necessarily the murderer — he may be acting for someone. It would be hard to imagine Patience married to such a man. Think of Davey's fear of him, and the glimpse I had made me shudder — I know, Sam, it was only a glimpse — but I had an impression of something unwholesome.'

'We need to do two things — find our unwholesome pedlar and find your Alice Drown. Either one might be able to point us in the direction of Patience's earlier life — and family, if she had one.'

'I wonder about the possibility of a child,' said Elizabeth. 'Perhaps he or she died. That may be why Patience left her husband.' Sam shot a concerned glance at her but she only said, 'It's all right, my dear. There are secrets here that throw light on the murder. I'm sure of it. Someone hated her — think

of what he did to her. Someone who felt she had betrayed him
—'

'Or someone who had something to gain from her death — who wanted something that her death might gain him,' said Dickens.

'Money?' asked Sam.

'Or,' said Elizabeth slowly, 'another, new wife?'

'An excellent point, Elizabeth,' said Dickens.

'It is and certainly worth considering. But now we must go and seek out Edward Drown.'

13: Jacob's Island

Dickens and Jones went out into the dark streets to make their way to Wapping Old Stairs where they would meet the two constables and their police boat. Their cab took them along busy Oxford Street, to Fleet Street, south towards the river down Farringdon Street and along Thames Street into the dark purlieus of Wapping High Street and the Stairs. The night was raw, and they could smell the river as they descended from the cab. They shivered in the mean wind blowing off the brown water as they went down the twenty-two stairs slimed with green and mud to stand and wait for the police boat. The water slapped against the various boats and hulks moored there. The muddy shore was strewn with washed-up objects waiting to be gathered next morning by the mudlarks, mostly children, but some women known as tide-waitresses who made their living by selling on the bits and pieces they found: part of an old cask, old rope, pieces of coal, bits of old iron, and whitened bones, whether human or animal Dickens did not care to think.

The rusty creaking of the inn sign above The Town of Ramsgate sounded eerily like the gibbet of nearby Executioner's Dock to where the notorious pirates were brought from the Marshalsea or Newgate to swing in their dance of death on the short, terrible rope; the bones he saw might well be those of some hanged man bound in chains, left in the water until three cold tides washed over him, eroding him to a swollen lump of decay for the fishes to eat. The thought made Dickens shudder. The silence was broken from time to time by some hoarse cry, the sound of glass breaking and running feet. Superintendent Jones stood impassive in the faded lamplight. He had heard it all before. He knew, as Dickens did, what went on in the maze of passages and tunnels behind them. This was a terrible place; in the alleys dreadful lives were suddenly stopped; children grubbed for a living in filthy gutters; women and girls were bought and sold; boys were abused, beaten and sodomised; young men were stabbed for the price of a tot of rum. Many tongues were spoken here; sailors came from China and lay insensible in rotten opium dens; there were Danes, Finns, Malays, Lascar seamen, exiles from Poland, Germany and Italy, all crammed in the narrow threads of alleys woven round the docks. And all Jones could do, and Dickens could do, was to save whom they could and bring justice to the dead whom they knew about which was why they stood in this darkness clinging about them like a filthy cloak.

They heard the working of oars in their rowlocks and the police boat appeared with its cargo of three constables including Constable Rogers, his eager face alight. Dickens and Jones climbed in, and the two river police manoeuvred the boat away from the shore. They had to cross the river against the tide, avoiding the traffic bearing down on them, the long lines of barges bringing goods to the docks. Looking back, Dickens could see Shadwell dock with its massive warehouses stocked with tobacco, wines, brandy, port, coffee and spices carried across the wide seas by sailing ships to be bought by wealthy men in their spacious houses and comfortable clubs not two miles from here but a world away. The boat rocked on the rolling water as the rowers pulled hard. Dickens held on tight as the slanting rain drove into their faces and the cold seeped into their bones. On the other side they passed the ironically named Cherry Garden Pier and Fountain Stairs, and worked their way up to St Saviour's dock, the inlet which led to Jacob's Island.

Jacob's Island, the haunt where Dickens's own Bill Sikes had met his maker, was dreadful enough in the day, but at dark it was grim indeed. It seemed colder here with the sleety stinging rain borne on the bleak wind. Now further up into the creek, the water was still. It was black, almost solid. Above it were grimy warehouses lining the water, looming tall like enormous gravestones, and cracked and blistered barges were moored at the warehouse quays. Deeper into the darkness and the smell of the graveyard drifted along the scummy water; it was a smell of decay, of corruption, a smell of sulphur gas created by the once white lead paint, peeling and black now from the doorposts and window sills. It was a stench of rotting fish and decayed carcases; whether human or animal, it was not bearable to think about. It was sickening; Dickens held his handkerchief to his mouth. The boat crept along in the half-light; a greenish, misty vapour hovered over the water like cobwebs. Sometimes the water seemed clogged with red where the leather works poured out their noxious liquids, as though blood had congealed in it. Lights bobbed in occasional barges and boats, peering through the vapour like bleared eyes. Dickens thought of the quiet, old abbey of Bermondsey whose monks had built St Saviour's dock when the sweet tributary of the River Neckinger had flowed into the Thames. He thought of Elizabeth Woodville, Queen to Edward IV, sequestered in the abbey five hundred years ago, praying for the deliverance of her two boys, Edward and Richard, from the hands of the crookback. Crookback, Crookface, he thought again of the man who haunted their dreams, half expecting the twisted face to emerge from the miasma of smell and mist to sing its ghastly song.

The place was a jumble of rickety houses and bridges leading into grimy courts and impossible alleys which twisted and turned and came back on one another so that you could never find anywhere nor ever get out. There were innumerable secret doors and passages linking attics and roofs, the lairs of thieves and murderers. The houses, some dating as far back as the reign of Charles II, held each other up like drunken wretches — if one falls the others do. Some had wooden balconies accessed by crazy staircases with gaps where the stairs and railings should be, some of which stopped suddenly in mid-air as if they had forgotten where they were going. Some had galleries precariously hung over the stinking ditch. It was impossible to tell what held them up. There was a woman hanging out a quantity of yellowing linen on a cracked balustrade. They could make out a white face in the mist. The constable steered the boat closer so that he could shout to her, 'Edward Drown — you know him?'

'Down there,' she called, 'three or four 'ouses along.' Her voice echoed across the water, then the mist closed round her, and she vanished like a ghost.

They crawled along the water, past the ancient inn, so aptly named, The Ship Aground, whose denizens were no doubt drinking themselves to death within — better than death by cholera, thought Dickens cynically. Something slipped into the water, a rat perhaps. A drunken man — or woman — lay insensible, the head inches from the stinking water. They slid along the oily water and saw a man in a boat at the next landing. He was stowing away some baskets, a few miserable household articles, a couple of cane chairs, a trunk and some threadbare blankets. A woman came out of the house carrying a child in her arms.

'Edward Drown?' shouted the constable.

The man looked up and stared at them suspiciously. "'Oo wants ter know?' he asked belligerently.

'Superintendent Jones of Bow Street,' Jones called out. 'I need information — about your sister. We'll come onto your landing.'

The constable manoeuvred their boat so that they could step onto the landing where Edward Drown waited sullenly, and his wife shushed the child in her arms.

'Are you leaving here?' asked Dickens looking at the possessions on the landing.

'Gettin' out,' said Drown tersely, 'before we die 'ere. Lost one child to the sickness already.' He was thin but strong-looking, with the same flashing dark eyes that Dickens remembered in his sister. There was determination in him; the urge to survive was alive in those eyes.

'Where will you go?'

'Goin' fer a job at the Pool — longshoreman, I am. Oughter make a decent livin'. Got lodgin's in Gravel Lane wiv the wife's ma.' He jerked his head at the young woman whose narrow, pale face looked out from the folds of her hood. She smiled at them, glad to be going. Dickens felt pleased for them — he could see the golden head of the child peeping out from a grubby little cap. One saved, at least. A thin little cat suddenly appeared and jumped lightly into Drown's boat. Drown looked at as if he might chase it away. He looked at his wife.

'Oh, all right then. It can come.' His gaze was tender as he looked at his wife and child.

'What about Alice?' asked the woman, shyly, ''As somethin' 'appened?'

'No. We just want to find her. She may have information concerning a missing woman.'

'She came 'ere a few weeks ago. Give us money. Told us to get out and save that child. Good girl is Alice.' He said the last aggressively as if the superintendent had other ideas.

Dickens smiled. Alice was a good girl for all her petty thieving and loose living. He remembered her bold, generous laughter.

'I don't doubt it,' said Sam, 'but we need to speak to her. Do you know where she is?'

'Theatre. Victoria. Gotta job, she 'as, singin' and dancin'. That's where money came from, if you woz wonderin'.'

'I wasn't. Thank you for your help.'

'Good luck,' said Dickens. Drown grinned suddenly, his face transformed from sullenness to good humour.

'Aye, we'll survive. I'll see ter that.' Dickens had no doubt that he would.

They climbed carefully into the launch; the constables pulled at the oars and turned the boat to face the dark tunnel of warehouses and the black stretch of water which would take them back to the Thames and Wapping Stairs.

'It is now eight o'clock,' said Jones.

'To the theatre then,' said Dickens, glad to be on land again, however muddy and dreary. 'I could go at half time — for nine o'clock. It'll be half price,' he added with a grin.

'I'll not come with you — Alice will prefer to talk to you alone. You'll get more out of her than I would.'

Dickens and Jones with Rogers took a cab back to the Strand where Jones and Rogers got out to walk to Bow Street; the cab took Dickens across Waterloo Bridge where he hoped to find Alice Drown at the Victoria Theatre.

14: Alice Drown

Dickens made his way through the New Cut market lined with hawkers and traders selling everything in a mad tumble of temporary stalls: fruit and fish, boots, baked potatoes, bonnets, brushes, live chickens and dead ones, eels and whelks, night caps, lace caps, old clothes and new, battered steel helmets and rusty swords with basket hilts. Dickens imagined himself brandishing one in a duel on stage. '*Behold I have a weapon*', he quoted, grinning at his fancy. Brass-voiced women shouted their wares, beaten children and dogs howled, gin-soaked customers staggered singing crazy ballads, knocking into stalls and passers-by with equal indifference. At the theatre, the half-price audience was pouring in as the full-pricers poured out into the glittering gin palace opposite.

Dickens paid his shilling and sat down at the half-way point in *The Brigand's Chief* when the wife of the chief dashes in, wielding a blue wooden dagger with which to despatch her treacherous mate. Seeing the fair captive — how she came to be there, Dickens could not quite follow, but no matter, the sight of her brings tears to the wife's two black eyes. It seems that she is, in fact, the wife's long-lost daughter. The daughter is dragged away. The wife returns, plunges her dagger into the breast of her miscreant husband, a ghost appears clad in a fetching bit of sheeting — nobody knows whose ghost it is, but, again no matter, justice is done and the audience, including Dickens, roars its approval.

The play was followed by burlesque sketches and songs with girls in satin dresses, and with bright rouged cheeks. Dickens leant forward — it was hard to tell, but one of them might be

Alice Drown — perhaps the one on the end who rolled her eyes and tossed her dark hair, kicking higher than the others to display a pair of sturdy legs sheathed in black stockings.

After the burlesque numbers, Dickens went round to the stage door where just within there was a sallow-looking man with yellow fangs who looked like a kind of Cerberus — the doorkeeper — guarding whatever lay in the dingy corridor beyond his little box. Dickens asked for Alice Drown, and was rewarded with a wink and a nod to the corridor. He pushed his way through a crowd of players coming out, their glamour gone in the miserable light which cast a grey pallor over their faces now that the powder and paint had been wiped off. A friendly girl pointed him to a door. 'In there,' she said, giving him an appraising look. She opened the door for him, saying to someone inside, 'Alice, dearie, it's yer lucky night. Gentleman fer yer.' With that she went off, rolling her hips and giving him a wave over her shoulder.

The green room was a dilapidated apartment with a thick, dusty carpet that had once been patterned, shabby, once green velvet curtains, a spotted mirror over the fireplace with notices in the side of a chipped, gilded frame which gave instructions about rehearsals, and a cheval glass in a mahogany frame for the players to see their costumes. The air smelt of powder, dust, sweat and stale scent. Nevertheless, for Dickens, backstage was still, despite its tawdriness, a place where secret, magical transformations took place. He loved being out front, but being backstage was to be in on the secret, to be part of the magic, to be able to be transformed into someone else, into many different selves, each man in his time playing many parts. That was what he loved, forgetting himself, becoming someone else, as Alice Drown was doing, standing before the mirror, powdering her face and swishing her satin skirts. She saw him in the mirror.

'Hello, Charlie,' said Alice Drown mischievously. 'How d'yer find me?'

'I found your brother.'

'Come ter take me back?'

'No, Alice, unless, of course, you wish to.'

'No fear. I'm doin' well 'ere. Makin' my own way, ta very much. I know yer meant well but some of us ain't suited for the quiet life.'

'You didn't fancy Australia, then?'

'It's a long way from 'ome, Mr Dickens, an' I gets seasick on the river steamers. No, it wasn't that so much as yer promisin' we'd all get married and live 'appily ever after. Not fer me, Mr Dickens. Kids, neither.'

'Why ever not, Alice?' Dickens was surprised. It was one of his cherished schemes that the young women who came to the Home could be offered the incentive of a new life, the potential for marriage to an honest man, and children, a family life. That was what made Urania Cottage different — the promise of a better life.

'I seen too much. I was oldest of ten — two of us lived. I seen eight of 'em die, the last born dead an' took my ma with 'er. After that Pa died an' me an' Eddie woz left on our own. That's when we come to London — born up Chertsey way — to live with our aunt. Mean old skinflint she was. 'Er 'usband was a brute, as well. I don't like ter tell yer wot 'e did to me. Put us ter work as soon as — well, I ain't seen many 'appy couples. Why'd it be different in Australia? Look at Eddie and that wife of 'is — lost one kiddie already. I seen too many kids dead, Mr Dickens, an' I likes my own way. You got kids?' she asked with a shrewd look at him.

'Eight.'

'Blimey. You bin busy. Wot's yer wife think of that? Or didn't yer ask er?' She chuckled richly, and too knowingly. Dickens thought of Catherine passive on her sofa, passive in his arms. What did she think? He couldn't answer. Alice took pity on him.

'Sorry about runnin' off — I knew yer'd try ter make me stay. I got me own life, Mr Dickens. I earns my own money and that's 'ow I like it. An' I like it 'ere — it may not be much, but on that stage, I can be someone else — someone different from that raggedy girl from Chertsey way.'

Dickens understood, of course he did. He saw how the satin, garish as it was, suited her better than the neat uniform of Urania Cottage.

'So wot can I do for yer — yer didn't come jest to pay a social call, did yer?'

'No, I came to find out if you ever knew a young woman called Patience Brooke, whether you told her about the Home.'

'I did — I didn't know what else ter do with 'er — she wozn't goin' ter last out on the streets. Wot's 'appened to 'er?'

'She's dead.'

'Gawd! 'Ow?'

'She was murdered — her throat cut, and I want to know who did it — and why. Can you tell me anything about her?'

Alice stared at him, her eyes wide with horror. 'Not much. I found 'er in the street — half-starved she woz. I could tell she was a lady even though she 'ad nothin' with 'er — not a thing, Mr Dickens, 'cept the clothes on 'er back. I took 'er 'ome — couldn't leave 'er there could I?'

Dickens did not doubt that she could not. He waited for her to go on.

'I fed 'er up a bit. She was all fer goin' but I says, "where to?" She didn't know so she stayed a bit. I got 'er some work, sewin' an' that for the costumes but yer know, Mr Dickens, she 'ardly told me anything — not that I asked much. Why should I? I 'ad my own secrets — yer remember about the 'at and the red feathers — well I woz young and foolish — an' it made me go straight. Still, anyways, Patience stayed till she woz better, an' then I thought of you.' Her eyes twinkled at him. 'Just the place for a girl like Patience. I told 'er not to say 'oo sent 'er an' she never did, did she?'

'No, she did not. I thought she might — in time.'

'So did I — but yer know though she woz quiet and modest an' that, she wozn't weak — when she said she woz goin' I knew she meant it.'

'So, you can tell me nothing about her? I have a suspicion she might have been married, had a child perhaps.'

Alice thought, her brown eyes narrowing, 'Run off from a brute of an 'usband, yer think?'

'Could be.'

'She never said nothin' about bein' married, but she liked kids — my landlady, Mrs Cross, 'as two boys — little 'uns. She used ter look after them sometimes — to the manner born, Mrs Cross said — oh, blimey, it fits don't it? — but why'd she leave a kiddie?'

'I don't know. Now think, Alice, was there anything she let slip — however small?'

'I asked her once where she come from — woz she from London, and she said, "a long time ago" — but it couldn't 'ave been that long — she woz young. An' we woz once talkin' about where she might go an' she says she lived at somewhere called Polly something — I can't remember the name — then she shut up quick. I'm sorry, Mr Dickens, but that's all.'

'Was the word "polygon"?' Dickens hoped, holding his breath.

'Might a bin — funny old word innit. Is it a place?'

'It is — up in Somers Town. I lived there once myself.'

'Well I 'ope it's the place. An' I 'ope you finds 'ooever killed 'er. I liked 'er. I thought she might do all right in Australia — but it wozn't ter be, woz it?' She sounded sad. 'Wot a world, eh?'

What a world indeed, thought Dickens as he stood in the corridor. He had wished Alice the best of luck. She had turned down the money he had offered. 'No, Charlie, buy some sweets for all them kids you got!' She laughed at him but kindly, shook out her satin skirts, showed him a black-stockinged leg and went out, ready for her last call. He heard her laughter float back to him as she disappeared along the corridor.

15: A Pair of Black Eyes

'The Polygon,' Sam Jones repeated. Dickens had told him what Alice had said the night before. It was Wednesday morning and they were seated in Jones's office at Bow Street.

'Up at Somers Town. I lived there once — as a boy. It was what you might call shabby genteel — respectable people down on their luck. Hoping for better times,' Dickens said, remembering his father whose fancies of a cultured life of ease had so often come to nothing. 'And a few artists and writers, musicians and so on.'

'I'll get Rogers to look about the Polygon — see if there's anyone there who might know of Patience Brooke. He can go in plain clothes — a lawyer's clerk asking about the family. Let's hope that really was her name. If it wasn't then that's a dead end though there might be something in Rogers's idea about the missing persons notice — a bit unlikely, I know. What about Crooked Face? Are you going to see that lad of yours, Scrap? I had thought of putting a constable on the watch for Crook but we don't want to spook him. Your lad won't be noticed. If he sees him, then it's time to leave it to us. We don't know yet what we're dealing with.'

'I'll go to the shop now and see if there any developments. I'd like to know, too, about that father of theirs and who is really looking after them.'

'Elizabeth said she would go there. She might be able to find out something — just her sort of thing — abandoned children. She has a very tender heart, and she's good at getting them to tell her things — Posy, for instance.'

'Yes, she has. You are fortunate, Sam, in a wife who is beautiful and intelligent,' said Dickens, 'and if they are in need of help, she would be the right person to gain their trust.'

Dickens went out into and through Covent Garden towards Seven Dials and Crown Street. The shop was empty of customers, but the proprietors were at their counter. Scrap came in a moment later — not in so much of a hurry as usual, it seemed. He carried a brown paper bag which he placed with an air of triumph on the counter.

'Currant cake,' he declared. 'Not broken bits neither. Bought it — wiv me earnin's.' He looked at Dickens. 'Want some?'

'I'll get a knife,' said Eleanor as she opened the bag and took out a handsome round of cake.

'Got one,' said Scrap, fishing in his pocket and bringing out a rusty article which looked too blunt to slice even an egg.

Eleanor said tactfully, 'I'll get a bigger one.'

She came back to cut the cake into five equal portions which she placed on a plate she had brought in, and offered the plate to Dickens first. 'Our guest first — family second.' Scrap looked delighted.

They ate slowly, savouring the sweetness, apart from Poll who swallowed hers in one gulp.

'Poll,' said Eleanor reprovingly. Poll hung her head.

The bell jangled as the door opened to admit Elizabeth Jones.

'Why, Mr Dickens,' she said. 'I took your advice and came to buy some supplies.'

'May I introduce a friend of mine,' said Dickens. 'Mrs Elizabeth Jones and these are my friends, Miss Eleanor Brim, Tom, Scrap and Poll. I recommended her to your excellent shop.'

Four pairs of eyes looked at Elizabeth.

'Pity you dint come sooner. You could 'ave 'ad some cake. Real cake, not broken bits,' said Scrap proudly.

'What do you need, Mrs Jones? We have an extensive stock — all colours of ink for a lady, and some very good pen-wipers, paper, of course, good pens,' said Eleanor, the businesswoman.

'I should like to see some inks, and some pen-wipers, please.'

Whilst Elizabeth approached the counter, and Eleanor busied herself with various boxes, and Poll waited for her instructions, and Tom finished the crumbs of cake, Dickens motioned to Scrap to come nearer the door.

'Any news?'

'Seen 'im — at Gray's Inn like you sed. Picked 'im up end of Whetstone Place and dogged 'im up Brown Street.'

'He didn't see you?'

'Ol' Crookface?' Dickens couldn't help smiling at Scrap's apt choice of name. He had thought of it, too, when they'd been to Jacob's Island. Scrap continued, 'Nah, course not — 'e niver looked be'ind 'im anyways. Ugly cove, int 'e? Face all twisted. Bin bashed abaht a bit, shouldn't wonder.'

'You didn't see where he came from in Whetstone Place?'

'Nah — lots of alleys off there — could a come from any of 'em — but I saw where 'e went, dint I?'

'Where?' This could be the breakthrough.

'Inter some offices. Lots o' signs on 'em — names an' that. Could show yer if yer wants.'

Dickens hesitated. He did not want to meet the man, yet he wanted to know which offices he had gone into.

'Right,' he said. 'You go on ahead. I'll meet you at the entrance to Gray's Inn. You approach me as if you are asking for something then point out the building. We must be careful, Scrap, we don't want him to see us together.' Dickens was improvising. He didn't want to be seen walking with the boy — it would look odd, even suspicious, and he did not want Crookface — Scrap's name was useful as well as apt — to see them, either. He didn't want to put the boy in any danger.

Scrap was looking at him with wide, excited eyes.

'I'll meet yer back 'ere arter you done yer investigatin'.'

Dickens turned back to the counter where Elizabeth was examining the inks and pen-wipers. He had an idea. 'Mrs Jones, I have an errand to do with Scrap. I wonder if you would wait for me here then I can escort you home. Would that be all right, Miss Eleanor?'

Elizabeth understood his stratagem for her to get to know the children better. Eleanor seemed pleased to have such an elegant customer.

At a nod from Dickens, Scrap went out. Dickens followed and saw him running along Crown Street from where he would, no doubt, criss-cross the maze of alleys which would lead him to Whetstone Place and across High Holborn to Gray's Inn. Dickens went at a more sedate pace through to Endell Street and Drury Lane down Parker Street then through Whetstone Place where he kept his eyes open. Whetstone Place — he could not help wondering whether somewhere in a court or passage, the murderer was sharpening his knife.

He saw Scrap lounging unconcernedly at Gray's Inn gate. As he approached, the boy held out his hand. Dickens felt in his pocket for a coin to give to the beggar boy who winked at him. Dickens dropped several coins which rolled conveniently into the gateway. The boy was on his hands and knees scrabbling after the scattered money. Dickens followed and at the inner entrance of the gate which opened into the courtyard of the inns, they stood together apparently fumbling with the money. Scrap who was enjoying the pantomime — as was Dickens —

pointed to a doorway of one of the gloomy eighteenth-century buildings, and whispered, 'That one — 'e went in there, I'm sure.' Then he was gone.

Dickens walked quickly as if he were bent on business at the offices. He knew Gray's Inn well; when he was fifteen, his mother had taken him to see Mr Blackmore, a partner in the law firm of Ellis and Blackmore, and he had been engaged as a clerk at ten shillings and sixpence a week. Oddly enough, it was at the time he and his family had lived at number 17, the Polygon, and he remembered that it had taken him half an hour to walk to Gray's Inn on six days a week. And, the building which Scrap had pointed out was the building where he had dwelt among the red seals and dusty parchment. Not that it was the labour of the blacking factory, but it was dull work, carrying papers to and from other dusty offices, copying documents with ill-tempered quills, registering wills, and keeping account books. He laughed as he remembered that on the very first day he had arrived with a black eye — a big rough fellow had knocked his hat off and he had retaliated with a blow only to receive a punch in the eye.

He would look at the names of the companies on the brass plates and report back to Sam. He walked briskly and came to the steps leading up to the offices just as a man came hurrying out. The man came down the steps, brushing past Dickens, knocking into him briefly. Their eyes met for a few fleeting seconds then the man rushed on. It was only a second or two, but Dickens had held the eyes, and had seen the grey crooked face before it turned away. His quick eye had caught the impression of a black coat buttoned up to the chin, and a hand raised as if to cover the face. Dickens dared not stay to see where he went. He hurried up the steps, through the door and into the familiar hallway. He must wait. He must seem as if he had business there. His heart pounded as he stood looking through the hallway. He was not sure — but in those moments of brief contact, he thought that there had been recognition in those black, impatient eyes, eyes with no depth in them to be looked into — just as he had imagined Mr Murdstone's eyes, and he had been aware of that sense of something unwholesome he had felt when he had seen the face in the crowd in Whetstone Place. He stood, thinking. It could be imagination, but it was possible that the man recognised him. The Reverend Goodchild had seen him at the end of January, as a pedlar then, in his churchyard. He must have watched the Home — perhaps he had seen Dickens there.

Dickens waited — he could not go out. Crookface might be waiting, watching. The hall was empty so he sat down, trying to look as though he were waiting for an appointment. He looked at his watch — if anyone asked, he could say he was early for an appointment at Ellis and Blackmore. No one came. He would give it fifteen or twenty minutes. Suppose Crookface came back? Dickens stood up, uncertainly. If Crookface worked here then he might return — and soon. He looked out through the door then darted back, afraid he might be seen. He could not stay here, exposed. He remembered that there was an unused cloakroom down the hallway — perhaps it would be open.

He tiptoed down the hall where the cloakroom was situated under the stairs. He slipped into the darkness; the mouldy air had the same damp smell he recalled from years ago — sometimes the clerks were sent to store boxes there. They were still here. He could see their square, sharp outlines in the gloom. He thought of all those lives imprisoned in those black boxes, people dead before their cases were ever resolved, wills never proved, properties unclaimed, bank notes mouldering in vaults, ragged deeds and parchments, sealing wax dried to the colour of crusted blood, tattered red ribbon, food only for the mice, all caught up in the strangling ropes of the law.

He had a desire to laugh, realising the ridiculousness of his situation — Charles Dickens confined in a dusty cupboard, hiding from a man with a crooked face, but, still, if the man recognised him and made the connection with Patience Brooke then he might, in the superintendent's words, be spooked. Dickens hoped that in his rashness he had not damaged their investigation. He tried to see the time, holding his pocket watch close to his eyes. He did not know how long he had waited or how long he ought to wait. He could not stay here all night, he thought ruefully. He would have to risk it. He could go out a different way, not through the main gate but one of the side alleys which led into Portpool Lane. He opened the door, listened, scuttled out to the rear entrance of the building and squeezed out into a little court out of which a passage led to Portpool Lane. He hoped to God he would not meet Crookface.

He knew his way: from Portpool Lane into Leather Lane then High Holborn to the back of Lincoln's Inn, avoiding Whetstone Place, hurrying into Portugal Street, through the alleys into Wild Street and then back to Crown Street. He walked fast as if pursued. He stopped to cross Wild Street, the crowd swirling round him and the traffic rushing by. He imagined that twisted face peering out from some corner watching him. The idea was so strong that he could almost sense him, could almost feel his breath at his back. The traffic parted; he crossed and was away into Crown Street, entering the shop to the sound of the jangling bell.

Elizabeth was sitting on a chair with Tom on her knee, Poll at her feet; Scrap was at his ease on the floor tickling the dog's ears and, sight of sights, Eleanor Brim was sitting on the counter, her legs dangling. Elizabeth Jones had done her work well — she was at her ease, too. He thought of Patience Brooke with James Bagster's little maid on her knee, Patience who was dead and whose child, if there were one, might still be waiting for her. He very much wanted to know what Elizabeth had found out about these seemingly parentless children. Scrap looked at him enquiringly; Dickens gave him a nod as if to say that all was well. Elizabeth stood and sat Tom on the counter. She picked up her parcels.

'Mr Dickens and I must go now, but I should very much like to come to see you again,' she said. 'My husband writes much — I shall be in need of paper and pens for him soon enough.'

'You will be welcome,' said Eleanor. 'Thank you for bringing your friend, Mr Dickens.'

Dickens and Elizabeth went out. They walked a little along Crown Street in silence until Dickens asked, 'Did you find out anything?'

She smiled, 'I did. It all came quite naturally — the mother is dead. Eleanor remembers her but Tom does not. He is only five, and she died when he was about two. Eleanor Brim is ten and between her and Tom there was another child, a sister who died, and the mother died soon after the birth of a baby brother who died, too.'

'No wonder she is so grave and sensible. The father is living?'

'Yes, but he is ill. Somewhere at the back of that shop lies a sick man. What I think is that he has periods of sickness during which time Eleanor Brim takes charge. She pretends that he is out on business and that she is serving for an hour or two. There are suppliers to whom he owes money —'

'Ah, the man in the white waistcoat — someone was in the other day when I got there — an angry man — I wondered about that.'

'I think that is where Scrap comes in — he sees himself as their protector. I thought I would return tomorrow with something for the sick man — some fruit, perhaps. I'll buy some paper for Sam, too. I hope to find out more, perhaps to help in some way. Eleanor Brim is a brave little girl but she has too much responsibility. If I take over the watching of this little family, you can concentrate on the case of Patience Brooke. I take it that was your business with Scrap.'

'It was, and I am going to see your husband now to —' He broke off. What if the crooked man were really there? What if that breath on his neck was the breath of the real man? He had to go back.

Elizabeth gazed at him in wonder, seeing the panic in his face. 'What is it, what have you thought?'

'I must go back to the shop — I'm afraid — go to Bow Street, bring Sam — tell him Crooked Face saw me. He'll understand. Quick as you can, please.'

Elizabeth hurried off — she didn't need to ask more. His face had told her. Dickens felt foolish for a moment — the man had become his bugbear — he was seeing him at every turn. Never mind, it might be foolish but it might not. He hurried on. Near the corner of Crown Street, he heard the dog barking. It was Poll — the sound was high, angry, unceasing. Rounding the corner, he saw that someone, a man dressed in shabby corduroy trousers, a battered waistcoat and rough shirt, had hold of Scrap, dragging him into an alley a few yards along from the shop. Scrap was shrieking, cursing and struggling. Eleanor was trying to follow and a tall, thin man was holding her back. People in the street had stopped, wondering what was happening, but not doing anything.

Dickens ran, shouting, 'Stop him!' But the crowd did not know if he meant the man or the boy. He shouted again. 'The boy!'

A man in a top hat detached himself from the crowd. He dashed into the alley. As Dickens approached the man emerged with Scrap shaking himself as if he were just rescued from a pond.

'Coulda saved meself. Taken by surprise, that's all. Kicked him where it 'urt, though.' He grinned at Dickens.

The man in the top hat looked at Dickens. 'I know you, sir. I am glad to meet you. Your books give me great pleasure. The Artful Dodger, perhaps.' He glanced at Scrap.

Dickens smiled, 'Not quite. You have given *me* great pleasure in saving my young friend here.'

'The other got away, I'm sorry.'

'Could you describe him?'

'Tall, thin, black eyes, dressed like a labourer, ragged corduroy trousers, greasy waistcoat, dirty shirt and jacket with holes, wretched boots, scarf over his face.'

'You didn't see his face clearly?' Dickens asked. Was it really him? Could it just have been a man who wanted a boy, or just a thief, thinking Scrap might have a bit of money?

'Not really — the scarf, you know.'

'Thank you, anyway.'

They shook hands and the man disappeared into the crowd. Dickens and Scrap turned to go into the shop.

'It woz 'im, Mr Dickens, I knows it.'

'How?'

'Could smell 'im — knew 'is eyes. 'E woz after me — I knows it.' Scrap was determined.

'I think I know it, too.' He might have donned yet another disguise, but Dickens did know. It had to be. That flash of recognition at Gray's Inn, that sense he had of being followed. How the devil had he disguised himself? He was like a conjuror — now you see him, now you don't.

Inside, Dickens saw Eleanor and Tom standing with the tall, thin man. His hollow cheeks and dark eyes told that he was ill, but the red in his face showed that he was angry and afraid.

'Mr Dickens, my daughter has told me of your visits, but I do not understand what has passed here today — are they in danger?'

'My fault,' said Scrap, miserably, ''e musta seen me. I musta bin careless — sed 'e 'adn't seen me but 'e 'ad — sorry, Mr Dickens.' He looked as if he might cry, so distressed was he at his failure.

'No, Scrap, it was not your fault but mine. He saw me at Gray's Inn. I was the careless one.'

Eleanor said, 'Poll saved him — she barked so we knew —'

Poll — where was she? Dickens and Scrap dashed from the shop. They did not care if ten or twenty twisted men should be after them. Poll must be got back. They turned into the dim, greasy alley where Scrap had been dragged. It was narrow and filthy, lined with tumbledown houses and shops. Children played in the gutter, bedraggled women sat on front steps and men lounged in doorways. Dickens slid in the mud as they ran to the end where the alley twisted away into an even narrower passage. Scrap grabbed his hand, and with the other Dickens regained his balance by touching the dirty wall. They ran into the passage, Dickens gasping for breath. The passage curled into a little courtyard where they saw Poll barking furiously at a blank wall.

'Poll, Poll!' cried Scrap. 'Poll!' Poll turned and trotted to them. Scrap scooped her up. 'Let's gerrout of 'ere. This way.'

Dickens had not seen the opening out of the court into what seemed like nothing but a tunnel, but Scrap knew his way. They could not run here — the ground was slimy and the walls oozed damp. The dark enclosed them suddenly. Dickens felt suffocated. He hoped they were not trapped in this filthy dungeon. He glanced fearfully behind, but there was no following step, only the sounds of shouts and voices raised, coming up from subterranean rooms where, no doubt, families crouched in misery, eking out their terrible days. Scrap was moving faster now as the tunnel widened out, and then there was light, another alleyway and the blessed release into Crown Street.

''E musta gorn over the wall — tha's why Poll woz barkin.' Scrap stopped as Dickens caught up with him. Spring-heeled Jack, he thought.

They went back to the shop where Poll was greeted as a heroine, and Dickens was greeted by an angry thin man.

'Thank you both for bringing her back, but, Mr Dickens, please, tell me what this is all about!'

Dickens was saved from the necessity of answering — he hardly had the breath — by the jangling of the bell and the entrance of Superintendent Jones, Elizabeth and Constable Rogers.

'Rozzers,' Scrap said. 'Wot they want?' He was suspicious.

'Police,' said the thin man. 'What on earth —'

'You are Mr Brim,' said Elizabeth. 'I was here before, talking with your children.'

'Our friend,' said Tom.

'Yes,' said Elizabeth, 'and we are to help.'

'I think we need to explain,' said Sam. 'Is there somewhere?'

Mr Brim indicated that they should go into the parlour at the back of the shop. Rogers was to stay in the shop with the children and Poll. Scrap, who was apparently glued to Dickens, went in with them, determined to hear what "the rozzers" wanted and to have his say.

'Now, I have been patient enough. Into what danger has Mr Dickens put my children?' Brim's voice was sharp with fear.

The story was told by Superintendent Jones, whose calm authority kept Scrap quiet: the murder of Patience Brooke, the suspected role of the pedlar who was also a lawyer's clerk and a wretched-looking street man, Scrap's role as a spy, Dickens's accidental meeting with the man with the crooked face, their suspicions that he had tried to kidnap Scrap — perhaps for information, and the possibility that he might return.

'You mean that he could come back here — he could harm one of the children?' asked Mr Brim.

'I don't know,' Jones said frankly. 'It is possible.'

'What then do you intend to do? I will tell you my situation honestly. My wife is dead. I have been ill — poor Eleanor has looked after me and the shop — and Scrap here has been our guardian. I do not like to leave the children alone, but I have to keep the shop open. I am recovering now, but I cannot deal with such a danger.'

Elizabeth stepped in. 'May I make a suggestion? Mr Brim, you have been ill — you need more care than Eleanor can provide. Your family may be in danger. I should like to offer —' she looked at Sam who nodded — 'room at our house for you and the children until my husband believes that the danger is passed. I could look after you — I have nursing skill. You could rest and the children would be safe.'

Mr Brim looked astonished. 'I could not. It would not be right. In any case, the shop...' he faltered.

'I think you should close the shop — at least for a few days,' said Jones. 'If he comes back and finds you all gone then he will not come again, I think. In the meantime, I and my men will be looking for him. When he knows, and he will know, that he is a wanted man, he will stay away from here. Mr Brim, you must let us keep your children safe.'

'You must,' interrupted Dickens. 'I feel this is my fault and —'

'No, Mr Dickens, from what you have all told me, it was accidental. You have been kind to my children — and a good customer — from what I hear,' Brim said wryly, 'and you, Mrs Jones — such a quantity of ink!'

Elizabeth smiled, 'You will come then?'

'I will — and I thank you.'

It was settled. Clothes and other necessities were packed into bags. Eleanor and Tom were excited to be going on holiday, Poll, too. Rogers was despatched for a cab, and they were all installed under his protection. Only Scrap stood back, a little forlorn. What was he to do?

Elizabeth saw. 'Scrap, can you come? I will need you — for protection.'

Scrap darted forward. If he was needed, well. He jumped in, all smiles. The cab drove away leaving Dickens and Jones on the street.

'That lad — has he no home?' asked Jones.

'He mentioned a father, but I wonder —'

'Let us hope that no irate parent comes looking.'

'Somehow, I doubt it.'

They walked away back to Bow Street. Scrap and the children were safe, and Mr Brim would improve under Elizabeth's care. Dickens saw the set of Sam's jaw. 'We need to find him, Charles, whether he is the murderer or not.'

The evening was closing in, casting its shadows over the little courts, alleys and passageways, darkening them even more. Dickens thought of the tunnel and his momentary suffocating panic. He was glad of the superintendent's solid figure next to him. He thought of Crookface, now in his lair, cheated of his prey. They would hunt him down as he had hunted them, and he would tell them what he knew about the terrible murder of Patience Brooke.

16: Blackledge

'Scrap knew him,' said Dickens, 'despite the scarf that covered his lower face. I'm inclined to believe him. I knew him at Gray's Inn. It was just for a moment, I know, but it was the face of the man in the crowd — and I think he knew me — you know that start of recognition, too quick to be controlled. He must have seen me at the Home. It was my mistake to have gone to Gray's Inn.'

'But it was his, too, if you think about it — he took a risk and he failed. All your impressions may have been fleeting — even the touch of his breath on your neck — but he was at the shop, I don't doubt. No, that momentary flash in his eye tells us for sure. I think he did know you from the Home, and he made the connection with Patience Brooke. He followed you, and he tried for Scrap to see if he knew anything about you.'

'Could he be the murderer? His trying to take Scrap suggests that he may be desperate.'

'He could be, and when we find him, we'll ask him, shall we?' Jones's smile was ironic. 'It's time I put some men on this — at night at any rate. We'll go to Gray's Inn and make some enquiries — I don't care if he sees us. All right, he might run and we might not find him, but we need information about him — we could do with knowing who he works for — he must work there or have business there, and we might find an address — someone might know something. And, I have something else to tell you — about Rogers's visit to the Polygon.'

'I had forgotten about that with all the excitement. What did he find out?'

'Two things: first, the residents of the houses he visited, telling his story that he was from a lawyer's office enquiring about a family and a legacy, were a bit suspicious — apparently someone had already been asking — last summer, they thought —'

'Someone looking for Patience? Was it?'

'Could have been, the descriptions were vague. Someone said "queer-lookin' cove", that sort of thing. It probably was him. But there is more — Rogers was asking about a family by the name of Brooke, and no one remembered the name. He asked about a family with a daughter. No Brooke.'

Dickens was disappointed. But the superintendent had more. 'Rogers started to make his way back, disappointed, as I see you are, but he is an intelligent man, and he thought about the names he had been given of families that had lived there: the Woods, the Grimstones, the Halliwells,' he paused, enjoying Dickens's impatience, 'and the Rivers.'

'Rivers?' Light dawned. 'He thought —'

'He did — shrewd fellow — Patience Rivers perhaps became Patience Brooke. So he went back to ask about the Rivers family and he found out. The family did live at the Polygon, they did have a daughter called Patience. The parents died — this was about three years ago — Patience would have been about eighteen — and she left. No one knew where she had gone — into service, they thought, but, and this is the best bit, they remembered a servant, Annie Saywell, who now lives with her daughter in Snide Alley off Purchese Street, just by the Cock Tavern. And there we must go, too, but daytime would be best — we do not want to frighten the woman by banging on the door at night. In any case, I want to see what we can find at Gray's Inn.'

'Now?'

'Yes, if you can.'

They walked from Bow Street, cutting through a narrow lane to Drury Lane through Kemble Street up Gate Street and along Whetstone Place.

Dickens wondered if the crooked-face man were here somewhere. It was dark now, the gas lamps were lit and people were going home, clerks from Lincoln's Inn with parchment faces hurried on, a thin, pinched-face girl, shaking with cold, offered matches for sale, a stout woman puffed as she passed them carrying bundles of washing, cabs rolled grumbling down the street, their lamps winking as they went by at the slab-faced girl in draggled red skirts standing on the corner outside the public house. Inside, Dickens could see the bar with its bottles and decanters of brightly coloured cordials, and the moon-faced barmaid serving brandy and water to a man in a white waistcoat — Eleanor Brim's irascible customer, perhaps. They passed a chop house with its sanded floor and straight-backed wooden seats where two of the clerks were taking their supper.

They came to Gray's Inn and walked to the offices where Dickens had waited in the cloakroom. Upstairs they went to the first door which opened into a small panelled room where a young man was writing. He looked up, his bright face helpful in the gaslight.

'Ambrose Tiplady, Ambrose Tiplady at your service, service.' He was about sixteen, about the same age as Dickens was when he copied for his living here. Mr Tiplady had fair curly hair, a smooth unshaven face, and shining eyes which looked at them hopefully.

'I am Superintendent Jones of Bow Street and this is my friend, Mr Charles Dickens. We are looking for someone.'

Ambrose Tiplady's eyes shone even more brightly, pink flushed his cheeks, and his mouth opened wide at the mention of Charles Dickens. He simply gazed. The open mouth emitted a squeak first, then he managed the words, 'Charles Dickens, Charles Dickens —' he scrabbled at the desk and offered a book — 'Charles Dickens,' he repeated. 'I have — been — er — have been — reading — reading — Charles Dickens — you are he?' He indicated the book, a copy of *Dombey and Son*. '*Dombey and Son* — fine — death of Paul — dreadfully sad — oh! — Charles Dickens!'

Mr Tiplady could say no more. Overcome by confusion, he continued to stare. Dickens offered his hand to the boy. 'How do you do, Mr Tiplady, I am very glad that you are enjoying the book.'

Putting down the book, Tiplady managed himself well enough to take the proffered hand. Sam Jones, who had been much amused by all this, cleared his throat. Tiplady, still holding on to Dickens's hand, looked at the superintendent as he might have looked at an elephant in the room standing with an archangel. Dickens extricated his hand.

'Oh, I beg your pardon,' said Tiplady, 'I am so —'

'Superintendent Jones and I are enquiring after a man who might be a clerk in any of these offices. You might be able to help us.'

'Certainly, by all means, certainly, decidedly, certainly.'

Dickens wondered if his propensity for repeating himself were the effect of a career in the law — ten words where one might have done. 'He is a man with a distinctively crooked face.'

'Crooked face, crooked face, distinctively,' said Tiplady, giving in to his habit.

'Yes,' Jones said, forbearing to repeat the words, hoping his brevity might rub off.

'Blackledge, Blackledge, that's his name, his name.'

Dickens exchanged a look with Jones; at last a name, an identity.

'Can you tell us any more about him?' Jones asked, 'As briefly as you can. We have not much time.'

'Certainly, certainly,' Tiplady blushed, aware suddenly that he was doing it again. 'He's a clerk for Ducat's — Mr Ducat's office is upstairs.'

'How long has he worked for them, do you know at all?'

'A year or so, I believe. He was here before I came.'

'Do you, perhaps, know where he lives?' asked Dickens.

'I am afraid, afraid not — I do not know him really — I don't — he is —' Tiplady broke off in confusion.

Dickens put the question. 'You do not like him?'

Tiplady blushed again. 'I would not want to be unfair or unkind —'

No you would not, thought Dickens, but you did not like him just as I did not nor Scrap.

Tiplady continued with a rush, 'He is unpleasant, sneering — he acts as if he knows something that I — or others — do not. He has money, too. More than most.'

'I have seen him briefly,' said Dickens kindly, 'and I didn't like him either.'

They thanked him for his help, told him not to mention their conversation to anyone else, and made their way up the ill-lit staircase to Ducat's office.

They hoped that Blackledge — a decidedly appropriate name, a scraping, rasping sort of name, thought Dickens, who could never begin a novel without the names, for without names there could be no characters — would not be there. If he were, then Jones had said they would invent some business about a missing person. 'Thin,' Jones had admitted but it would have to serve.

There was a musty old clerk with a face like shrivelled parchment who coughed dustily and did not know, could not say, doubted, felt it unlikely — another circumlocutionist — that Mr Ducat who, of course, was an extremely busy man, many calls on his time, could, or even would, be able to see them. Jones insisted, and the little man, bent over like a question mark, disappeared into an inner office. He returned, looking anxious. Mr Ducat could, would, give them a few minutes of his time. He motioned them to the door and in they went.

Mr Ducat, senior partner of Ducat, Sterling and Cash, looked as prosperous and polished as his name. Ducat was a man who was well paid to cherish the secrets of his wealthy clients. His desk was neat with papers carefully piled, sealing wax, a handsome silver ink stand and a couple of golden sovereigns which gleamed in the dim room. *Sealed bags of ducats, double ducats*, thought Dickens, remembering Shylock crying through the streets of Venice after his missing daughter. Ducat stood up to meet them, tall, sleek, handsome in a predatory way. His smile was easy. Like Ambrose Tiplady, he wished to be of service; unlike Tiplady, his eyes betrayed caution, the well-oiled wheels of his mind turning quickly.

'Thank you for giving us your time, sir,' said Jones, carefully erasing any hint of irony, and looking as deferential as he ought to be as a mere policeman. 'My friend, Mr Dickens and I wish to know something of your clerk, Mr Blackledge. We think he may have information that could be useful to us concerning a confidential matter which pertains to Mr Dickens.' Jones could circumlocute with the best of them when he needed to.

There was a calculated bewilderment in Ducat's smile. 'I know Mr Dickens, of course. I am very happy to meet the author of so many wonderful books but I do not know in what way my clerk' — the emphasis on the last word was clear — 'could be of assistance. Is it in connection with his professional duties? If there is anything to do with Ducat's, I should be happy to help you. I can hardly think that he would have information about any client of ours which I do not know about.'

Ducat wanted to know. He would be concerned if Blackledge had any secret dealings with any of the important clients. Dickens's heartbeat quickened. Perhaps Blackledge did have dealings with an important man — a man who knew something about Patience Brooke — blackmail, he thought suddenly.

Jones was apologetic. 'I am sure it has nothing to do with your business here, sir, but we would like to know something about him. Anything you can tell us may be useful.' Jones felt he was treading on the slippery edge of ice at the circumference of a pond — he wanted information without having to disclose information.

Ducat was reluctant, but he knew they would not tell him anything more. He was aware of the superintendent's rank, and he was aware of the fame of Charles Dickens. Who were his solicitors? Dickens would be an important client if a firm could get him.

'Mr Blackledge has been with us for over a year. He is a most capable man, most assiduous in his work —'

'The nature of which is?' Jones interrupted. He was becoming impatient, but his tone was smooth.

'Well, he would copy deeds, wills, conveyances, all kinds of documents. He would sometimes see clients on matters of routine — documents that might need to be read, signed; he might give advice — that sort of thing.'

'Would he meet any of your more distinguished clients?' asked Dickens. 'He is clearly a man you value.'

'Yes, he would, if the matter were only routine as I have said; for example he has recently been working on deeds connected with the Crewe family,' Ducat paused, afraid he had been indiscreet, then recovered. 'But I am not sure, Mr Dickens, Superintendent, how this can help you at all.' He was polite but it was clear that he, too, was growing impatient.

'You are right, sir, I am sure the matter does not touch your business. We simply wanted to know a little about Mr Blackledge and you have painted a picture of a most reliable employee. If you will keep our confidence, I am sure that Mr Dickens will not object to my telling you that the matter is to do with a distant relative of his — we had an idea, no doubt erroneous, that Mr Blackledge may have known this person. We will not keep you any longer. Goodnight, and thank you, sir.'

They bade farewell to the dusty clerk and made their way down the stairs in silence. They did not exchange a word until they were safely through Gray's Inn gate.

'Have you thought of the stage, Sam, as a new career? We could form a new company, Dickens and Jones, tragedy, comedy and humility our specialities.'

Jones laughed. 'Did I overdo it?'

'Not at all. I almost believed your story about the distant relative — I daresay I have them. Not that I want them. I have quite sufficient importunate near ones. I loved "no doubt erroneous" — I really thought we were wrong for a minute.'

'We didn't get his address, but I thought we ought to get out of there before he smelt too big a rat — I could sense him sniffing a small one!'

'Do you think it gets us anywhere? I did have one thought —
I wondered about Blackledge's connection with important
clients — blackmail, I wondered.'

'Did you notice that he slipped out the name Crewe? That
might be useful.'

They walked on back to Bow Street. Dickens turned over the
name 'Crewe' in his mind. It was a name he knew well.

17: Memory

Dickens had parted from the superintendent and made his way home to Devonshire Terrace where he expected guests for dinner.

All the time during the dinner at which he sparkled as usual, a thin dark thread of thought ran at the back of his mind. Looking at the distinguished guests, and the table with its pyramids of bright fruit, the candles rising out of the artificial flowers, their reflections glittering on the glasses and silver, he was remembering his grandmother, the housekeeper at Crewe Hall for the aristocratic Crewe family, and his grandfather, the steward. It amused him that, in a cynical, if painful way, those seated there knew nothing about his grandparents in service more than forty years ago nor about his maternal grandfather, Charles Barrow, caught out in defrauding the Navy Pay Office. He knew that sharp-tongued Jane Carlyle, there tonight with her husband Thomas, laughed behind his back sometimes. He had been told that Edward Fitzgerald had thought him a snob for calling his son after Tennyson. They could not know that he was well aware of his desire for substance, for the material things with which he wanted to weight himself down? He wanted to make assurance double sure, otherwise the dark might close in and all that he had gained might vanish. Beneath the glittering surface of his fame, as if deep in dark water, lay the memories of the Marshalsea and his father's disgrace; Gower Street, the home with nothing left but a few chairs; the trips to the pawn shop; a family so reduced that his mother and the younger children were forced into the prison; and he left to drudge in the blacking factory and to pay for his own bread and cheese, lounging about the streets as forlorn as any vagabond. And now the name of Crewe had risen out of the dark water like a spectre come to haunt him.

Later in bed, Dickens lay awake thinking about the Crewe name and the link to Blackledge, and if there was a connection to Patience Brooke. It was uncanny and disturbing the way in which fragments of his own life touched the murder — it had occurred at the Home set up by him, the song Davey had heard, Blackledge at Gray's Inn where he had started his working life, Patience Brooke at the Polygon where he had once lived, and now the Crewe name. We are all connected by fate, without knowing it, he thought, fate so strangely entangling these very different lives. People supposed to be strangers suddenly brushed by us, looming out of the crowd to disturb us when we least expected them.

He slept at last, but restlessly, and in his dream he was in that suffocating tunnel with Scrap who vanished into the shadows, leaving Dickens to face the figure that followed them, the man with the crooked face and a knife in his hand who dissolved into another shape, a man whose face he did not know but who pursued him through a maze of strangely empty alleys that seemed to go down and down, never ending, never reaching the light.

Dickens awoke on Thursday morning still beset by the thoughts and dreams of the night. He took his daily shower, went in to breakfast where the busy domestic scene steadied him. Later, sitting at his desk in the study, he thought about the Crewe family. It was forty years ago. What had it to do with him now? There was no need to tell the superintendent about his connection with the Crewes — not that Sam Jones would judge him. If ever there was a man without pretension, Sam

Jones was he — a staunch friend who judged men by their deeds not their name or fame — a man with a face that had nothing to hide, but showed himself exactly as he was. But there was in Dickens's mind, still, a niggling worry about his links to the case. Perhaps Sam ought to know. At the very beginning, they had wondered if the murder had been intended to discredit Dickens and his work at the Home. He was sensitive about the past — was someone trying to dig into it and to wound him? When he thought rationally, it seemed unlikely. If they found Blackledge, then he would know.

He looked at the blue slips of paper on his desk, conscious that he had written nothing. There was a letter from Mrs Morson in reply to his own that he had sent by hand, telling her what they had found out about Blackledge. She was grateful that he had persuaded Miss Coutts to let her employ James Bagster's sister. Things were quiet; even Isabella and Sesina were behaving themselves though Lizzie Dagg was still depressed. Mrs Morson hoped to see him soon and would he write with news about Patience when he had some. Dickens was relieved; at least there was no pressing need for him to go to Urania Cottage just yet.

At Bow Street, Sam told him that Rogers and another man were keeping watch for Blackledge at Gray's Inn. They were to follow him if they saw him to try to find out where he lived. If they did, then that night would be the time to beard him in his den. In the meantime he and Dickens would go to Snide Alley to find out what Annie Saywell could tell them about the Rivers family.

A cab took them to Eversholt Street by Euston Station with its huge iron roof and great Doric portico. The Polygon was as shabby as Dickens remembered. Snide Alley by the mean-looking Cock Tavern was even shabbier. The dwellings here were a mixture of small cottages, broken-down sheds and disused stables. Superintendent Jones asked a boy playing with stones in the gutter if he knew where Annie Saywell lived. They were directed to the last cottage in the alley after which they could see a patch of unenclosed yellowish grass strewn with bricks and bits of timber, and where, improbably, a donkey was tethered. Annie Saywell's cottage was small, two rooms by the look of it.

'Let us hope she does,' said Dickens.

'Does what?' asked Jones, puzzled.

'Say well,' Dickens replied, his eyes telling that he hadn't been able to resist the pun.

'Very droll, Charles,' Jones replied though his smile showed he was amused.

He knocked on the door which was opened by a sturdy woman of about forty years dressed in black with a cleanish apron covering the dress. She eyed them suspiciously.

'We are looking for Annie Saywell,' said Jones. 'Is she in?'

'And who might you be?' asked the woman, stepping forward to prevent their coming closer.

'Superintendent Jones from Bow Street. We want to ask her about the Rivers family. Your — er — mother — used to work for them, I believe.'

'Yes. You'd better come in then.' She opened the door and they stepped into a tiny room with a ceiling so low that they had to stoop. The room was lit by a smoky oil lamp. It was a dark day and little light found its way through the one bleared window. A small, older woman of about sixty was sitting at the table folding piles of laundry. She looked at them with curiosity.

'Policemen wanting to know about the Rivers family, mother,' the daughter spoke loudly. Annie was deaf.

154

'Oh,' said Annie, doubtfully, her face crumpled like a linen dishcloth.

'We want to know about the daughter, Patience, if you can tell us, Mrs Saywell.' Jones raised his voice so that she could hear.

'Somethin' 'appened to 'er?'

'She is missing and we would like to try to find her,' Jones said. It was not necessary to talk of murder. 'Tell us about the family, if you will.'

'Sit down, please. Emma put the kettle on. Can I give you some tea?'

'Thank you,' said Jones as they took a chair each at the well-scrubbed table.

Emma was busy at the fire while Annie Saywell set out cups. The china was pretty but there were only two saucers and the cups did not match. Jones was patient while the tea was made and served, though he could sense Dickens's desire to get on with it.

'Now, Mrs Saywell?' Jones's voice was kind. Kindness and patience would coax Mrs Saywell to tell them all she knew.

'Mr Rivers taught music — they 'adn't much but they was good people, clever, you know, educated. Mrs Rivers was sweet, pretty, but she wasn't in good health. What they call delicate. They 'ad no servants, but me an' a little girl sometimes. I didn't live there — I lived 'ere with Emma and me 'usband. 'E's dead now. They was kind — you know, they'd give us food sometimes, an' a shawl or dress or something.'

'And the daughter, Patience?'

'She was a clever girl, musical, too. She went with her father sometimes teachin' in grand 'ouses — sometimes it was grand 'ouses, sometimes just ordinary folk. She was pretty, too, in a quiet way — not flashy.'

'When did you stop working for them?' asked Jones.

'About five years ago. Broke me leg — on the ice — it never mended.' She lifted her skirt to show the twisted limb which had never healed since an incompetent doctor had tried to set it.

'What happened to the family afterwards?'

'Mr and Mrs Rivers died — pneumonia in that bitter winter. Patience went to work as a governess or sum such in one o' them grand 'ouses. She came 'ere to tell me she was goin'. I was fond of Patience. Felt for 'er — she was 'appy at 'ome.'

'Did you hear from her again?' Jones sounded quite calm. Dickens felt a fluttering in his own chest but he sat still.

''Ad a letter sometimes. She told us she was all right, teachin' and that, and then after about a year, she wrote an' said she was getting married but that was it. After that, nothin'. That must 'ave bin three or so years ago.' Annie shook her head, puzzled still by the lack of communication from the girl she had been fond of.

'Mebbe too grand to write to us,' said Emma unexpectedly. There was a hint of bitterness in her voice.

'What makes you say that?' asked Jones.

'I dunno — just thought she'd married class, mebbe. She 'ad somethin' — yer know — not ordinary.'

That was true, thought Dickens. Patience was not ordinary. That was why he had agreed to let her stay at the Home. She had tried to disguise herself, tried to be effacing and quiet, but Emma was right — she had something.

Jones asked carefully, 'Do you happen to remember the name of the family she went to work for?'

Annie Saywell thought about the question. 'Crewe.' The name hung in the air. Dickens had hoped, just for a moment, that it would be something else so that the Crewe family could stay hidden — in that long distant past.

'Has anyone else been here to enquire after Miss Rivers?' Jones thought that if someone had been at the Polygon then he might have traced her to Annie Saywell's.

'There was a man from a lawyer's, 'e said. 'E asked if I'd heard from 'er. 'Ad she visited, or been to visit. I said not since she'd left to go to 'er governessin'. 'E didn't say what 'e wanted Patience for just that 'e 'ad news for 'er.'

'Can you remember what he was like?'

'Queer lookin' — mouth all twisted, but 'e was polite. Said 'e was sorry to trouble us. Didn't come back.'

'Thank you for your time, Mrs Saywell,' said Jones as they prepared to leave.

''Ope yer find 'er, sir, she was a good girl to me.'

18: Lantern Yard

Dickens was silent as they drove back to Bow Street. Sam wondered what was on his mind, what had been said at Snide Alley which made Charles so thoughtful, but he waited. Dickens spoke at last.

'The Crewe family, Blackledge and Patience are all connected, and I have been wondering —' he broke off, uncertain how to go on — 'I have been thinking whether there is any connection to me.'

Dickens explained how he had thought about the way in which the case touched his life: the Home, the song, the Polygon, Gray's Inn and the Crewe family.

'I can see the first links, but how is the Crewe family connected?'

'My grandparents worked at Crewe Hall, steward and housekeeper — forty years ago.'

'But you have no recent connection with the Crewes?'

'No — as you can imagine, I have not advertised the fact that my grandparents were servants,' Dickens admitted. Somehow, it was not as important as it had seemed in the restless night before. That was Sam — he asked the important question, paying no attention to the fact of Dickens's grandparents as servants.

'So, forty years ago, your family was connected to the Crewes? I can't really see a link to Patience's murder. As you said, no one knows of the connection. It would be devious indeed if someone were to murder a girl at Urania Cottage with a view to exposing your humble roots. No, I think Patience's murder is to do with Patience and her past.'

'When you put it like that…' Dickens felt a little foolish.

'I think,' said Jones briskly, 'that Patience may have married "class" as Emma put it, and it would seem that something went dreadfully wrong. She left her husband, disappeared, was traced to the Home by Blackledge, was murdered, possibly by Blackledge, so that her husband could be free — to marry again, perhaps.'

'There might have been a child, and that makes me wonder what must have happened that she left a husband, a child and a more than comfortable life to end up on the street where Alice Drown found her. I wonder whom she married in the Crewe family?'

'We can find out — I'll get Rogers to do some digging. Meantime, we're still in search of Blackledge. We must see if Rogers is back.'

Rogers was back, but there had been no sighting of Blackledge. He had enquired for him of the bent clerk at Ducat's. The senior partner was out so the clerk was more forthcoming; it was clear that he did not like Blackledge and was not sorry to believe he might be in some trouble. He gave Rogers an address: Lantern Yard, off Wellspring Lane, a tributary of Whetstone Place. Rogers, in his plain clothes, would return to keep watch at Gray's Inn at about five o'clock to see if Blackledge had arrived at his offices at all. Dickens and Jones would wait for him in a chop house near Whetstone Place. They would see Rogers there and he, they hoped, would tell them where Blackledge had hidden himself. If he had not seen him, then they would try to find his lodgings.

The chop house was busy at five o'clock as the clerks came in for their meals of mutton chops, kidneys, mashed potato, a pudding of Banbury cake, all washed down with pale ale. Dickens and Jones took a table by the window nearest the door. They bought a sausage roll apiece and a cup of tea, quick to consume if they needed to dash out. They watched the street through the blurred window, noticing the faces in the gas light. There was no familiar crooked countenance but he could have slipped past in the surging crowd. They hoped not. They chewed as slowly as they could and took sips of the tea. The face of Rogers suddenly loomed up like a drowning man's in the steam of the window. Out they went.

'No sign,' he said. 'Not been there all day.'

They went down the alley to find Lantern Yard. There were a few houses surrounding the small courtyard out of which another alleyway led. It seemed an odd place for the lawyer's clerk to live, especially if, as Ambrose Tiplady had said, he had money. It was not the worst of places — those would be found deeper in the maze, but it was on the downward slope from barely respectable to disreputable. A scrawny woman with a tight bun of mousy hair and a harassed face was coming from the other alleyway. She turned as if to go into one of the shabby houses. Rogers asked for Mr Blackledge.

She pointed to a house on the other side of the court from her own. 'Lodges there.'

They turned to the left to examine the property. It looked as though the house had two rooms upstairs and two down. The downstairs rooms were all in darkness, but there was a little light coming from one of the upstairs rooms. Rogers tried the front door, turning the knob. The door opened — perhaps someone had just come home upstairs. The door of one downstairs room was open; it was empty apart from a few broken chairs and a mattress. Rogers tried the other door which was locked. While Dickens and Jones waited in the empty room, Rogers went round to the side of the house in search of a window. A few minutes later, they heard the opposite door open. They crossed the little corridor, glancing up the staircase briefly, and went into Blackledge's lodging.

The room was surprisingly clean and bare except for two neatly made up beds and a small deal table at which there were two wooden chairs. At the foot of one of the beds was a large wooden chest, the sort that a seaman might use. A cupboard of old oak hung in a corner. The window through which Rogers had climbed was grimy with a threadbare curtain stretched across it on a string. It looked as if no one lived there, as if it were waiting patiently for someone to make a fire in the small grate, light the one candle in its tarnished brass holder, and set out a comfortable tea on the table.

There was nothing to see except what was in the chest. Rogers opened it and they stared inside at the clothes piled there. Rogers lifted out a ragged pair of corduroy trousers, a worn waistcoat and rough shirt. Dickens recognised them. 'That's what he wore when he was trying to take Scrap.'

Oddly, there was another, similar outfit of ragged trousers and waistcoat. The colours of both sets were similarly faded to the colour of mud. Underneath these were a canvas jacket, and a red woollen scarf.

'That's what Sesina described the pedlar as wearing,' said Dickens. 'I wonder where the tray is.'

Jones indicated that Rogers should look under the beds. Under one he found a stout tin cash box, but that was locked, too. Shaking it produced the rattle of coins inside. The front door opened. They waited, but the footsteps went upstairs. They heard voices from upstairs, a woman and a child's then a man's gruffer tones. It was time to leave. Rogers slid the cash box back under the bed. They would have to come back later.

As they turned to go, they saw hanging on the back of the door the black lawyer's coat that Dickens had seen him wearing in the crowded street.

'I wonder what he is wearing now. Or rather I wonder *who* he is now — our man of many disguises,' Dickens whispered.

'It is curious,' said Jones.' I wonder why he needed two workman's outfits.'

'Fastidious, perhaps,' said Dickens, 'though neither looked particularly clean.'

'We'll come back later. I'll get Constable Feak to keep watch. There will be a couple of constables on the beat round here. He can ask them to keep an eye out. If Blackledge comes in, Feak can run to Bow Street in ten minutes, and we can hurry back.'

It was about seven o'clock now, and they did not know how long they would have to wait. Perhaps he would not come at all, perhaps he was elsewhere in another disguise and the lawyer's suit was never to be worn again. The cash box, however, suggested that he would come back for his money, but when?

Dickens and Jones returned to Bow Street and the warm fire in the superintendent's office. Tea was brought, and they settled to their waiting.

'Does the cash box mean blackmail?' Dickens reflected. 'What is his relationship to the Crewe family? He traced Patience — we do not know how — to the Home. Was it under the instruction of her husband with whom he had come into contact at Ducat's? Did Blackledge kill Patience for money — was that the money in the box? Did Patience's husband kill her and is Blackledge blackmailing him?' He tried to tease out the various threads of the story.

'Ambrose Tiplady said he had money — was he in the pay of Crewe for a time, earning his money by trying to trace her?' offered Jones.

'One of them killed her, but which?'

'Perhaps he'll tell us — when we find him. What do you know of the Crewe family?'

'Not much — as I said, my grandmother worked as their housekeeper nearly forty years ago — I've not paid them much attention since. They have an estate in Cheshire and there was a London house. It's odd but my father did not talk about them much though he was a boy there. I suppose he was a bit ashamed. I did wonder though if the Crewes had any hand in getting him a job in the Navy Pay Office at Somerset House. It was a good step up for him.' If only he had lived within his means, Dickens thought moodily. It was, no doubt, a melancholy truth that even great men have their poor relations, but he could not help wondering why so many of his should be so impecunious.

'You don't know anything about sons or grandsons — Patience's husband would have to be a grandson or cousin, I imagine if he is of a similar age to Patience.'

'We can find out about the family in Burke's Peerage — see who has the title and if there are sons.'

'And we can get some information from the town house. Rogers is good with servants.'

'He's a busy young man — and an engaging one.'

Rogers came in. Feak had reported in. Blackledge was at home — and would be receiving guests though he did not yet know it. Feak had hastened back to his guard post at the end of Wellspring Lane. He was sure he had not been seen and in any case the sight of a policeman in Whetstone Place would not have been out of the ordinary. The other three set off briskly. Feak reported that after Blackledge had gone in, he had dared a look at the house. Through the front window he had seen candlelight, but he had moved off for fear he would be seen.

All four went into Lantern Yard and saw the candlelight flickering. He was there. Feak went round the back; Rogers took his station at the window through which he had climbed. Dickens and Jones approached the front door which was ajar just as if someone had gone out. The door to Blackledge's room was open, too. There was not a sound from within. They waited. Upstairs a child was crying. The sound was heartbreaking as if the child knew all the sorrows of the world. Jones touched the door gently and it opened soundlessly. They stepped forward. There was no one inside — only the candle burning in its brass holder. The chest was open and they saw a jumble of clothes — one of the workmen's outfits was gone. But someone had been there with Blackledge — there was a bottle of wine on the table and two glasses. The door to the oak cupboard was open.

'He must be nearabouts — otherwise why leave the door open? Let's go and look.' They turned to go out, noticing that Blackledge's lawyer's coat was not on its peg. Was he wearing that on top of the workman's outfit? Double disguise? Where had he gone?

Rogers and Feak joined them. They turned on the bull's eye lamps and went into the narrow lane which turned suddenly at a right angle into another narrower alley from which various tunnels and passages led off in different directions. There were the usual wrecks of houses and tenements reeling against each other, and it was dark, too dark to see much. Which way to go? They hesitated, uncertain. Then they heard something.

The superintendent stopped and put his finger to his lips. They froze. It was a snatch of a song, the song of poor Edmund. It stopped suddenly so it was difficult to tell where it came from. They strained to hear. Somewhere someone was running. Was it Blackledge? Had he known that Feak was following him? They heard the steps receding from them and then nothing. The alleys were silent; they were deep in the maze. Jones signalled to Rogers and Feak that they should take two of the alleys, his eyes asked Dickens if he would go down with Feak, and he would go straight ahead. The two constables took out their truncheons. Jones drew a flintlock pistol out of his coat pocket.

Dickens followed Feak as lightly as he could into the mouth of the tunnel to the left of them — it was too like his dream to be comfortable; the passage sloped downwards to God knew where. Feak walked carefully, holding his lantern up. Dickens's lamp swayed in his nervous hand and cast shadows on the walls, misshapen forms which brooded over him. The buildings almost touched in the middle over his head. Something scuttled over his foot. Feak turned off into another passageway, leaving Dickens alone. The lamp shook even more and the shadows closed in. There was a shape of something on the ground ahead. Dickens found he had not the courage to go forward; he felt that same suffocation that he had experienced in the tunnel with Scrap, as if thick breath were clotted in his throat. He lifted the lamp to see that the passage ended in a black, blank wall, looming at him like a threat. He could hear the slow drip of water; the walls were pressing in on him. He felt the trickle of cold sweat like an icy finger at his back. Where was Feak? He took a step back, and felt the mud ooze under his boot, the heel slipping so that he almost fell.

Then, suddenly, horribly, the thing on the ground reared up, a confusion of rags and bones, a living skeleton, a thing from a nightmare. It charged at him. There were naked arms and legs, and in the quivering light Dickens saw briefly a simian face, burning, terrible eyes and a wide open mouth which shouted, 'I am Legion!' The figure barged past, knocking into him so that he almost lost his balance, his feet sliding in the mud. He scrabbled for something to hold on to and the lamp fell from his hand. Blackness descended on him like a thick blanket tossed from above. Then there was a shout. It was Rogers, his voice high and urgent, coming from somewhere else. At that moment his hand found Feak's thick woollen sleeve.

'All right, sir,' whispered Feak. ''Oo woz that?'

'Not our man.' Dickens's voice was hoarse, but surprisingly steady after his terror.

Rogers called out again. Dickens and Feak hurried out of their alley. Where was the superintendent? Footsteps, hurried. A light. Sam Jones appeared, his face white in the flickering lamplight.

'We've found him — dead.'

Dickens followed Feak, his feet clumsy in the mud, slime and broken stones. Halfway down the alley which Rogers had taken, he saw the constable kneeling by a form sprawled on the ground. Sam and Feak were there holding up their lamps. Dickens approached, and all four looked down at the crooked face with its pitiless eyes staring, ghastly in death. Blackledge appeared to have two mouths, one twisted in the rictus of death and the other a gaping red beneath the chin. Dickens could see that his throat had been cut and the blood had poured out, staining the grimy stones, running still to create pools round Rogers's spread coat.

'Feak, use your rattle — raise up the other constables. We need help here.'

The high roaring of the rattle sounded. Soon, heavy feet were heard trampling down towards them, and the two other constables appeared with their lights. Faces appeared at some of the windows, and a knot of people appeared at the entrance to the alley, attracted by the sound of feet and the rattle. Feak told them to go in. They went reluctantly, muttering about the 'perlice', and they heard whispers: ''Oo's dead?'; 'Stabbed, I think.'

'I want you to deal with the body, Feak, with the help of these two. Rogers you need to go for the police wagon. Take him to the morgue. Mr Dickens and I will have a look round. Oh, and Rogers, look in the pockets. We could do with his keys. Then go and lock up his room, and bring them back to me before you go to the station.' Jones hoped the key to the cash box would be there, too.

Rogers found the keys and dashed away. Dickens and Jones stood looking at the body of the man they had hoped would unlock the mystery of the murder of Patience Brooke. It was too late — the crooked face would reveal nothing now. But the ugly gash at the neck told them, without doubt, that Blackledge had not killed Patience, the same hand had destroyed both. In death he looked no different; no sense of peace had softened the features. He looked, if anything, angry, the twisted mouth seeming almost to snarl up at them as if it were their fault that he had been cheated. Superstition had it that on the victim's eyes would be stamped the face of his murderer. Who was it that he saw? Dickens almost bent over Blackledge to see if those open eyes could show them the face of the killer.

Rogers returned with the keys. The door to that strangely impersonal room was locked now. It could yield up few secrets except perhaps what might be in the cash box. Dickens and Jones went along the alley and into another, but it was hopeless. There were too many places where he might hide, and anyway, the sound of running footsteps they had heard told them that the murderer had gone.

They left Feak and the other two to watch over the corpse while they went back to the house. No need for caution now. They went in. To their astonishment, a young woman was sitting at the table sipping a glass of wine. She was attractive in a hard way and reasonably well-dressed in a dark red velvet jacket which accentuated her curves and a velvet skirt which fell in folds to the floor. She wore a black feathered hat which sat on black tightly curled hair. The immediate effect was of unexpected elegance in this mean room. Her astonishingly blue eyes were immediately suspicious.

'Wot you doin 'ere? Police ain't yer.' Her look at Jones was hostile. 'Where's Alf then? You got 'im for somethin'?'

'I am Superintendent Jones of Bow Street, and yes, we have got him. How did you get in? What is your business here?'

'Obvious innit.' She laughed. 'You ought ter know that, Mr Superintendent.' She held up a key.

Jones smiled. 'I think I can guess. Were you to meet him tonight?'

'Yers, 'e said 'e 'ad some business, but we'd go out for a bit o' dinner — 'e's good ter me is Alf. Generous yer know.' She smoothed down her velvet skirt, not new but good second hand. It was elegant in its way if a bit worn in places where the nap of the velvet had been rubbed. She was obviously pleased with it. 'Alf's got money. We woz thinkin' of movin' on ter somewhere better — America, pr'aps but 'e said 'e 'ad business to finish off first. I woz waitin' — I wanted somethin' better even if —' She broke off, suddenly uncertain.

'What sort of business?' Jones asked not expecting her to know much.

'Wiv is partner, 'e said.'

'Have you met this partner?'

'Yers, 'e's a toff — pretends e's not but yer can tell. 'E puts it on — wearin' rough clothes, talkin' like us. They go out sometimes, Alf an' 'im, sort o' in disguise.'

'Name?'

'Dunno — Teddy, Alf calls 'im. Might be 'is real name, might not. Didn't care though. 'E was rough at times even if 'e was a toff an' 'andsome as a prince.'

'Rough? In what way?'

She looked down; Dickens thought he saw a faint flush at her neck. Perhaps she wasn't as hard as she wanted to be.

'Alf wanted me to be good to 'im — yer know, Teddy. I didn't wanter but Alf said 'e 'ad to keep in wiv 'im cos o' the money so I let 'im —' she looked at Dickens — 'yer don't wanter know what 'e did ter me. I didn't tell Alf cos — I don't know — I thought —'

'He'd be angry with Teddy — it might cause trouble between them?' Dickens asked.

'Not really. 'E'd be angry wiv me, I thought. 'E's good ter me, 'e is,' she insisted, 'but I've to do wot 'e says. I 'ave ter — if I wants —' unconsciously, she smoothed her velvet skirts again. No doubt for the first time in her life she had something to wear that wasn't coarse wool or cotton. Dickens feared that the price for the velvet and feathers had been too high. His fears were confirmed in her next words.

'Teddy 'e likes 'em young, yer know. I 'ad ter bring young uns 'ere so that 'e could — yer know —' she looked miserable now — ''e could be cruel, that Teddy. Frightened 'em — frightened me sometimes, too.' She rubbed at her arms and one hand twisted round a wrist as if in memory of being tied there. What had been done to these girls in this room which was so innocuous, without any imprint at all of what had occurred there? She shook herself so that the memory fell away like a discarded scarf. 'Still we're gettin' out of it soon. Wot you done wiv Alf?' She remembered that they had got him.

She had to be told. 'What is your name?'

'Wot's that ter you?' She was angry again now. 'Louisa Mapp.'

'I'm sorry Miss Mapp, but Mr Blackledge is dead.'

'Dead? 'Ow? When?' The colour drained from her face as swiftly as her hopes of a better life drained away.

'He was murdered — not long ago — down in the alleys. His throat was cut.'

'Gawd,' she said, 'oh gawd — woz it 'im — Teddy? 'E's vicious 'e is. Dangerous. Yer catch 'im?'

'We were too late. He got away.'

'Too late — yer woz — too late for Alf — and for me.' Tears welled up, and she looked what she was really — just a girl who had had hopes and lost them. The hardness had gone from her face. It was pinched with disappointment. Dickens thought of the Home — would there be a chance for her there? He would find her again and ask her. Her concern for the young girls she had brought here showed that she had some feeling left — it had not all been taken out of her by two brutal men. He did not doubt that Blackledge had been violent with her even if she pretended to herself that he was good to her.

The tears ran through the paint, and underneath they saw how young she was — seventeen, perhaps. How old were the young ones that she had brought here?

'Yer'll get 'im?' she asked.

'Tell us anything you can about him,' Jones asked, 'anything. Where did they go in their disguises, for example?'

'Down ter Ratcliffe 'Ighway — Johnstone's — yer know it.'

They did — one of the notorious opium dens down in the East End, not far from Wapping Stairs, another labyrinth of squalor and degradation. It seemed that both Teddy and Alf had liked to live dangerously, and one had been murdered. Perhaps Teddy was the more ruthless or simply got in first. Whatever had happened, neither could let the other live.

'Did you know Teddy's other name?'

'Nah, niver said it ter me. I'm just Teddy, 'e sed. Sed it as if it woz funny, yer know. 'E'd old yer down and stroke yer wiv is knife — just Teddy, 'e'd say, laughin' like 'e 'ad a secret. Sang sometimes, too when he woz doin' yer. Nasty it woz — creepy, as if 'e wanted ter use the knife for somethin' else. Cut one of the little girls once across the throat — terrified she woz but 'e laughed. Give 'er two shillin's. Two shillin's,' she said bitterly, 'when 'e had thousands.'

'Can you remember the song, Louisa?' asked Dickens gently.

She sang the words that Davey had written down, '*Thrown on the wide world, doomed to wander and roam, Bereft of my parents, bereft of my home.*' The words sounded low and plaintive in her mouth; she was singing for herself, and as she sang, the tears ran down her face. She put her head down on the table and wept again for all she had lost before she had come to the streets. What a mockery Teddy had made of that song.

Dickens put his hand on her shoulder. He looked at Sam seeing in his face his own pity for the lost innocence of Louisa Mapp and those other little girls who had been brought here to please two depraved men. Louisa Mapp had not told them half. Presently she stopped and looked at them.

'Gotter go,' she said. 'Yer don't want me no more? If yer do I'm at Bell Lane, Mrs Cutler's 'ouse.' She wanted to get away from them. They had seen too much. She adjusted her velvet jacket, rustled her skirts, straightened her shoulders, looked at them with a defiant stare from her bright eyes, and was out before Jones had time to ask for anything else. Dickens admired her courage — she was going out into the dark, but her hat was straight and she stood erect.

'It was he who sang as he killed Patience.' Dickens's voice was tight with anger. He had thought Blackledge bad, but this was worse. Teddy was a brute in every way, callous and laughing as he had hurt these girls. They had to find him. 'Teddy is the Edmund of the song — he must be. So, surely, it follows that he is Edmund Crewe. I wonder what the song means to him. What must he have done to Patience? No wonder she ran away.'

'We have to find out all we can about him. We can't say definitely yet that he is a Crewe, nor that he killed Blackledge. The connection between them is a fact — that much Ducat told, but it's not much use. We have to find him, rattle him — if he can be rattled — and watch what he does.'

'Why kill Blackledge?' asked Dickens. 'I mean now — what prompted it?'

'Perhaps Blackledge knew we were on to him and told Teddy. Someone might have said we were at Ducat's.'

'Not Ambrose Tiplady?'

'I don't think so nor Ducat, but his clerk might have mentioned to someone that the police had been there, and if Blackledge saw Feak he might have thought he was in some danger. And we do not know what else they have been involved in. They could have taken other girls anywhere. They could have killed before Patience. Blackledge might have

172

warned him, thinking they were in it together, not realising the danger he was putting himself into, not realising that Teddy would kill him just as he would a rat. He should hang — when we get him. Now, let's have a look at this cash box.'

Jones slid it from under the bed. The other key on the string opened it. Inside there was cash in sovereigns and notes, altogether about three hundred pounds. And there were some letters addressed to Mr A. Blackledge at the Western Central Post Office at Holborn and marked 'to be collected'. Jones opened one of these. 'He had a wife — and a daughter.' He scanned the contents and handed the letter to Dickens while looking at the other two.

'She wants to know when he is coming home. She asks him to send some money as she is a little short and the butcher needs paying. The child is well now after suffering from a winter cold,' Dickens gave a précis of the contents.

'These are along the same lines. She is glad he is doing well in Town, but hopes he will come soon and, again, she tells him she is in need of money. The address is Brick Holes, Shepherd's Bush — very interesting.'

'I wonder if he went home at those times he was watching Urania Cottage — I bet that is where his pedlar's tray is,' Dickens said.

'We'll have to go and see her — tell her he's dead, and tell her about the money. It is hers — if they are actually married. Let us hope so. This death will be reported to the Coroner tomorrow — we can't keep this one quiet. There'll be an inquest, but it will be adjourned — pending further enquiries by the police, so I'll tell the coroner. So time is still on our side. Feak, Rogers and I will give the bare evidence. You won't have to — I'll see to that. I don't want Teddy to know about you — you'll be the one to do the asking about him — he must

173

belong to a club — he must go out into society — that's where we can find out more about him. Then, when we know a bit more, we can go and tell him his wife's dead. See how he responds to that. We'll take the cash box with us and those clothes. We need them as evidence. Can you carry the box? I'll send Feak and another constable back tomorrow to talk to the neighbours — they might have seen Blackledge with Teddy. Someone might know something useful about them. We'll meet tomorrow after lunch time. I'll have reported to the coroner by then. Have you a Burke's peerage?'

'No, but I know where to find one. I'll look up the Crewes by tomorrow afternoon.'

They went out into the rainy night. The alleys were quiet now and their footsteps echoed behind them as they left Lantern Yard. They glanced up the lane to the alley where Blackledge had died, but there would be nothing there now except the blood staining the stones. Most of it would be washed away by the rain, into the sewers, away to the river, and at last to the sea itself. *Making the green one red*, quoted Dickens to himself. All that blood, and Patience's too. *Blood will have blood.*

19: Brick Holes

Dickens walked from Bow Street to Devonshire Terrace. He thought of Edmund Crewe and Sam's grim portent that Crewe would hang. His own anger had matched Sam's when they contemplated what had been done to those young girls, children really, what had been done to Patience, even the murder of Blackledge though he was a crook. He understood the desire to see that man punished, to see him suffer as his victims had suffered, but he wondered what difference it would make. He had written letters to the *Daily News* in 1846 arguing against the death penalty. He had argued that the watching of such scenes led to a disregard for human life, a coarsening of the souls of those who saw the spectacle. He had seen, and had not forgotten the jeering, bawling callousness of the crowd at the hanging of Courvoisier. He did not believe in it as a deterrent; the threat of hanging had not deterred Edmund Crewe — Dickens thought that the ever-beckoning shadow of the gallows would tempt the murderer on to defy it, to laugh at the phantom even if it should catch up with him. This, he thought, would be the psychology of Edmund Crewe — insolent, dissolute, brought up to believe he was invincible, reckless, and without feeling for his fellow men or women.

The house was quiet at this late hour; the children would be safe in their beds. He thought of those little girls abused by Edmund Crewe, and Blackledge, probably, even if Louisa Mapp did not want to believe it. They were perhaps twelve or thirteen, only a year or so older than his Mamie and Katey still playing with their dolls and toy theatres. It would be Mamie's birthday soon. What would she like? Papa to be there, he knew, and he resolved to be present. To bed.

The next morning, after Dickens had worked on his manuscript, he walked down to the offices of *The Examiner* to consult Burke's peerage which told him that Sir Hungerford Crewe was the third baron, grandson of the first baron, Sir John Crewe, for whom his grandparents had worked. The country seat was Crewe Hall in Cheshire and there was a town house in Grosvenor Street. He was not married so there was no heir yet. There was one sister, Annabella, unmarried also. No Edmund — so who was he?

He went on to Bow Street. Feak had been sent back to Lantern Yard and Rogers would go to the Crewe Town House; he would be investigating burglaries around the neighbourhood. It would be helpful to talk to the servants and ask if they had seen anyone suspicious. Rogers, that inventive young man, would find a way to worm information from some unsuspecting kitchen maid, so Sam said. Dickens told him the address and away he went.

Dickens and Jones made the familiar journey to Shepherd's Bush by fly which was quicker. They asked about the location of Brick Holes. It was not far from Sepulchre Lane. Dickens wondered if Mrs Blackledge were one of the congregation, one of the elect. They found Brick Holes, another gloomy yard off Angel Lane, parallel to Sepulchre Lane. Where the angel was in the dark griminess of its lane was difficult to tell — perhaps in chapel with Godsmark — or, not — if it had any earthly common sense. Brick Holes was tidy enough despite its name, a bit like Lantern Yard, poised between propriety and disgrace. There were neat enough children playing in the courtyard and in a grassy plot seen through the gap between two houses, and two women in aprons chatted over their laundry baskets. They could see poles and lines in the little plot beyond — perhaps the Jopps had been selling their wares here.

'Mrs Blackledge?' enquired the superintendent of the two women. The smaller of the two stepped forward, anxiety creasing her thin face. She was young, perhaps late twenties, but worn-looking, faded in her old brown dress, the colour of which emphasised the sallowness of her complexion. She was no oil painting, but neither was Blackledge. She would hardly compare to the voluptuous Louisa Mapp in her red velvet, worn though it was.

'Yes?' she asked. 'What do you want?'

'May we go inside, Mrs Blackledge?'

'Mary, keep an eye on Rose for me will you?' She spoke to her neighbour. Her voice was low and pleasant, educated.

'Yes, dear. 'Ope everythin's awright.' The woman, Mary, looked curiously at the superintendent.

Mrs Blackledge took them inside the cottage. It was clean, neatly if sparsely furnished with a couple of armchairs by the low fire, a table with four chairs round it. There were books on the table, a pen and some paper. Was she writing to her husband again?

She looked at them, her colourless eyes wide with fear, her thin lips slightly parted. Dickens looked at Sam. It would be hard to tell her — he was glad that he didn't have to do it.

'It is bad news, isn't it? He's dead, isn't he?'

'I am afraid so, Mrs Blackledge.'

Ironically, she asked the same questions as Louisa Mapp had. Two women, so different, but the same in that their hopes were blasted.

'How? When?'

177

'Last night. He was found dead near his lodgings in Lantern Yard. He was murdered.'

Her head went down but she was too shocked to cry. Only a dry sob like a cough escaped her. They waited for her to recover. Her eyes were dry and she blinked as if they were full of grit. It was curiously different from Louisa Mapp's noisy grief. It was difficult to tell what she felt.

'Tell us what you can about him, Mrs Blackledge.'

She looked puzzled. 'I don't know — you mean about his work, about him, what?'

'His work?' asked Jones. He thought she might go on unprompted to tell them about him as a husband.

'In London. He went to work there about two years ago. He didn't want us to go until he had a better place to live and earned more. I wrote to him at the Post Office. He said in London he had to change his lodgings too often to give me an address. He worked for a good firm — he had prospects, he said, but we had to be patient.'

'Have you always been here? What did your husband do before he went to London?'

'We came up from Portsmouth. He worked for the Navy Pay Department, but there was some trouble — the accounts didn't add up. They blamed Alfred, but they couldn't prove anything. It was unfair. Alfred said he couldn't stay where they thought he was dishonest so we came here and stayed with my sister until we rented this house. Alfred went to London — the Pay Office gave him a reference — they could not prove he had taken money.' Her sallow face was flushed. Like Louisa, she did not want to believe he was crooked.

How history repeats itself. Dickens thought of his grandfather, Charles Barrow, another fraudster of Portsmouth who was caught and proved guilty. He felt sorry for this mouse of a woman who had no idea of what her husband had really been. And another link to his own life — was this case destined to make him remember what he had buried so deeply?

'Did he come back often?' Jones asked.

'No, he said he had to work hard there, study the law in his time off if he wanted to get on.'

'Has he been back in the last few weeks?'

'He came back a couple of weeks ago, and also at the end of January.'

'Why?'

'He said one of the clients at the law firm had asked him to do a bit of work. The client wanted him to find out about somebody. It had to be secret — like detective work. He laughed about it — said he would make a bit of money from it — to add to our savings.'

Dickens glanced at Jones. He knew what the superintendent's next question would be, and he hoped he knew the answer.

'Did the detective work involve disguise?'

She looked astonished and afraid. 'How did you know?'

'What disguise?'

'He dressed as a pedlar. He left his tray here. Rose played with it, pretending to sell me ribbons and things. She liked a piece of black velvet ribbon to tie round her neck — pretending she was a lady at a dance — in her white nightdress — you know. He was annoyed about that. Told her not to touch the tray, not to take it outside — ever. She was frightened. I put it away — upstairs. He took the ribbon away from her — I don't know why he had to do that.'

'May we see it?'

She nodded and went out. They heard her slow tread on the wooden staircase. She came back with the tray and they looked at the pincushions, bits of lace and ribbon. Dickens stared at the black velvet ribbon, a piece of which Patience had bought, and which she had worn with her white dress in Mrs Morson's dream.

'You can take it. I don't want it here, now.'

A little girl of about eight came in. 'Ma,' she said, 'it's too cold to play out.' She saw Dickens and Jones and looked at them uncertainly, and at the pedlar's tray.

'We'll take it. Rose, would you like some of the black velvet ribbon?' Jones asked her, pointing to the coiled velvet in the tray.

She shook her head. 'Pa'll be angry. I can't have it.'

'It's all right, love, Pa won't mind — now.' Mrs Blackledge was gentle.

Rose came over and took the ribbon. But it wasn't the same — the joy had gone out of it. Dickens could see that it was worth nothing to her now.

'There's pink ribbon, too,' he said, remembering Mamie and Katey with pink ribbons in their curls. 'It matches your name. Why not take that?'

She gave him a smile which gave a fleeting beauty to the little pale face with its slightly twisted mouth. She took the ribbon with her left hand, holding it carefully like a gift.

'Take your ribbon upstairs, Rose, and put it in your treasure box. These gentlemen will be gone soon.'

She smiled at Dickens again and went out; they heard her feet skipping on the stairs.

'Was your husband left-handed?' asked Jones.

'Yes. Why?'

'I just wondered. Rose is.'

'She is — it makes things difficult for her. I wished she wasn't so like him — in looks, I mean...' She looked sad.

'Did her father love his daughter?' asked Dickens, thinking of the pinched little face.

Mrs Blackledge looked hurt, but not because of the question. 'I don't think he did.' That was all. She said nothing else, but it told the two men that Blackledge had loved neither of them, and Dickens thought they would be better off without him. What might he have done to his daughter had he lived, or would he really have gone to America without them? Probably, and without Louisa Mapp, as well.

'What happens now?' she asked.

'There will be an inquest in a few days which you will have to attend. Have you anyone who can come with you?'

'My sister will come.'

'There is some money. He had about three hundred pounds which will come to you.'

'Thank you.' She looked drained. She could not yet take in what the money might mean to her. Blackledge had done more for her in death than he had ever done in life.

Jones had to ask. 'You don't know who he was trying to find or where he went?'

'He told me nothing about it. He just came, as I told you. He stayed the night both times and went back to London on the Saturday — to report to his client, he said.'

'And he didn't say who the client was?'

'He did not — only that he had plenty of money, and that Alfred would do well out of it. Did he kill my husband because of what he found out?'

'We don't know. We will try to find out.'

'I hope you will. Alfred did not deserve to be murdered whatever —' she stopped, and in the silence that followed they knew what kind of husband he had been.

'We should go now. Perhaps your sister will come,' said Jones.

'She will. She is very good.'

'Goodbye, Mrs Blackledge. We are very sorry to have brought such news.'

'Goodbye.' She turned to Dickens. 'Thank you for the pink ribbon. It was a kind thought.' She looked at him. 'Have I seen you before? Your face is familiar.'

'I don't think so,' said Dickens who had seen the books on the table. *Oliver Twist* and *Nicholas Nickleby*, the edition in which there was an engraving from his portrait by Daniel Maclise, painted in 1840.

They went out of Brick Holes watched by the inquisitive Mary, turned out of Angel Lane and made their way to Lime Grove and Urania Cottage.

'Well, we can be sure Blackledge did not kill Patience. At least that poor woman won't have to learn that her husband was a murderer,' Dickens said, thinking about the revelation that Blackledge had been left-handed.

'And Crewe can't pin the murder of Patience onto Blackledge — that's something he might have tried.'

As they walked to the Home, Jones said he would go to see James Bagster in the garden. He wanted a word about security, and he would seek out Constable Jenkins to make sure he was keeping his eye on the house.

Dickens said, 'You think he might come here?'

'He might — he's been here before, he thinks he has got away with murder, more than once. He knows what kind of house this is. What a temptation for him, all these girls whom you are trying to reclaim and he could ruin.'

'I have thought about him, too; I think he is arrogant, I think he believes his position in society will protect him from suspicion. I think he could be reckless, too.'

'Let us hope that recklessness might be his undoing — you must tell Mrs Morson to be vigilant, too. The girls are always accompanied are they not?'

'Yes. She can tell James Bagster's sister to be watchful and to take note of any strangers on the grounds; that since Patience disappeared more care must be taken. I don't want the girls to be unduly alarmed nor reckless themselves. I worry that the excitement of knowing that there is danger might have the opposite effect from that which we want — there are those that might put themselves in danger by looking out for him, if they know that someone dangerous might come.'

'You mean someone like Isabella Gordon?'

'Precisely. She is bored here and inclined to make trouble, perhaps by simply frightening the more timid girls, pretending to have seen him.' Dickens thought of what Mrs Morson had told him about her behaviour with Sesina which might have been just trouble-making. 'She's just the sort to go looking for excitement.'

'Pray then that he confines his depravity to London, and that he realises that coming here would be too risky.'

'I hope the very risk is not the temptation,' said Dickens. 'We have tried to protect the Home and its reputation and work. It would be dreadful if he were to do such damage that it would be impossible to go on.'

Dickens was afraid. He felt that the spectre of the crooked man who had haunted him had been replaced by something even more terrifying because he was, as yet, faceless.

Jenny Ding was there to let him in. Dickens, always perceptive, noticed that she was less lively than usual, rather pale; she looked as though she might have been weeping. He hoped it was something temporary, perhaps illness, perhaps her monthly health. He had hopes for her progress and success. She took his coat and hat as usual, and he tried to cheer her by commenting on her dress.

'Blue suits you, Jenny. It matches your eyes. Mrs Morson gives me excellent reports of you in your lessons.'

'Thank you, Mr Dickens. I'm tryin' 'ard.' She smiled at him and looked better for it. She was young, he thought, and easily upset and, probably, just as easily cheered up.

Mrs Morson was in the kitchen. There was the making of soup for the poor and the baking of bread and cakes for the house. The cheerful domesticity reassured him. Even Isabella was busy. He smiled to see her concentrating on taking a batch of scones from the oven. Davey was sitting at the kitchen table. Isabella took one of the scones to him.

'Try one o' mine, Davey boy. I'm the best cook, ain't I? Careful, though, it'll be 'ot.' She put the hot scone on his plate and ruffled his hair. She wasn't all bad, Dickens thought, there was a rough affection for the boy, a kindness which endeared her to him. She went back to the wire tray and took a piece of another which she gave to Sesina, putting it on the girl's full red lips, making the sound of a kiss as she did so. It was flirtatious but, then again, it might just be the same sort of affection she had just showed to Davey. She was hard to read, so mercurial was she.

She saw him and came over with a piece of the scone. 'Want a bit, Mr D?' she asked. 'Piece of me scone?' she added cheekily, about to put it in his mouth. He took it in his fingers, but he was well aware of her teasing eyes. How easily she could put herself in danger.

'It's very good,' he told her.

'Best cook me. I like a man with a good appetite.'

By the cooking range Sesina laughed, and some of the others did. Isabella was popular with some — she was full of vitality and wit. Dickens couldn't help liking her, but there was always a question mark over her.

Isabella went back to the range where she and Sesina giggled together. What secrets did they have, and what was the real nature of their intimacy? It was a concern, and he could see the reflection of his own thoughts in Mrs Morson's troubled eyes as she came to stand by him. They went into Mrs Morson's sitting-room.

'What news?' she asked.

'I wrote to you that we had found the pedlar and discovered his name was Blackledge. The superintendent had him watched and we found out where he lived, and followed him there, but we were too late — he was murdered. His throat was cut just like Patience.'

She looked horrified. 'What does it all mean?'

'We believe he was working for someone he had met through the law firm. He had a wife who lived here at Shepherd's Bush, and she confirmed that he had been looking for someone on behalf of one of the company's clients.'

'Looking for Patience? Who?'

'We discovered that Patience was married — or, at least, she had written to a former servant that she was to be married.'

'A servant?'

'Yes, Patience's parents — both dead, we found out — were genteel folks. The father was a music teacher. We traced this servant who told us about her family and this possible marriage — we think to someone wealthy and possibly connected to the Crewe family — there is a Sir Hungerford Crewe, third baronet. We have not proved it all yet but we think we will.'

'This is very difficult to take in — you are telling me that she ran away from this husband who tried to find her, using the pedlar — this Blackledge.' She was silent, working out the implications. He waited. 'Blackledge has been murdered so it follows than that Patience's husband must have killed her and he is still free. Do you think —?'

He knew what she was thinking. 'We don't know. The superintendent is with James Bagster now asking him to be vigilant, and he is going to see Constable Jenkins on the same errand. I just want you to be extra careful — tell James's sister to watch them well when they go out. You can just tell her that you do not want anyone else to go missing, tempted by Patience's running away. That's the best I can do — we don't want the girls made restless and frightened by knowing a murderer is on the loose, especially when what we believe is based on conjecture not hard fact. We don't want one of them running away because she is frightened nor do we want someone like Isabella to be telling lurid stories or even taking it upon herself to go looking for trouble.'

'James could sleep in the house, and Davey. He has been staying with James in his rooms over the stable since Patience was killed. I could move them both back here. The girls need not know — he could come in after they have gone to bed and leave before they rise.'

'A good idea. Do it — make sure he is armed with a stout stick.'

'I can't keep them in — I wish I could, but there's no reason to do so. They only go out in fours so it should not be too difficult for me or Ellen Bagster to keep a close eye on them when we do go out. Oh, Mr Dickens, how I wish this was over — poor Patience, what trouble she brought with her.'

'I know, but we can only be careful. Write immediately or send Davey if there is anything.'

'I will.'

They stood and she came to the front door with him. He mentioned Jenny Ding. 'Yes,' she said, 'I have been a bit concerned about her. She is usually so cheerful but she's growing up and it's not easy for any of them — we think that we can offer them a glowing future, but they are uncertain of what they want, afraid of leaving here, and marked by their pasts.'

'I know,' he said. She understood them, probably more than he. She lived with them and observed them every day, and she was a woman. She had had to grow up, too. She smiled at him. 'I will try to keep them safe.'

He could depend on her, he knew that. She was not easily frightened.

'So will I, and the superintendent. We will catch him.' He clasped her hand before he went round the side of the house to meet Jones.

They were back at Bow Street by five o'clock. Constable Rogers was ready to report what he had found out about the Crewe family. His story about the burglaries had got him into the kitchens where he was able, over a cup of tea, to find out who lived at the house and who were the regular visitors. Sir Hungerford Crewe lived sometimes in London, but he spent a good deal of time at his northern estates in Cheshire and Staffordshire. His sister lived with him and they had plenty of guests, distinguished members of the upper classes, bankers and politicians. He was a member of the Royal Society and the Society of Antiquarians so a good many learned men came to dinner, according to the housekeeper.

'Any other relatives?' asked Dickens eagerly.

Rogers grinned. 'I didn't ask too much — didn't want to seem too nosy, but I kept me eye on the house and when one of the maids came out, I spoke to her, pretendin' I was on duty an' I asked her if she was all right and hoped she wasn't frightened by wot I'd told 'em. I walked with her a bit an' asked some more about the family.' His eyes gleamed. 'I asked her were there any black sheep — we was getting quite friendly by then, me and Mollie Spoon.' He grinned again at their waiting faces.

'And there is a black sheep — and his name is?' asked Jones.

'Edmund Crewe.'

'Known as Teddy.' Dickens felt triumphant.

''Xactly!'

'Had she met him?' asked Jones.

'She saw him. Handsome, she said, tall with yeller hair — looked a nice gent, she thought though the housekeeper, a stern sort o' body, told her handsome is as handsome does. I changed the subject then, askin' her how she liked her place and that so she wasn't suspicious. She liked it fine, she said. Sir Hungerford was a good master and they was all pretty comfortable there. And on that happy note, I left her.'

'You did not find out where he lived, by any chance?'

'Sorry, sir, shoulda said. She said he lived in some smart apartments somewhere. Didn't know where 'xactly, but shouldn't be too difficult to find.'

'Well done, Rogers, once again. Your cunning does you credit,' Jones said laughing. 'You'll be a detective yet.'

'Thank you, sir. Do you want me to find him?'

'That's the question. Timing is all. At some point we want to break the news of his wife's death, see how he reacts, but I would like to know more about him. Mr Dickens here will be our spy. Charles, it is time for you to go into society but where to start?'

'He'll belong to a club — sure to, and I must get myself into it. I know which ones it won't be — I belong to the Garrick and the Athenaeum. It will not be a political club — he is more the gambling and drinking sort, and there is Boodles which has been labelled a den of vice. And there are others which might suit the reckless type. I shall find out. And so doing, I should be able to find out where he goes, who he sees, what is his reputation. Trust me for that. I shall make enquiries this very evening.'

'The electoral register should give us Crewe's address. Rogers, you can research that tomorrow. Have you heard anything from Feak regarding Lantern Yard?'

'Nothing, sir. No one's been there. He spoke to the neighbours, the family upstairs. They knew about Blackledge being murdered. Told 'em the police was watchin' the place, and that it was likely he was murdered by someone he knew, and the police was investigatin', but they was to tell him if they saw anyone. They told him who the landlord was an' he went there and told him he couldn't let it until we'd finished with the place. He wasn't pleased, but Feak insisted. Told him to keep away until enquiries was finished.'

'Good. Now I am going home to see my wife and my house guests. We should be able to let them go home soon. I can reassure Scrap and Mr Brim that Blackledge will trouble them no more, and when my Elizabeth thinks Mr Brim is well enough he can open his shop again. Charles, you will no doubt have some more stationery to buy, and perhaps you can persuade some of your writer friends to do business there — it will make up for his days of lost trade.'

'I will indeed. I shall go home, too, see my wife and children. On the way, I'll call upon my friend Mr Lemon, editor of *Punch*, who will be able to tell me something about the kind of club which will attract a man like Edmund Crewe.'

20: Rake's Progress

Dickens walked to the office of Bradbury and Evans in Lombard Street, his own publishers and those of *Punch*, a magazine in which he took enormous delight, especially when it advertised his works. Two recent cartoons satirising the government had included references to the Artful Dodger and *The Haunted Man*, his last Christmas story; both had given him great satisfaction. He was not himself a frequenter of gaming clubs. He preferred the company of his friends, men like Forster with whom he established the Trio Club with only themselves and Thomas Beard. He meditated on the idea of the gentleman's club, thinking wryly to himself that gentlemen were precisely very often what the members were not, especially young men like Edmund Crewe. However, he enjoyed the dining club, The Parthenon, where Mark Lemon offered to dine with him, after which they would visit Boodles in search of Crewe.

They dined on oysters, turbot and beef with a good bottle of claret. Dickens explained that he wanted to find Crewe in relation to a girl missing from Urania Cottage and that he was working with Superintendent Jones of Bow Street about whom Mark Lemon knew.

'Helping the police with inquiries, eh?' said Lemon.

'I am,' said Dickens, 'thinking of setting up in the detective line with a large brass plate. Terms: ten guineas to find your lost cat, dog — or child — if you should want it back.'

Lemon laughed and regaled him an advertisement he had put in *Punch*. 'I could not resist it. Listen to this: "Wanted: a place of solitary retirement by a person thirty years of age who wishes to exclude himself from all society and live as a hermit for any period not exceeding seven years, on suitable terms!" It's true as I sit here — from the *North British Advertiser.*'

'I wonder if the suitable terms means that he pays or the employers pay. What would be the duties of a hermit? Do you suppose he inhabits a grotto, emerging daily for the edification of noble persons who visit the spacious park? I think I might advertise myself — seven years solitude would mean more than a bit of peace.'

'Charles, you wouldn't last a month — you would miss the entertainment of your witty friends, like me for instance!' Lemon's round, falstaffian face beamed.

They talked of *Punch*, of friends, of crime and punishment, the time when Dickens had been accused of being a felon by a pickpocket who had tried to steal Lemon's watch. In court, the criminal had tried to turn the tables on his accusers. He identified them as a couple of swell mobsters, and insisted, much to Dickens's amusement, that he had met Dickens in prison doing six months. Then it was time to go.

They found at Boodles in St James's Street a young friend of Lemon's, Oliver Wilde, who knew Edmund Crewe. 'He doesn't come here so often now — doesn't always pay his debts, y'know.'

They did know.

Oliver Wilde told them that there was a club popular with young bloods and that Edmund Crewe was often there. It was called The Polyanthus. Wilde offered to accompany them. It was not far, just across Piccadilly in a side street off Dover Street. Wilde could introduce them to the club where they might take a glass of champagne, and Dickens could see if Crewe were in the gaming room. That was where he could usually be found. Dickens repeated a vague tale that he wanted to identify Crewe in connection with a matter of some delicacy — Wilde did not seem surprised so they set off to The Polyanthus.

'It's all right, Tyce,' Wilde said to the servant, 'I've brought two friends for a drink. Champagne, if you will.' At the entrance to the gaming room, Wilde pointed out Crewe to Dickens and went to sit in the salon with Lemon.

For the first time, Dickens saw the man whom they believed had murdered Patience and Blackledge. He was, as Rogers's parlour maid had described, attractive, fair-haired; in fact, he was more than just attractive. His oval face was finely modelled, the lips full, almost feminine, and the high cheekbones giving the face the look of a sculpture. His hair was swept back from his high forehead in waves and he looked, though he was seated, as though he would be tall and strong. There was nothing which marked him out as a murderer, nothing, at this distance at any rate, of the unwholesomeness of Blackledge. Were you to identify one of them as a killer, you would have chosen Blackledge rather than this fair young man with his ready smile. He was smiling as he lost his game, carelessly throwing his cards onto the table, grinning ruefully at his companions and raising his glass ironically to the winner. Unlike Blackledge, Crewe was right-handed. The long hand that now held a champagne glass had held the knife at the throat of Patience Brooke, had pressed the point into the soft flesh, and drawn the swift blade from left to right. It must have done.

Dickens turned away, sick at heart, and went into the salon to join Mark Lemon and Wilde. Dickens hoped that they might hear some gossip. Crewe came in and lounged with two of his companions on comfortable sofas from where they called for champagne. Crewe declared that he was ready to go home, that he had a particular engagement the next day with a young lady. The others laughed.

'Caught her, yet, Crewe — is she ripe for plucking?' This from a slight, dark young man with fine features beginning to coarsen, no doubt, from drink.

'I'll beg you not to discuss my future wife so basely, Lovelace, I may have to call you out — and I'm a better shot than you are.' He aimed an imaginary pistol at Lovelace who fell back on his sofa as though hit.

The third of the group, a red-headed burly young man, worse for drink, was more aggressive. 'She's not accepted you yet an' I don't think she will. What's her father say — does he know about your money situation, eh, Crewe?'

Crewe's good humour turned to anger, and Dickens saw, as the young man stood up and seized the red-headed man by his lapels, that his face was dark with temper. 'Shut up, you brute — I tell you it's all right. She loves me and my money ain't your business. Look to your own, Carew.' He shook Carew roughly and slouched back moodily onto the sofa. Carew looked equally sulky.

Lovelace offered, 'Shall we go on, then, somewhere less public, somewhere we can have a bit of fun?'

Crewe said bad-temperedly, 'I've told you I'm going home. You two go where you like — to the devil, if you will.'

He rose and made his way out of the salon to the hall where he was helped into his greatcoat by the obliging Tyce to whom he gave a coin. He went out, stumbling a little down the steps. Dickens and Lemon rose to go. Wilde finished his champagne and stood, too. He indicated that he would go into the gaming room. 'I pay my debts,' he said. They bade him goodnight and went out.

Crewe had not gone far. He was leaning against the wall getting his breath. Dickens and Lemon stood uncertainly on the steps. Would he take a cab or would he walk? It looked as if he would walk. He turned into a narrower street. Dickens was struck, as always, with the contrast between the smart streets they had traversed, Piccadilly, Pall Mall and St James's Street and the squalor that was so close, the smell that was under the nose of the wealthy, a smell which they liked to believe a nosegay or two could disperse. Riches and poverty, vice and virtue, innocence and guilt all crowding together in the teeming city. Crewe shambled on; from time to time a woman would approach him, hoping for a customer. He waved them off, scattering coins at them in careless mockery. Once, he turned round to watch a little barefooted girl go by, and in the lurid gaslight Dickens saw his face — the face of a ruined angel. The terrible light showed what he really was. *The rake's progress*, he thought. Crewe had advanced detestably through all the stages of cruelty to murder itself, and he had murdered his own soul in the process. They followed as Crewe walked by the homeless vagrants, indifferent to the child crying in the gutter, not seeing the scrawny dog which looked at him with terrified eyes and cowered against a wall. A stout bundled-up woman walked past in a dress the colour of mud with a matching bonnet and shawl so that she looked as if she might have risen from a nearby ditch, and smelt so, too. She stared at Crewe but he pushed passed her. 'Poor creetur,' she muttered and went on. What had she seen in that beautiful face, ruined by the hideous light?

As they followed, Mark Lemon was able to tell him something of the taunting Carew whose family he knew, and to whom he could take Dickens should he wish to meet them at an evening reception. It would be easy — who would not want to meet the great Charles Dickens? It was an idea — Crewe might be there — in pursuit of his, as yet unknown, lady-love.

The narrow lanes led them at last into the light and into Burlington Gardens.

'He'll live at the Albany, I'll bet,' said Lemon.

And he was right. They saw him turn right in front of the Albany, home to sixty-nine bachelor apartments known as sets where young men lived in rather cramped rooms, yielding space for fashion. It was enough. The two friends parted on Piccadilly, taking separate cabs to their respective homes.

It was late now; Dickens was ready to go home, but he thought, as got into his cab, that he might call at Norfolk Street. If there were a light downstairs he would knock and hope that Sam would come to the door.

Leaning across the railings which enclosed a tiny patch of garden, he knocked lightly on the downstairs window with his stick. A light showed that someone was still up. Sam was not unused to receiving callers at late hours nor was Elizabeth. Sam appeared at the door and Dickens came quietly in. They went into the parlour where they had dined two nights before. Sam had been sitting by the fire with his brandy and water. Accepting a glass gratefully, Dickens sat down in the chair opposite Sam, and felt the glow of the fire warm his boots.

'Constable Dickens reporting, sir,' he said smiling as the brandy and water slipped pleasurably down. 'I bring great tidings. I have been out and about in clubs and cabs, taking a peek at the life of raffish young men — what larks! I never was raffish myself. I should like to have been, though. Too late now for us, Sam.'

Jones laughed. 'You found him and you know something important.' He saw the eyes alight with knowledge, despite the tiredness round them.

'I have and I do. He lives, as we might have expected, at the Albany. I saw him at The Polyanthus Club, playing cards amiably enough. He is an attractive young man, as the maidservant told Rogers, but he has a temper. He went off in a surly mood after one of his friends taunted him about the girl he wants to marry.'

'Did he now? It's as we surmised; having disposed of a first wife, he now looks for a second. That's why he had to find her.'

'I believe so, and he was annoyed when his friend rattled him about money, the implication being that he, being short of it, was looking to marry it. A living first wife might have got in the way though I wonder who knew of it. It cannot have been common knowledge if he has been pursuing another. Perhaps his marriage to Patience was kept secret — she would not have been, perhaps, a socially acceptable wife. A youthful indiscretion — one that he regretted.'

'And Patience, too. She left him and we have an idea why — his treatment of those girls and Louisa Mapp told us enough.'

'We have his motive, that's the thing. His motive to kill her was that he needs to marry again. But what was his motive in tearing open her dress, unbinding her hair and daubing her in that crude rouge? What was his motive?'

'To suggest that she was a prostitute, that she was one of your fallen women and that she was killed by some angry pimp?'

'Yes, and because she was not,' said Dickens. 'She was virtuous and he had degraded her or tried to. Perhaps he could not — I thought there was steel in her. And she insisted to me that she was not a prostitute even though she would tell me nothing else. She resisted him. He could not break her and she escaped him. He could not support that so he destroyed her.'

They were silent for a while. Dickens closed his eyes. As the fire died down, the coals slipped making a sound like a hoarse shushing. Beneath the ash, red glowed, dimmer but still alive. Sam Jones regarded his sleeping friend, his eager, restless vitality dimmed in sleep. What a man, he thought as he looked at the face in repose with its broad forehead, firm nose and sensitive mouth. A genius, and a good man. He thought how Charles Dickens's life had touched so many others as if threads unwound from his fingers stretching out endlessly. Yet, Sam sensed an aloneness in the sleeping figure. Perhaps we are all like that in sleep. He had watched Elizabeth sleeping after Edith's death, and had felt he could not reach her. He had watched Scrap, too, the sleeping face just a child's when the knowingness of life had gone out of it.

Another coal shifted in the fire. Dickens woke to find Jones offering him another brandy and water. He wondered at the kindness in his eyes.

'Tomorrow,' said Jones, 'I'll send Rogers back to the Crewe town house. He ought to ask Miss Mollie, the maid, about the rumours of marriage.'

'Ah, the shining Miss Spoon. Did I detect a glimmer of a liking there from Rogers?'

'I wondered about that — it won't distract him though. One of my best lads is Rogers — I hope she's a decent girl.'

'Sounds like it from what he said. Anyway, Mark Lemon says he can get me an invitation to the house of one of Crewe's companions at The Polyanthus — a young man called Carew. It might be useful to find out who the lady is. I tell you what, I could find Oliver Wilde, Lemon's friend, and ask him. I could do that tomorrow.'

'And when we have found out, we can go to the Albany and see Crewe. It's time we came face to face with him, even though, as yet, we can't prove he is a murderer.'

'At least, when he knows that we know he was married, and that the fact of his marriage would come out at an inquest, it might change his mind about another marriage. From what I heard earlier, the girl's father would not be pleased to know about his impecunious state. He would be less pleased to know that Crewe was secretly married when he was courting his daughter. We might save her.'

'True, and our visit might alarm him — he might do something foolish like try to get away. I don't know. I just wish we had evidence.'

'Perhaps Louisa Mapp could help us — we could see her again.'

'We will. Tomorrow, by the way, Elizabeth is to take Eleanor and Tom, and Poll, of course, back to the shop. Mr Brim is a lot better, but he is fretting about his business so Elizabeth will act as chaperone whilst Miss Eleanor serves the customers. Elizabeth can deal with the man in the white waistcoat — she told me about that — she can pay him off, if necessary. Brim won't like it — too proud — but Elizabeth will deal with that later. Scrap, of course, is to be the bodyguard.'

'That is very good. And those children?'

'Are enjoying their holiday, bouncing about the garden at the back with Poll and Posy who seems to have forgotten that she is a lady of position in the house. It is good to see them. Scrap is always on watch, however — takes his duties seriously.'

'Until tomorrow then. I will call at Crown Street after I have pursued my enquiries for Mr Wilde. Goodnight, Sam. I am sorry I kept you up so late.'

'Shall I walk with you?' Jones asked, concerned by how exhausted Dickens looked.

'No, get thee to bed. The walk is not far.'

'Goodnight, Charles.'

Jones watched him go along Norfolk Street towards Park Square, a solitary figure in the night.

Dickens walked home. At Devonshire Terrace, he stood for a moment looking up into the sky where the cold moon gleamed, remembering how he and his sister, Fanny, used to wander at night about a churchyard near their house at Chatham, looking up at the stars and wondering at their distance. Well, Fanny was far away now, dead of the disease that would kill Francis Fidge before the summer, and the little crippled boy, Harry, her son, dead, too. He went in.

21: Missing

On Saturday morning, Elizabeth Jones took a cab to the shop in Crown Street. Mr Brim had been given instructions to stay in bed and to be tended to by Posy; he had submitted to the combined persuasion of Eleanor, Elizabeth and Posy, too. And he had professed himself reassured by Scrap who had declared, 'Yer don wanter fret, Mr Brim, cos Mr Dickens sed that Ol' Crookface is gorn far away and can't 'urt us. Anyways, yer got me to look after 'em, an' Mrs Jones, 'ere, well she's a lady an' she can tidy shop and fings, but I'll be on guard — me an' Poll can see orf any villuns.'

The shop was re-opened, the man in the white waistcoat, somewhat dashed by Elizabeth's authority, was paid his dues, and Poll and Scrap took up their station in the doorway where they were found by Dickens who had thoughtfully purchased another cake for their morning refreshment.

'I owe you some money, Scrap,' he said after greeting Poll with a pat on the head.

'Nah, Mr Dickens, I bin treated these last days. No need.'

'But you have been on duty. The superintendent told me. Reassured, he was, when he had to go to Bow Street. Two shillings, I think. You're in employment now. Can't turn down your wages. We have a contract.'

'Oh, well, if yer puts it like that.'

'I do,' said Dickens, handing over the two shillings. 'The job's not over yet — at least until Mr Brim comes back.'

They went in. Dickens declined to stay for cake, but he enquired for ink and paper.

'Are you sure, Mr Dickens?' asked Eleanor.

'I am, Miss Eleanor. I have much writing to do.'

'About Jip?'

Dickens had almost forgotten that he had promised a good dog in his new book. 'Yes, indeed.'

'What is he like?' asked Tom Brim, suddenly popping up.

'He is — er — a spaniel,' Dickens improvised, 'yes, a pretty little spaniel with silky ears, and he is very clever, of course.'

'As clever as Poll?' asked the little boy. Poll growled slightly.

'No, no. He has not had the opportunities that Poll has had.'

Elizabeth smiled at him. She loved the way he entered into the child's world, and the seriousness with which he answered their questions. Dickens chose his ink, blue, and his paper, another quire, and left them to their cake.

He walked on to Lombard Street and obtained the address of Oliver Wilde, a handsome set of apartments on Regent Street. Thither he went and found Mr Wilde enjoying his coffee.

'A late night?' Dickens asked.

'An early morning, rather, but I pay my debts, as I said.' He grinned and asked Dickens what he could do for him. A nice young man, Dickens thought, looking at his rumpled hair and open face.

'I wondered if you knew anything about Crewe's marriage plans.'

'Ah,' said Oliver. 'There is talk. He is pursuing a young lady, a very young lady, as a matter of fact. She is only eighteen. She is the daughter of Mr Topham, a banker who has a fine house in Hanover Square. You may have heard of him. He is famously rich and she is his only child. Laetitia, she's called. Lovely name, is it not.'

Dickens heard the wistfulness in Wilde's voice. You may be successful yet, he thought before replying, 'I have heard of him — does the young lady return his affections?'

'How could she not? He can be very charming and he is a good-looking young man. All the ladies rave about him, though —'

'There is a but?'

'Well some of us who know him don't like what we know — he gambles, as you saw, and he drinks and he can be a nasty piece of work if crossed, but she doesn't know all that. Who could tell her?'

'Her father must have heard things.'

'I think he has. There is talk of her going to Paris — I hope she does — with an armed escort,' he said fiercely. 'I'd be prepared to guard her against that man myself.'

'I hope so, too,' said Dickens. 'Perhaps when she comes back, things will be very different — don't give up.'

Oliver Wilde was quiet. Dickens could see that he was concerned. He prepared to go but the young man stopped him.

'Mr Dickens, do you know something about him? Why did you want to see him last night? Do you think he is a danger to her? Would he harm her? — I mean, suppose he were to do something dreadful if he knew her father was going to take her away. He is capable of anything, I think. We all know that he has money troubles, and that Sir Hungerford is losing patience with him. Oh, God, Mr Dickens, what can I do? — I'd do anything for her —' Wilde blushed.

Dickens felt himself in a quandary — he could not lie to Wilde. If Crewe did try to take Laetitia, then the young man would certainly blame him, yet he could not tell Wilde the whole story. He would have to tread carefully.

'I do not know, Mr Wilde, what he might do. Perhaps you could keep a discreet eye on him. You might watch his behaviour if you see him at a social occasion, but you must not be rash. All that you have said is speculation — you must not let him know you are watching. You might hurt Miss Topham's feelings. I beg you, be discreet. If you are concerned or you hear anything then come to me and we will see her father.'

Oliver Wilde promised that he would not be impetuous. Dickens went away, but he was not entirely certain that Mr Wilde would exercise caution. That he loved Laetitia Topham was as obvious as it was clear that he did not like Edmund Crewe. He felt anxious that he had created a complication as if the case were not complicated enough. He could hardly have told Wilde that Crewe was a suspected murderer, but had he put the young man in danger? He had to hope that his reference to Miss Topham's feelings would prevent the boy from acting rashly, and what would Sam think?

Dickens took a cab to Bow Street to give the superintendent his news about Crewe and Laetitia Topham. He explained what he had felt necessary to tell Oliver Wilde. Jones agreed that the young man's fearful questions had had to be answered, and that they could only hope that Oliver Wilde would be cautious. Jones's practical common sense and ability to accept things as they were was reassuring, as always, so they went for lunch at the Piazza Coffee House then went back to find that Rogers had come from the Crewe town house. He had found out much the same thing: the talk in the kitchen was that Mr Edmund was to marry a rich heiress and all his money troubles would be solved. There had been a row with Sir Hungerford though the details were not clear — probably about money, Mollie had said. She thought it all very romantic. Talk was that the young couple might run away because Mr Topham, her father, cast in the role of villain, did not approve. Rogers did not know how much was true, but it made him think about the poor young lady.

'I see,' said Jones, 'You think he might run off with her to get the money. It's time we scared him off. Interesting,' he said to Dickens, 'that Mr Wilde had expressed the same idea.'

As he spoke, the door was flung open, and a harassed-looking constable came in, followed closely by a frightened-looking Mrs Morson.

'The lady, sir, she wouldn't —'

'It's all right, Semple, I'll deal with it.' Semple disappeared. Dickens and Rogers stood, appalled at what they saw in Mrs Morson's face.

'Jenny Ding is missing.'

'Oh, God,' said Dickens, 'he has her.'

Mrs Morson sat down; she was white and shaking. Dickens took her hand. Jones took charge. 'Rogers, take a constable with you to the Albany. Tell him about Crewe, what he looks like and so on. There'll be a porter, ask him if he knows if Crewe is at home. If he is not, leave the constable on watch for him. As you go out, get Feak and another constable, Stemp will do, and tell them to get to Lantern Yard immediately. He needs to have a look through that window you climbed through. Tell him to be careful not to be seen. If Crewe is there, Stemp must come back here for me. Come back from the Albany as soon as you can.'

Rogers wasted no time. Jones turned to Mrs Morson. 'Tell us what happened. Do you know that she was taken?'

'No, we do not, but after what Mr Dickens told me at the Home, I thought —' she broke off, uncertain now, hoping that it might not be so — 'I had been out with some of the girls to the village. Ellen was with some of the others in the kitchen. Jenny was about, in the kitchen, then in the parlour, then in the hall, reading her book. She liked to wait there to answer the door — I did not think to warn Ellen about that — but would he just come to the door? Anyone might have answered.'

'When was it realised she was missing?'

'When I came back, I knocked at the door — I could have let myself in with the girls, but we had parcels and I knew Jenny would be there — but no one came so I knocked again. Eventually Ellen came and I asked where Jenny was. Ellen thought she might be in the parlour. She was not. I went upstairs, but she wasn't there either. I questioned the girls, but no one had noticed. Isabella thought she might be out in the garden with James or Davey, or in the stable. She wasn't — they had not seen her — and they didn't know how long. I had been out for two hours — she may have been gone since I went.' Mrs Morson stopped to wipe her eyes. 'Oh, Mr Dickens, you told me to be careful. I should not have left the house.'

He pressed her hand. 'But, we had James Bagster sleep in the house, and we could not expect Crewe to come in broad daylight — we did not expect him to come at all — it was just precautions.'

'You do not think she has just run away?' asked Jones.

'On the way here, I thought of that. She had been unusually subdued, unhappy. I thought — I said to Mr Dickens that she was growing up. We talked about it.'

'Could he have approached her — in the village? Could he have persuaded her to go with him? It is all so unlikely — why would he do this?' Dickens felt frustrated. None of it made sense except — he thought of that ruined angel's face. What recklessness possessed it? 'When could he have seen Jenny?' he asked.

'Tuesday, Wednesday? Ellen took Jenny, Isabella, Esther, and Lizzie Dagg to the village — they pair off sometimes to go into the shops. It would be easy for a pair to split up.'

'What if —' Dickens's mind was racing — 'what if Crewe approached the older one, say, Isabella, flirted a little whilst keeping his eye on the younger. Suppose Isabella, or whichever one it was, told Jenny not to tell — that's why she was upset — suppose he did come to the door, persuaded her to come out to take a message for Isabella and then just took Jenny?'

'We have to assume he has her,' Jones decided, 'and we must act on that assumption. Feak hasn't come back so I assume that Crewe is not at Lantern Yard. Where's Rogers? He should be back by now!'

On cue, Rogers arrived to tell them that Crewe had not been seen at the Albany, and that he had left the other constable there.

'Rogers, I want you to go to the Home with Mrs Morson, and I want you to find out if any of the girls knows anything, if any stranger approached them. Tell Jenkins to start searching. Bagster can help — anywhere down the lane where he might have taken her. I doubt they'll find anything. He'll be back in London, but it has to be done.'

Rogers and Mrs Morson left. 'We go to Lantern Yard,' said Jones. 'I'll get another couple of constables to go with us. We could do with Scrap — he can get into places we can't and he's invisible. No one will notice one more ragged boy wandering in the lanes.'

'Will he be safe?'

'He's resourceful and clever — he'll know his way round those alleys better than Crewe. We'll tell him just to keep his eyes and ears open. Will you get him from Crown Street?'

At the shop, Dickens told Elizabeth quickly that Sam needed Scrap. She understood, her eyes telling him that they should take care. Scrap understood that Dickens had urgent need of him. He dashed into the back of the shop, emerging with an old cap of Mr Brim's which he jammed on his head. Outside the shop, he bent and daubed his face with a bit of mud — he knew he looked too clean. Dickens and he took a cab from Shaftsbury Avenue to Whetstone Place from where they hastened down to Lantern Yard, passing one of Sam's constables.

Feak was at the entrance to the yard, and further down, they could see another constable waiting. Inside the house, Jones was just emerging from the empty room opposite Blackledge's. 'Nothing,' he said.

They went into Blackledge's room which smelt stale after being locked up. But it told them nothing. It was just empty, keeping its secrets as it had done before.

'Scrap, we are looking for a girl, about thirteen, small, dark hair, wearing a blue dress. Neat — not a girl from the alleys — she will look different so you'll know her. She might be with an older girl, dark hair, red velvet jacket and skirt. I want you to scour these lanes, go where we cannot go, ask — any children playing, any mothers — people you think will answer — you know the type — tell them she's run away. Listen in at the cellars, back yards, but do not do anything. If you see or hear anything come straight back. There'll be a constable here. Wait for us. It will be dark soon. Listen out for the clocks. It's now four o'clock. When you hear six striking, come back anyway. We'll be here. Go now — and Scrap, don't put yourself in any danger — don't ask the wrong people.'

'I knows wot yer means, sir. No need to worry abaht me. I'll be back by six.' He took off the clean shirt Elizabeth had given him, and put his shabby jacket back on. Seeing their faces, he said, grinning, 'Gotter look the part.' They went to the door with him and watched him go, kicking stones and whistling like any urchin with nothing much to do.

'I don't think Crewe has been here,' said Jones. 'I spoke to the neighbours upstairs. They haven't heard anyone downstairs. We need to find Louisa Mapp. He might have been to her. She said she lived at Mrs Cutler's in Bell Lane.'

They went out. Feak and the constable in the lane were to search as well as Scrap and the constable who had stood at Whetstone Place was to stand guard at Lantern Yard. They hurried down Serle Street and into a knot of lanes off Carey Street where Bell Lane lay. It was rather wider than the lanes they had walked through and led out to Hough Street. Jones knew the house. It looked respectable enough if you did not know what it was for. It was one of a terrace, double-fronted with a railed area in front, and steps up to the front door. They knocked. Jones did not stand on ceremony. 'Police to see Mrs Cutler.'

He was in through the door before the waif-like servant girl had a chance to answer. The hall was lit by gas. It was square with a red and cream tiled floor, and a couple of chairs by a fireplace — the fire not yet lit. There was a palm in a brass pot at the bottom of the stairs and a table with a lace cloth. Dickens was amused at the gentility of it all, and noted with interest an inviting velvet chaise-longue in the room whither had gone the startled waif in search of Mrs Cutler. A young woman came in after them through the open door. They looked round quickly, but it wasn't Louisa Mapp. The young woman looked surprised and curious, but went upstairs without a word, glancing back once in a slightly anxious way.

Mrs Cutler came, a tall, handsome woman in her thirties, he guessed. Her dress was of some dark green, heavy material and it fitted her well. She was confident, too, and gracious, as if she were welcoming them to tea. She moved well and seemed to glide towards them. Her voice was educated though monotonous as if she had prepared her words beforehand.

'Superintendent,' she said. 'How may I help you?'

'We are looking for Louisa Mapp, and it is urgent. I cannot give you any details. It is not, I think, anything to do with your business here, but we need to find her. Is she here?'

She did not blink at the word 'business', but replied in her colourless tones, 'No, she is not. I have not seen her since Thursday. She came back late at night. In the morning she was gone. I do not know where.'

Dickens was surprised at how precisely she spoke. He had thought she would be rough and hard; he wondered what had brought her to this way of living. It was as if she were not real, that she had manufactured herself, a large doll devoid of feeling.

Jones asked if she knew whether Louisa had any family. Mrs Cutler did not, but she would ask one of her other residents, Mary Lyons, who had been friendly with Louisa. She went out of the room and they could hear her calling for Susan, presumably the waif.

'Residents!' laughed Jones. 'Born actress, this one — I wonder what happened to the real Mrs Cutler.'

After a few minutes, Mrs Cutler came back with the girl they had seen go upstairs. She looked nervous when Mrs Cutler told her that the police wished to speak to her about Louisa. Jones sensed that she would tell them nothing if Mrs Cutler stayed. He could not afford to be tactful so he told her bluntly that they would like to talk to Mary alone. Mrs Cutler was gracious once more. 'Certainly, Superintendent, as you will.'

Mary was Irish and beautiful with her creamy skin and green eyes. She was also frightened now she was alone with them.

'Tell us about Louisa. It's very important that we find her. A young girl is missing. Where has she gone?'

Mary knew about Blackledge. Louisa had told her that he was dead. Louisa also told her that she wanted to get away, find somewhere else to lodge.

'Get away from what?' asked Jones sharply.

'I don't know — she was frightened of someone.'

'Who?'

'I don't know. I think he was a gentleman, a toff, she said. A bad 'un she thought, but Blackledge'd look after her, she said. Then when she came after he was dead, she said it was better I didn't know where she was going, but that she'd try to come back and see me.'

There was no time for more — they knew of whom she might be frightened. Now there was Louisa Mapp to worry about as well as Jenny Ding. One last question.

'Did she have parents, family — where?'

'Covent Garden — mother and sisters, brothers. I'm not sure. She went there sometimes.'

'Where?' Jones almost shouted.

'Off Floral Street — Lavender Alley, I think.'

They hurried away, not bothering to speak to Mrs Cutler.

Dickens began, 'So, she was frightened enough to leave the formidable Mrs Cutler. I wonder if Crewe went to see her, to find out what she knew about Blackledge's death. It would be logical for her to go home, to hide there, but if she is not there, then, surely, there is every chance that he did find her, and perhaps took Jenny to her — if he thought she was still on his side or he could frighten her.'

'We must go back to Lantern Yard quick as we can — we'll check if Scrap's been back or if Feak has found anything.' They were racing now, rushing up the length of Serle Street. At Lantern Yard, the constable told them that no one had been back. Jones instructed him to tell Feak that they would be back by six o'clock. It was past five now. It would take about ten minutes to Floral Street.

Away they went again, striding out, their fast-coming breath misting as they went, too quick to speak, hastening through Kemble Street, Bow Street, Covent Garden, Floral Street where they ducked into the ginnel where one gaslight guttering like a corpse candle showed them the entrance into the stinking alley with the inappropriate name.

'Mapps?' Jones asked a man coming out.

'Down there.' The man pointed to some steps leading underground, no doubt to some squalid, malodorous cellar where more than one family would live.

Mrs Mapp was so unlike her daughter that it was tragic — impossible to tell her age, she might have been forty or seventy, so much a wreck of a woman she was, so emaciated that her face seemed to have fallen in around a toothless, gaping hole of a mouth. They knew at once that Louisa wasn't there. The dwelling was only one room with a few pitiful broken bits of furniture. There was a straw mattress on the floor, its insides spilling out; there were some wretched worn blankets piled on it. Lying underneath was a girl of about ten or so — she might have been older. Her hair was stringy, wet on the dirty rags which made her pillow. Her eyes were closed and her breathing was hoarse and laboured.

Mrs Mapp stared at them. They had come down the greasy steps, their feet clattering as they came and stood now, too large, in the dingy cellar. Her eyes darted to the bed and to the door. She was terrified. It was as if she expected an attack, that they would leap on her — perhaps someone had done that before? Was there a Mr Mapp? Dickens wondered.

'Mrs Mapp,' said Dickens as Jones moved back towards the steps. He knew she was frightened of his size. He didn't blame her. He felt enormous in this confined space. Mrs Mapp stared uncomprehendingly at Dickens as though she did not recognise her own name. The girl in the fusty bed coughed and whimpered in her sleep. Dear God, thought Jones, the misery of it all.

'Mrs Mapp,' tried Dickens again. 'We are looking for your daughter, Louisa.'

The woman burst into tears, terrible hacking sobs. They were astonished. What on earth did this mean? Jones felt a second's terror. Was Louisa dead?

Dickens was appalled, too. 'Mrs Mapp, tell us. Where is she?'

She looked at them with her tragic eyes which he saw were Louisa's eyes. 'She 'ant come. She said she'd come. She woz bringin' money.' She looked at the bed. 'I need the money. She's gotter come.' She wept again, her despair filling the room in a long wail of grief and abandonment. 'Why don't she come? Why don't she come?'

There was nothing more to say. Dickens took some money from his pocket, and taking her hand, put the coins in it. It was the hand of a starved bird. I can't stand this, he thought. Mrs Mapp stared at the money. She could hardly understand.

'We will find Louisa for you,' he said. 'She will come.'

Mrs Mapp did not answer. They went up the steps and out into the air which, stale as it was, seemed at least breathable after the foetid stink of the cellar. They stood, shaken by what they had seen, but it was pointless to talk about it.

'Back to Lantern Yard,' said Jones. 'This is a mess. A dead end, every which way we turn. God knows where she is. She could be dead, and Jenny Ding, too.'

Dickens felt for him; he knew how what they had seen had horrified them both. They had seen much already yet the misery here was somehow overwhelming. His money might do some good for a short while, that is if the woman were not too stupefied to spend it. Those two would probably die in there. Once he had seen, in another cramped, vile underground room, a naked child dead for days, and the family too poor to bury it, the corpse left lying in the corner. Anger flared in him like a flame. He thought he could have killed Crewe there and then for what he had done. And then helplessness swept through him. He looked at Jones, standing in Lavender Alley, his eyes closed, with defeat settled on his face.

'On, on, we noble English,' Dickens roused him with a touch on his shoulder, 'once more unto the etcetera.'

Jones smiled at him. 'You're right. We are not doing any good here. Thank you, Charles. It's good that you are here.'

22: A Present for a Good Girl

It was beginning to be foggy as they came out of the lane. All the city clocks were striking six. Time ignored them and all the sufferings they had seen. What were human beings to Time, implacable and inexorable, striding on, dragging them in its wake? They went back into Covent Garden where the last stroke of six sounded from St Paul's Church, passive in its Palladian grandeur, surveying coldly the things in progress under its shadow.

Scrap was back, shivering as he put on his shirt, but his eyes were alive with news.

'You know where they are?'

'Nah, but two girls bin seen. Asked abaht a bit — kids an' that like yer sed, Mr Jones. Some kids sed they seen a girl, cryin' she woz. She want in a blue dress, just rags, the other one woz dressed the same like, but she 'ad dark 'air 'angin' down an' she wore an' 'at. Draggin' the little girl, they sed — in an' 'urry.'

'Louisa in disguise?' asked Dickens, knowing the two seen could be any two. There was much to cry about in this world.

'It's a possibility — Mary Lyons said she was frightened so if he brought Jenny to her, and she decided to run away, she would try to disguise them both, and try to hide somewhere. But —'

'I know,' Dickens interrupted, 'but it's worth a try, surely, Sam.'

Jones nodded. 'Where were they? Did these children say?'

'I went over 'Olborn, talked to the kids in the alleys off Eagle Street. Kids saw 'em near there.'

'When?' asked Jones.

'Couple o' hours ago probly. I came straight 'ere arter I talked to 'em.'

'So, maybe she's going north up towards the Foundling Hospital. Perhaps she knows someone up there, someone who'll take them in.' Dickens hoped it was so.

'Could be — I'll send a couple of constables to have a look up there. You never know, someone else may have seen them. They might, at least, be safe from Crewe.'

'What now?' Dickens asked.

'Anythin' else yer want me ter do?' asked Scrap.

'Yes, go back to Crown Street, and see them all home — don't want them wandering off,' Jones said.

'Gotter keep our eyes on 'em, I know.' Scrap winked, and went out to escort Elizabeth and the children back to Norfolk Street. Jones went out with him to give his instructions to the constables. Dickens stood, thinking about Jenny and Louisa Mapp, hoping they were safe somewhere in the shadow of the Foundling Hospital.

Jones came back and they sat down on Blackledge's chairs. 'What now?' he asked.

'What now, indeed?'

As if in answer to the question, the sound of running footsteps came, and the door was flung open to reveal a grey-faced constable whom Dickens had not seen before. Very much out of breath, he could only manage, 'Body, sir.'

'Where?'

Dickens stood up. Not Eagle Street. Not Jenny. It could not be, surely.

'Cursitor Street.' Just a few minutes from Carey Street and Bell Lane. Were Scrap's informants wrong? Had they simply seen an older girl and a child and Scrap, in his eagerness, had wanted it to be Louisa and Jenny, and, had they? Because they wanted them to be safe.

'Just one body?' Jones asked.

'Yes, sir, young female — throat cut.'

'What sort of girl?'

'Dunno, sir, just a street girl, hardly any clothes, yer know.'

They did know. They were out of the door. 'Feak, your rattle. We need more men.'

At the sound of the rattle, the superintendent's constables came in the instant. Two more followed. They had been on their beat along King Street. Two were to go up across Holborn to look round Eagle Street, and the other two with Dickens and Jones to Cursitor Street where they could rouse another couple of constables. Feak would stay at Lantern Yard.

The grey-faced constable, Stemp, told his story as they rushed to Cursitor Street, the fog descending now like a curtain. Stemp and his colleague had been looking about the lanes and courts when a lad, about eleven or so, had run up to them shouting about a body. He had vanished and they didn't wait to catch him. In a little yard off one of the alleys they had found her.

The constable led them through the suffocating nest of alleys where the fog hovered in front of them obscuring outlines, softening the jagged walls, creating an eerie silence in which their hurrying feet seemed to echo as though someone or something dogged their footsteps. Dickens could not help turning round, holding up his lamp, but seeing only the vaporous mist moving and coiling as if it were forcing them onwards. Stemp was uncertain now, shining his light on to doors and gaps in broken walls until they came to a set of steps leading into a tomb-like courtyard surrounded by high walls which gave it the look of a prison cell. There was an old well here, and a door in one of the walls which was half open, and through which they could see a small overgrown garden. She lay near the door. Jones lifted his lamp. Dickens followed him, his heart filled with dread at what they might see. She was on her front, one arm flung out, the other crushed beneath her. She looked like a discarded doll, too small to be Louisa Mapp. Very carefully, the second constable turned her over.

It was not Jenny Ding. The body was of a younger girl, just a child about ten years old. She was wearing a pitiful shred of a shift and nothing more, but the blood which had poured from the slashed throat was dried out, congealed in dreadful lumps. She had been dead for some time. In the yellow rays of the lamp they could see the bruised young-old face which bore upon it traces of rouge crudely rubbed into the thin cheeks. The shift was rucked up to her hips, and, sickened, they saw the bruising on her inner thighs. The constable pulled down the shift, and looked up at the superintendent, his eyes reflecting the pity and revulsion they all felt. No one had missed her, no one had reported her, no one had come to find her. She had been left in this grave-like place, forgotten.

Jones told the grey-faced Stemp to get back to Bow Street and make arrangements for the removal of the body to the morgue. The second constable, Dacre, was to stay with the body. The police rattle summoned another set of constables from their beat on Fetter Lane. They were to search the area and ask if anyone knew of her. They might find the boy, they might not. Stemp's description gave one useful detail. In the light of his lamp, he had a fleeting impression that the boy's face was pockmarked.

Dickens and Jones went into the rank, unweeded garden of the tumbledown house where no one lived. They poked about in the grass, turning over rusted iron pans, a few spoons twisted out of shape, shards of pottery, a bent candlestick, a few ancient boots, and most ironic of all, a little pot, broken at the rim, bearing the legend: *A PRESENT FOR A GOOD GIRL*. Dickens could have wept. Clouds of mephitic vapour rose from the swampy ground as they disturbed the rancid grass and soil. There was a stench of excrement, and a rat scuttled over their feet, its red eyes winking suddenly, maliciously in the lamplight. There might have been something tossed away by the murderer, but it was too dark and misty and they had not time. Jones could send officers to search in daylight. They went through the ramshackle house with its empty rooms and rotten staircase leading into the fog-bound sky. A rickety table and a few chairs were all that was left, and a blackened kettle on the broken-down range. Their feet crunched on glass and pottery, and then they were out through the drunken door hanging off its hinges.

'Curse this fog,' muttered Jones.

'Was it he, do you think?' asked Dickens.

'I do. When you think of what Louisa told us, and she did not tell us all, it's more than likely — the rouge tells us what kind of life that child probably led. The bruises tell us how someone had used her, and the slashed throat is his trademark, so to speak.'

'I wonder when — probably before Blackledge died, even before Patience.'

'Yes, she's been there some time — gave him a taste for it. We'll go to the Albany, see if he's there.'

'And we should go to Topham's. What if he has tried to get Laetitia Topham away? If he has, she is in danger. I do not think he would kill her but he would ruin her. If she went away with him, her father would have to consent to the marriage.'

'You're right, Charles. The Albany first, though.'

They were in Fetter Lane and found a cab to take them to Piccadilly and the Albany. The journey was painfully slow in the deepening fog. The constable on duty told them that he had not seen anyone answering to Crewe's description go in or come out, but he might have missed him, Jones thought. They would try. He sent the constable to ask, giving the usual story that he was pursuing enquiries about a robbery nearby. 'Best not to unsettle him. If he is there we can go up ourselves,' Jones decided.

They waited. The constable came back to report that he had been directed to Crewe's apartment where the manservant had told him that his master was out — he did not know when he would be back, nor where he had gone. The master did not usually tell him where he went.

'Topham's,' Jones said. 'Hanover Square, your friend Wilde said.'

They walked, peering into the fog, keeping on the pavement and following the lines of gas lamps, the lights a greenish haze scarcely penetrating the gloom. It was not far, just up Bond Street, and then St George's Street would lead them into the south side of the square. It was dead quiet here, the central garden enclosed by its neat iron railings, dark and silent under the thick curtain of fog. Somewhere in there was a huge bronze statue of William Pitt, upright in the act of speaking. Would that he could tell them whether Edmund Crewe had passed through the noble portico of one of the fine white houses that lined the square. Prince Talleyrand had lived here, and Sir

James Clark, physician to the Queen, was a resident. The Zoological Society had established its offices here in 1846. It was a world away from the verminous nests of Seven Dials, yet if one stepped from the silent square a few yards beyond, there would be found the same mean lanes and ruined tenements — plenty of specimens for the learned zoologists to debate on if they could bear the filth and degradation that swamped these human lives.

They approached the north-west side of the square out of which Tenterden Street ran where the Royal College of Music was. Dickens remembered walking through the square to the college every Sunday morning to collect his sister, Fanny. Then they walked to the Marshalsea Prison to visit their parents — he was twelve, and Fanny, thirteen; now Fanny was dead, and he went to receptions to the grand houses now where the gracious hosts and diamonded hostesses knew nothing of the boy who had sold his father's books to pay the rent.

They stood outside the brightly lit house. 'Charles, you must ask to see Mr Topham. No need to mention the police — yet. I'm sure Mr Topham will be delighted to receive Mr Dickens, even without an appointment. I'll bet his library is crammed with your books.'

A liveried, powdered footman answered the door. Dickens was quick to inform him that Mr Charles Dickens would like to see Mr Topham on a confidential matter. Even the footman, who looked like an eighteenth-century aristocrat finding himself unaccountably in the position of door-opener, was sufficiently impressed to let them in, though he could not resist a disapproving look at the superintendent whose name had not been mentioned. Still, he resisted the temptation to ask, showed them into the library, assured them he would fetch his master, whilst with an anxious frown explaining that it was near dinner time.

The library was exactly what a gentleman's library ought to be, thought Dickens, approving the sight of his own books on the table and the shelves as the superintendent had foretold. He could not resist looking at those on the table. There was a copy of *Dombey and Son* with a bookmark in it. 'Someone's actually reading it,' he whispered.

Mr Topham came in. He was tall and spare with a scholarly air about him. He looked distinguished with his grey hair and ascetic face and sober black suit. His eyes were grey, too, watchful and intelligent. No wonder they had seen through Edmund Crewe. Dickens had expected a man exuding prosperity, fat with riches and good eating, the kind of banker he would put in a novel, stale rather than fresh, corpulent rather than lean. Topham was the kind of man he would put in an historical novel, were he to write one. He had something of the Elizabethan about him, he thought, remembering a portrait he had seen of Sir Francis Walsingham.

Mr Topham was courteous though the watchful eyes expressed curiosity. 'I am glad to meet you, Mr Dickens. As you see, I have been reading your *Dombey and Son* — an interesting portrait of Mr Dombey, the businessman. One feels a certain sympathy for his — er — misguidedness, a disappointed man whose bitterness is, perhaps, understandable if not at all condoned.' He smiled. 'Forgive me, I do not suppose you came here for a critique of your novel.'

Dickens was astonished at his perspicacity. Critics had objected to what they called the violent change in Mr Dombey from harshness to penitence, and here was Mr Topham offering the very analysis which Dickens himself would have given. He remembered why they were there.

'Thank you for your kindness, Mr Topham. May I present Superintendent Jones of Bow Street? We would like to ask some questions about a confidential matter.'

'Then, please, sit down.' They sat on the comfortable leather chesterfield and Mr Topham took a matching chair. 'Now, how may I help you?'

'First, Mr Topham, may I ask, is your daughter here?' asked Jones.

'She is. At present, she is upstairs. Later, we are to go to a ball in Cavendish Square. Why do you wish to know?'

'Our investigation concerns Edmund Crewe.'

Topham's eyes revealed his feelings about Crewe, and there was an unmistakeable curl of disdain at his lips.

'Tell me.' He was brief, a man who would not waste words.

'Miss Coutts,' Dickens began — Mr Topham acknowledged the name with the faintest nod — 'Miss Coutts and I have established a home for fallen girls. A young woman called Patience Brooke was employed there as a kind of assistant matron. Last Friday, she was found dead at the Home. Her throat had been cut. The superintendent and I have good reason to believe that Patience Brooke was Patience Crewe, that she was Edmund Crewe's wife.'

Mr Topham nodded again but he did not speak; he merely waited for Dickens to continue, but he understood the import of the words, especially for his daughter. Sam continued the story.

'I have reason to suspect Mr Crewe of that murder and, possibly, others, but I cannot give you detail now. I believe he is a dangerous man.'

'Ah,' said Topham, 'I see.' His tone was calm but they could see the anger flare in his eyes, and then the fear and horror.

Dickens explained what Oliver Wilde had told him about Crewe and the rumours about his intentions towards Laetitia Topham. Jones told him what Rogers had discovered at the Crewe town house, especially the gossip that Edmund Crewe might attempt an elopement with Miss Topham.

'You think my daughter may be in danger?' He knew the answer, of course, but he wanted the superintendent to spell it out.

'I do,' said Jones firmly, 'which is why we are here — to warn you.'

'You have my profound gratitude, Mr Dickens and Superintendent Jones. I will tell you something of my daughter. You shall tell her something of what you know, but only that Crewe had a wife when he began paying attentions to her. She is young and intelligent — I have seen to her education — but she is also very sympathetic. A man like Crewe would know how to engage her interest and sympathy. In society, he is charming, he appears sensitive and well-read. He will have read your books, no doubt Mr Dickens, if only to impress my daughter. I am sorry; I did not mean that your books are not worth reading. I mean that he would have taken no lesson from them. The plight of Nancy or Oliver Twist or Little Nell would hold no interest for a man like him. Have you seen him?'

'Yes,' said Dickens.

'Then you will know what a handsome young man he is, and how easy it might be for him to masquerade as an innocent. Of course, I heard rumours, of course, I saw his eyes, and the way his temper flashed sometimes when he thought himself unobserved and, of course, I wanted to keep my daughter from him without wounding her feelings. It is the burden of every father to negotiate between his daughter and the man she loves, especially if he knows that man to be unworthy. But now, I think she must know that he had a wife, and you must tell her, Mr Dickens. She will know that you are without prejudice. I will bring her to you.' He went out to fetch his daughter.

Dickens said to Jones, 'I'll tell her about the wife, not about the murders, that is what he wants.'

'Yes, we do not have proof, yet, and when it all comes out she will know then, poor girl.'

Mr Topham came back with his daughter. Dickens exchanged a swift glance with Jones. Miss Laetitia Topham was very like Patience. There was a gravity about her, a quiet, and intelligence in her clear grey eyes. Her hair was brown and shining, looped into ringlets about her temples. She was not the fashionable young lady they had expected. She had not yet dressed for her ball and was wearing a plain grey velvet dress with a white lace collar.

'Mr Dickens, I am so glad to meet you. I have read your books. I cannot tell you which is my favourite, though the story of Little Nell went straight to my heart. As you see, my father is reading *Dombey and Son* — I am waiting for him to hurry up.' She smiled as she looked at her father and Dickens saw the love that passed between them. How difficult it must have been for him to watch as his daughter fell in love with Crewe. She continued, 'My father says you have something to tell me.'

She sat down, looking at Dickens with her candid eyes. He could hardly bear to tell her. Mr Topham sat, too, and motioned to Dickens and Jones to resume their seats.

'Miss Topham, we came here because we have found out something about Mr Crewe.' She was like her father, still and controlled. 'I met a young acquaintance of yours, Mr Oliver Wilde, who told me that Mr Crewe seemed to have become fond of you, and that there might be a question of marriage.' She made no sign at all but continued to look at him steadfastly. 'I have found out that Mr Crewe was married. His wife died last Friday.'

She understood that Crewe had pursued her before the death of his wife and all that it implied. To their surprise, she turned to her father. 'Papa, I would not have married him. I knew he did not love me. I could tell that it was pretence — he tried to disguise it, but I saw how, sometimes, he was impatient as if the talk between us was something he felt he had to do. He tried to disguise the fact that he was in a hurry. People talked, I know. They thought I was a silly young girl who was flattered by a handsome man, and they thought that he would do well to marry me.' She paused.

Mr Topham asked, 'Why did you not discourage him? Why let me think?'

'Papa, I did not know what you thought. You did not tell me. As to discouraging him, I thought I had by my being only pleasant. Mr Dickens, Mr —' she stopped, searching for the superintendent's name.

'Mr Jones,' he said.

'You are involved in this?'

'Yes, Mr Dickens and I had reason to find information about Mr Crewe.' He dared not say more, though it was clear that she was curious about his role.

'I was going to say that perhaps you do not fully know how difficult it is to be a woman in society as it is. We are expected to receive passively the attentions of any man who chooses to pay them. I suppose it is thought that we should be grateful — whatever kind of man he is. We are certainly not expected to make a scene. If I had shown dislike of Mr Crewe in public, then society would have assumed that I was acting a part to encourage him. I was caught in a trap created by the mores of our society — if I seemed to like him, I was a silly flirt, if I seemed to dislike him, I was the same. Papa, you have educated me to read, to think for myself, and yet you could believe that my head was turned by the first young man who came my way, a young man who was obviously a man who liked pleasure and parties and cards, and not much else.'

My foot, my tutor, thought Dickens, casting Mr Topham as Prospero. She was an astonishing young woman, and like Patience, for all her quietness, there was strength there. He thought about what she had said about society's attitude to women, and he thought with horror about what her life would have been had she married Crewe. But she would not have gone with him willingly.

'I am sorry, my dear,' said Topham, 'I said nothing for I thought I might hurt you by questioning your judgement about Crewe, and now I find I have hurt you by underestimating your intelligence.'

'You meant all for the best, but be assured, when I choose, if I choose, it will be a man you respect. How could it be otherwise when I have had you for my example?'

There was the glint of tears in Mr Topham's eyes and Dickens felt their pricking in his. She was a remarkable young woman. What man, he thought, would be her match? He wondered about the amiable Mr Wilde.

'You are to attend a ball tonight?' asked Jones, who had thought all that Dickens had thought, but who was still concerned that Crewe might be reckless enough to take her by force. 'Do you expect Mr Crewe to be there?'

'I do not know. Do you wish me to avoid him? That might be difficult for the reasons I have outlined before.'

It would be better, thought Jones, if she did not go at all, but how to suggest this without alarming her?

Mr Topham intervened. Knowing the truth, he was prepared to make the decision. She needed to be protected and to know more, and he knew now that she would understand.

'Mr Jones is a policeman. He is investigating a crime about which he believes Mr Crewe to know something, and he believes that it would be better if you did not meet Mr Crewe. I think it would be wise for us to send our apologies then you cannot be placed in an embarrassing situation.'

'I understand. Thank you for telling me, Mr Dickens. It was kind of you both to come. I hope we may meet again.'

'I hope so, too,' said Dickens.

Mr Topham came to the door with them, much to the surprise of the lordly footman.

'Keep her safe, Mr Topham,' said Jones.

'I will. And she will keep me safe, too, until she chooses the remarkable man who will be her husband — but not yet, I hope.' He smiled as he showed them out. 'Thank you for coming to me.'

They stood in the raw air, feeling the cold after the warmth of the comfortable library. The night was uncannily still, but they could hear the traffic in Oxford Street and Regent Street. The city was waiting for them.

'Back to the Albany, then. And one of my constables shall go to the ball — I will put a watch at Cavendish Square. We may not find him tonight in this fog. Where has he gone to ground in this teeming place?'

There was no news at the Albany. The risk was the same — if he were not there, then his manservant would surely tell him that the police had been there twice. The story of a robbery was thin — it would not serve again. When Crewe knew that they had been to his residence, he would vanish, surely, or would he brazen it out? It was impossible to tell. Dickens and Jones stood uncertainly. Jones decided. He would go; he would simply ask for Crewe, not saying who he was. Dickens would wait out of sight. If Crewe were there they would go in and challenge him about Patience.

23: The Actor

He was there. The manservant, a young man in a dark green livery, was reluctant to admit the superintendent. Jones had said that he wanted to see Mr Crewe on a matter of some delicacy; the servant hesitated, looking over his shoulder anxiously. In the pause, Jones stepped into the little hall. Seeing him do so, Dickens hurried along the corridor and followed him in. The servant was surprised to find that he had two uninvited guests. 'I will ask Mr Crewe if he will see you but I do not think —' he broke off, his anxious, young face creased with worry.

Dickens felt sympathy. He imagined that Edmund Crewe would not be an easy master; the young man had obviously been instructed not to let in anyone whom he did not know. The vestibule was too small for the three of them. It was a small panelled space with a console table against the wall above which was an ornate gilt mirror. Dickens had a glimpse of his own face, as anxious as the servant's. He was surprised to see how dishevelled he looked, his hair swept across his brow in untidy strands, his tie floppier than usual, and his eyes too wide in his pale face. Good Lord, he thought, I look like the murderer! The manservant regarded Jones's implacable face and, looking even more nervous, said he would enquire and went through the dark, heavy mahogany door into the room beyond.

Jones looked in the mirror and they stared at their own strained faces. The servant returned. Dickens and Jones went in to a small drawing room, furnished with a sofa in rich cranberry coloured velvet and two leather armchairs facing the burning fire. There was a larger console table in shining mahogany against one wall; upon it there were a tantalus, some decanters and some crystal glasses on a silver tray. On the floor was a richly patterned Turkey carpet and there was a small round table with two balloon-backed chairs. It was all very tasteful, exactly what a young man about town needed to be comfortable enough. There was a door at the far side of the fireplace leading presumably to the bedrooms. The servant disappeared through it, and as if by some mysterious act of prestidigitation, Crewe appeared in his place.

Crewe must have been in the act of dressing for he was coatless, though he was wearing an evening waistcoat, black trousers, and a white shirt with expensive gold studs and cufflinks. One hand was at his neck and a ruby ring shone in the candlelight. He simply looked at them and said, 'Well?' Dickens heard the sneer in his voice.

Jones spoke, 'I am Superintendent Jones of Bow Street and this is Mr Charles Dickens.'

'Dickens?' said Crewe. 'There were servants of that name at Crewe Hall, our family seat,' he added. It was a deliberate insult, calculated to wrong foot them. Dickens did not respond though he felt a tightening in his chest and his grip tightened on his stick — he would have liked to strike that insolent face with it, but he simply stood still.

The words hung in the air. Jones ignored the comment. For all his lazy insolence, Crewe's eyes betrayed his wariness, but only wariness — not fear. However, Jones's silence forced Crewe to speak again. 'My servant said you were here on a matter of delicacy. What is it? I have not much time — I should be at supper very shortly and then to a ball at Cavendish Square.'

'We are here to discover information about the death of a young woman, Patience Brooke, who was employed at a home for young women established by Mr Dickens and Miss Burdett-Coutts.'

'And what has her death to do with me, Superintendent? — I do not know the name, Mr Dickens; I am at a loss to understand how you think I could help you.'

Dickens answered, 'Miss Brooke's real name was Patience Rivers, and we were led to believe that she was your wife, and that you had a child together.'

The name Rivers had produced a tiny flicker in Crewe's eyes, perceptible to Jones who was watching him as a cat watches a bird. He saw how that flicker betrayed the swift working out of what to admit, what to deny. Crewe passed a hand over his high, white forehead, concealing his eyes. When he removed it, the eyes were now clouded. He sat down on one of the chairs by the fireplace. They waited. Dickens was intrigued — the man was an actor. What part would he play now?

'Please, sit down, and I will tell you what I can. You say Patience Rivers is dead?'

'She is.' It was interesting that he did not ask when or how, and interesting that he called her Patience Rivers not my wife.

'I am afraid,' Crewe began, 'that what I am to tell you does not reflect credit on me.' He looked up at them, his expression rueful, that of a man who regretted some youthful indiscretion, but who was prepared to admit it. 'Patience and I had a child together — she was my mistress for two years. I confess I did not love her as she loved me — there was never any question of marriage — my guardian, Sir Hungerford Crewe, would never have countenanced it. Patience was only the daughter of a music teacher. However, Patience wanted more of me than I could give. We quarrelled bitterly and she left. I have not heard of her since. Fortunately, she left the child with me. She is being looked after at Crewe Hall in Cheshire. I did care for Patience. I am very sorry to hear that she is dead.' He bowed his head, looking the very picture of remorse.

Jones was blunt. 'She was murdered last Friday — her throat was cut.'

'Good God — how terrible —' he faltered and looked down. Arranging his face, thought Dickens. Crewe looked at Jones, 'Do you know who did it?'

'We have our suspicions, but, of course, Mr Crewe, I cannot discuss these with you.'

'I suppose she might have found another lover — who knows?' Again the tone was regretful, and at the same time the meaning was that these things happen, that it was a pity, but it was nothing to do with him.

'Oddly, another girl is missing from the Home — a young girl of about thirteen years. Fortunately, we may have a witness whom we are going to question tomorrow. We think the young girl may have gone away with a man who may have been seen,' Dickens said, hoping perhaps to startle him into what? He did not know. Jones watched Crewe's eyes. They opened wide now, their look was puzzled, curious, always regretful.

'It is strange, is it not, but I am afraid I cannot help you there. I know nothing of your Home, as you call it. Why should I? Now, if you will forgive me, I should like to be left alone — you have given me grave news here. I may not have loved her as she loved me, but her death is a terrible thing.' He bowed his head but Jones saw the faint gleam of something in his eyes. What? Satisfaction? Something mocking? It was gone in a second.

'What will happen about the murder? Will there be an inquest? Shall I have to appear?'

'All in good time, Mr Crewe, we shall certainly keep in contact with you.'

'Good night, then. Thank you for telling me. I am sorry I could not help you more.'

They had no choice but to go. He would give nothing away. The longer they stayed, the more assured he would become. They went downstairs and out into Piccadilly where the late-night traffic made its slow way through the viscid murk.

'Damn him, damn him,' muttered Jones. 'We are no better off. If he is not Patience's husband — and that could be true — then bang goes his motive. It's all so vague. Oh, for a good, honest witness or a good honest piece of evidence. Why didn't he drop that damned ruby ring at the crime scene?'

'A damned liar, that's what he is. I know it,' said Dickens.

'Yes, I saw that gleam of satisfaction in his eye when he had finished his recital of his and Patience's relationship. He thought he had fooled us with his performance. What if they were not married?'

'I think they were — why else would he kill her?'

'Unless he thought she might come back for the child just as he was about to marry Laetitia Topham. It would still be awkward for him.'

'Awkward but not ruinous — he would be engaged to a rich man's daughter. He could explain the child away — an indiscretion, a youthful error, and he might appear to be someone who was prepared to face his responsibility by looking after the child. Whereas if he were found out to be a bigamist, that would be disastrous. In any case, I think it is all more complicated. I am not convinced about the marriage to Laetitia Topham — he must have known she would not accept him. He's cleverer than that and he must have known Mr Topham would be an obstacle. If he was going to take her, it would be to ruin her for the sake of it; he killed Patience because she escaped him, because he wanted to punish her by showing the world that she was a whore; he killed that little girl because that's what he does — he is depraved, he enjoys his killing. He enjoys, above all, his double life, outwitting us all. I do not think it matters whether he married Patience or not.'

Jones listened. 'You're right — it doesn't matter just now, at any rate, for if your analysis is correct, then we have still to worry about Jenny Ding and Louisa Mapp, and we have no idea where they are. The sighting of them by Scrap's informants might not be right at all, and we have no idea where else to look. I suppose we could go back and see Mary Lyons, see if she remembers anything else. I tell you what, we'll get a cab to Bow Street and I'll send a man to relieve Feak and tell him to come back to Bow Street then he can go to see Mary Lyons. Feak knows how urgent it all is. He's a good lad and will know what to ask. Save us the trouble.'

'Mrs Cutler will not be pleased to have another policeman at her door,' observed Dickens.

'Well, she can damn well lump it. If she keeps a bawdy house, however discreet, she'll have to put up with the risks.'

'What about Crewe?'

'God knows. We need a break. We need him to make a mistake. He might, you know. He thinks he's shaken us off. I said I would put a man at Cavendish Square — I'll make it two — in plain clothes. We need to have him followed if they can see their way in this damned fog. One can report in if he comes back to the Albany. Our constable here can keep his eye on the place. Crewe might stay at home tonight, after the ball.'

'Or, he might go looking for Louisa Mapp. You don't think he'll go back to the Home — should I have said that we had a witness? I just wanted him to know. What if I made a terrible mistake?'

'It would be too hazardous a journey in this. Anyway, he will not get in tonight — Bagster will see to that, and Mrs Morson. Rogers will come back to Bow Street, but I can send him again to the Home. He could stay there tonight. What about you, Charles — ought you to go home?'

'I'll come back with you to Bow Street and wait for Rogers, and for Feak's news from Mary Lyons then I will go home.'

Jones went to speak to his constable then wearily they walked to Piccadilly to find a cab. At Bow Street, Jones went to give his orders to the men who were to keep watch at Cavendish Square and to the constable who was to relieve Feak. They sat by the dwindling fire in Jones's office waiting for Feak to return. But when the door opened it was the rubicund face of Rogers that peered round it. He had come back from the Home.

'Found 'em?' he asked. 'Mrs Morson's right upset and James Bagster.'

'No, Rogers, we have not. Anything to tell us?'

'Yes, I questioned the girls, one by one, and you was right, sir,' he said to Dickens. 'One of them, Lizzie Dagg, said a man spoke to her in the village — said he asked directions — nothing else, but he give her the eye, she said, an' told her he'd see her again. Jenny Ding was with her. He said she was a pretty girl an' he'd buy her a present some day. They was thrilled, o' course, but didn't tell anyone. It was a secret between them, Lizzie said. She thought he might come, so did Jenny.'

'Did she describe him?' Jones asked. Could this be the break, the witness?

'Said he was a toff, tall, blonde hair, handsome, charmin'.'

It wasn't much, but they could bring Lizzie in tomorrow and question her more closely. Feak came back to report that nothing had happened at Lantern Yard. He went off to Bell Lane to see what he could glean from Mary Lyons. The constables came back from their searches near the Foundling Hospital. They'd seen plenty of ragged girls, but none, as far as they could tell, matched the description of Louisa and Jenny. It was a waste of time, Jones thought. The constables could have passed them in the fog. And they might never have been north of Holborn. And if they were dead, they could be anywhere. The constables could resume their search in daylight. In the meantime they would wait for Feak.

'Did you tell them to take care at the Home?' Dickens was still worried that he had made a mistake in telling Crewe they might have a witness. He could not shake off the dread that Crewe might go to Urania Cottage.

'Don't worry, Mr Dickens, the place is locked up, tight as a drum. Mr Bagster'll stay up all night in the kitchen, and I told Jenkins to stay in the hall by the front door. Crewe won't get in. Want me to go back, sir? I will if you want or I can stay here all night — wait for news of Louisa Mapp and the little girl. You could go home for a bit, sir.'

'Yes, stay here, Rogers. I am sure the Home will be safe tonight. I'll go home after we have heard from Feak. He should be back any minute.'

'Daft Lizzie Dagg,' said Dickens. 'I'm not surprised she was taken in. She's a lone lorn creature, desperate for love, poor thing. Plain as suet pudding, and simple. She wouldn't think of consequences. The secret weighed on Jenny, though. She was probably dreading his arrival — they'd believe it, they'd think he'd come for them, and Jenny would know they'd be in trouble. And when he did come, she just went out for her present! It was probably that easy. Oh God, why didn't she tell someone?'

'Torn between guilt and a desire to get that present, I suppose. He's a cunning bastard, knows exactly what would tempt a little girl. Oh, hell, where are they?'

Feak came back from Mrs Cutler's. Mary Lyons could tell him nothing more — she knew only where Louisa's mother lived, but nothing of any other places Louisa might have gone.

'I don't think we can do anything more now. It is too dark and murky to see anything. Rogers, if you will wait tonight and you hear anything from the men I have posted to Cavendish Square, you can send a message to me at Norfolk Street. I can come back quickly or if you hear anything about Louisa Mapp or Jenny. The normal police patrols will be out. They'll report in if they find anything.'

'Don't worry, sir, I'll send for you if there's anythin'.' Rogers looked at his chief, his dependable face resolute, revealing his determination to help. A good man, thought Dickens.

'If there's nothing, I'll be in as soon as it's light tomorrow. You can try to get some sleep, Rogers. Build up the fire. The night inspector will tell you if there's anything from the constables. I'll tell him to fetch you.'

Dickens and Jones went out into the night. Despite the fog, the pavement and carriageway of Bow Street Station were crowded now with the ragged assembly of those being brought in: yelling drunkards, belligerent ruffians protesting their innocence to the world; tawdry women in their shabby finery screaming at the constables trying to restrain them; children whose faces were already hardened by vice; pickpockets in shiny hats, whistling as they went in for the fiftieth time, not caring at all, some even glad that they would have a bed to lie on tonight; and a crowd of shirtless vagabonds enjoying the show, cheering as they saw a constable lose his pot hat which rolled to Jones's feet. He picked it up and handed it back to the man whose face was red with annoyance. A large woman in a garish yellow satin dress hanging off her great white shoulders called out, 'Wotcher, Sam, fancy a night in with me?' The crowd roared its approval as the woman sashayed towards Jones, her huge hips swaying.

Jones laughed. 'No thanks, Bridie, I'm engaged tonight.' He gave her a sweeping bow. 'Another time — you'll be back tomorrow, I'll bet.'

The vagabonds yelled insults at Bridie. 'Bridie O'Malley, queen of the alley.' She didn't care and made her magnificent way into the station with two constables as her liveried courtiers.

Dickens and Jones pushed their way through the hordes. The catcalls and yells faded into the fog as they crossed Long Acre and made their way up to Crown Street where the stationery shop was in darkness.

24: Footsteps in the Fog

There was no point in taking a cab — it was quicker to walk than ride. Even so they made slow progress along Oxford Street, passers-by materialising suddenly in front of them, their faces greenish-yellow in the lamplight then vanishing as if they had never been. They made a detour into Princess Street, went again into Hanover Square, its garden still mysterious in the dark. All was quiet. They were in Cavendish Square now where lights burned through the fog from the ballroom in one of the great white porticoed houses. Carriages were still arriving; others were stationary along the sides of the square, moored like ships in the waves of fog. There was a small crowd outside the house where the ball was being held, and people were still going in, women wearing diamonds and tiaras, carrying great fans of ostrich feathers, their hooped skirts swaying as they glided in. Some of the men were in scarlet uniforms, gold glittering suddenly as it caught the light.

Dickens and Jones walked on, wondering if Crewe were there smiling his lazy smile over the white shoulders of some fashionable beauty, his eyes searching the crowded room for Laetitia Topham. They were glad she was safe at home with her father. Jones walked with Dickens to the junction of Devonshire Street and Portland Street from where he could cut through Carburton Street back to Norfolk Street. They stopped at a lamp post.

'Go home, Sam, you look —'

'A hundred,' said Jones, grinning. His face was drawn in the greenish light.

'Not so much — ninety-five, perhaps. When we looked in that mirror at Crewe's I did not know who we were. Dear God, we looked like two fugitives.'

'Tomorrow, then. We'll try again to find Louisa and Jenny. Will you go to the Home to fetch Lizzie Dagg, try to talk to her?'

'I will come to Bow Street first to hear if there is any news then I'll go — she'll be frightened, but by the time I bring her, I may be able to reassure her that we just want information. I hope the fog has cleared by then.'

'I hope so, too. Don't linger now — get ye home, Charles.'

They parted. Jones was dissolved into the dense mist, vanished as though Dickens had dreamed him. He only heard Jones's tread echoing back through the foggy curtain that surrounded him. He felt inexpressibly weary as he made his way down a silent Devonshire Road, all its familiar solid shapes disguised in the fog which seemed, if possible, denser now, hemming him in, brushing his face with its damp cobweb touch. He crossed the road near a solitary carriage parked at the pavement as if it had been abandoned. The horse stood patiently in its traces, waiting, its breath wreathing into the fog. As he passed it, Dickens glanced in. It was empty. When he looked back it was gone into the nebulous murk as if it had never existed — a ghost horse and carriage. He looked up, half expecting to see it floating silently in the air, taking away its invisible passenger. The air seemed filled with phantoms. He went by a little passageway between two houses.

And then he seemed to hear steps other than his own, a soft creeping footfall following him. He whirled round, the bull's eye lantern held high. Nothing to be seen, but the wall of fog, so thick it seemed to press on his very eyelids, winding itself round his mouth like a filthy gag. Was that his breath or the other's coming raggedly, hoarsely? He went on. Impossible to hurry in the fog.

Where was the turning into Devonshire Place? He did not know. Had he passed it? He stopped again, holding his breath this time, daring the other to breathe. He caught the faintest sound as if his pursuer had halted on tiptoe. He imagined him in the dark, poised to attack. The gas lamp on the corner showed him Devonshire Place. He turned in there, reaching out for railings and walls, desperate to touch something real, something solid. He felt as if he might drown in this green sea of fog. He stopped again, holding onto the cold iron of a railing, straining to listen. The footfalls had ceased. He blundered on blindly towards the New Road where he must cross into York Gate, sometimes looking back, expecting the spectre to leap upon him with the knife in his hand. And then, horribly, he heard it as if from a distance. A voice singing a snatch of a song. The words *bereft of my parents, bereft of my home* drifted back to him as if borne on the swirling fog, the word *home* drawn out horribly, the sound mocking and caressing at the same time.

Home. Dickens was there. Home. Had Crewe been there? Mamie, Katey? Were they safe? He crossed into the terrace and pushed open the iron gate in the high wall. The garden was dark, the trees seemed to rustle, shadows moved. Who was there? Lights in the hall and in a window on the ground floor. He fumbled for his key, dropped it, hardly dared bend down to find it, listened, found the key by the boot scraper, and struggled with the lock. He was inside.

He hurried upstairs; there was a strip of light showing at the bottom of the drawing room door. He went up another flight to the girls' room. He stopped himself from flinging open the door, but turned the handle carefully, not breathing at all. He still had his lantern and in the dim light he could see the two figures in the two beds. He almost laughed with relief. Katey, Lucifer Box, had her fists clenched in sleep. What dream had fired her temper? Mamie's hair was dark against the white pillow, her face tranquil and innocent. He closed the door softly. Leaning against it, he felt as if his body might collapse, his limbs fold up like a puppet's.

The door, the walls were real. The ticking of the clock in the hall was real. What was out there was the memory of a nightmare. Had he heard the song or just imagined it? Was it the fog and that terrible sense of entrapment that had produced the footfalls and the voice? He did not know, but it had seemed real enough. He breathed properly at last and went down to the drawing room where there was a fire, and Georgy sitting quietly at her sewing.

She saw his white face. 'Charles, what is it? What has happened?'

He told her how he had thought he had been followed in the thick fog, how he had imagined being attacked by a thief or pickpocket, perhaps, and how the fog had changed everything so that he could hardly find his way home. He dared not tell her about Crewe and what he had feared for his own daughters, but he did say that he would tell John, the manservant, to be extra vigilant in case there were thieves about. He might not have imagined it, he said. One never knew. Georgina, sensible woman, said that Catherine need not be worried, and that she would tell the other servants to be careful, too. Georgina was Catherine's youngest sister who had lived with them since 1842, and had become, for Dickens, the mainstay of his household. He relied on her intelligence and common sense, and, in return, she adored him.

When Georgina had gone, Dickens stood looking out at the fog. Telling her of his fear when he had been out there had almost convinced him that the footsteps had been of a thief but, still, there was the voice. Had he really heard it? He could not be sure now, yet he could hear it now in his head, menacing and somehow mocking as they had heard it in the alley before they had found Blackledge. He could not be sure. The fog had changed everything; the familiar streets seemed to have vanished when he was out there. He thought about the empty cab, the horse standing ghostlike in the street. Had Crewe left it there so that he could get away with Mamie or Katey? It was too horrible to contemplate. Should he have gone for Sam? He did not think he would have found his way to Norfolk Street. He dared not go out there again.

He stood staring out into the night wondering if Crewe were still out there somewhere in the dark, his ruined face desperate and reckless. What was Sam thinking now? Was he lying wakeful, looking into the dark, thinking about tomorrow and whether they would find Louisa Mapp and poor little Jenny Ding? He closed the curtain and shut out the dreadful night.

Sam Jones had found his way home. He let himself in quietly. In the kitchen he saw Scrap huddled by the door, watching and waiting. The dog was with him, listening, too, its ears cocked.

'Scrap,' he whispered, 'what is it?'

'Thort I 'eard somethin' — out there — a noise, dunno — coulda bin a cat.' He turned his anxious eyes to Jones's. 'Didn't go out — thort it best ter wait. Gorn now, though.'

Jones crouched beside the boy and listened, too. There was only silence. He rose and unlocked the door, peering out into the garden swathed in the deep mist. He stepped out onto the damp paving stones outside the door and went quietly across the grass. The back gate was shut. He stood listening to his own heartbeat in the silence. He could hear the faint clip-clop of a horse's hooves. A late cab, he thought, perhaps returning to Oxford Street having dropped off its passenger. He went back into the house.

'Nothing,' he whispered to Scrap. 'No one about. Probably a cat. Get some sleep now.'

Scrap curled up with Poll on his makeshift bed. Jones went into the parlour where the fire burned low. He would stay on the couch tonight, ready if any news came. He put more coal on the fire, and sat thinking about Edmund Crewe. He thought about the look in his eyes when he thought he had deceived them — a look of secret satisfaction, a look Jones had seen before in another man — Stephen Wilton, Edith's husband, Stephen Wilton whom he had disliked. When Edith had died giving birth to her dead child, Jones had listened to his expressions of grief. He had seen him make that same gesture as Crewe's, the covering of the face, the lowering of the head, and he had caught just for a moment that glitter of something false. They had not seen Stephen again. With the money he had gained by Edith's death, Elizabeth's money that she had settled on her daughter, he had moved to Manchester, and, they heard, he had married again. And they had nothing — only the emptiness in Elizabeth's eyes for a long time afterwards. Crewe's look had told him — the man had cared nothing for Patience. He had wanted her dead. But a look was not evidence. Lizzie Dagg had to tell them what she knew, and they had to find Louisa Mapp and Jenny Ding. Let them not be dead.

He stared into the fire. Then the door opened and Elizabeth came in. She saw his stricken face as he turned to her. She came to sit beside him on the couch.

'You were thinking of Edith.'

'How could you tell?'

'Sam, I watch you as you have watched me, each thinking we could hide from the other, thinking to spare each other. I have seen the concentrated anguish in your eyes, and I have known that it was not of a case that you were thinking though, God knows, I see you suffer for the victims of the crimes you uncover. No, I know when you are thinking of our dead girl so tell me.'

'I saw Patience Brooke's husband tonight and he thought we were deceived by his expression of regret, but I saw the gleam of triumph in his eyes and so did Charles. I had seen that momentary glitter of satisfaction in someone else's eyes —'

'Stephen Wilton. I know he didn't love Edith — he was fond of her, perhaps. He did not want the child, he wanted something more, more money, a greater social position, and when they both died, he was sorry in his way, but I saw that he was glad, too, to be rid of the responsibility. Oh, Sam, I saw it all, too, but I could not speak of it — what good would it have done? It was bad enough that she was dead, and her child, without my having to say aloud that he did not value her.'

'No, he did not, and I cannot forgive him for that. I am haunted by the thought that she knew it, that she was unhappy. I wish we had stopped her. Tonight Charles and I met a father and daughter who did not speak of their true feelings — the father was afraid to hurt his daughter, though he hated the man he thought she loved. She might have married this man and it would have been too late.'

'I don't think Edith was unhappy. Remember, she had the child to look forward to. Stephen was not cruel to her — he was kind enough in his way. It was not what we wanted for her, but how could we have stopped it? She loved him and she was happy. She might have become unhappy, but she was not then. I would have known. If only I could have given you another then we would have —'

Elizabeth wept then for the other children she could not have had. Sam took her in his arms.

'You gave me yourself, my Elizabeth, and I have loved you above everything.'

'And I you.' They sat on quietly as the fire died down.

After a while Elizabeth spoke again. 'And we have these others to care for now — Posy, of course, and Eleanor and Tom — and Scrap, too. When they go home, I shall continue to visit them and we can keep watch over them. Mr Brim is a sick man, Sam. I think those children may need us soon.'

25: Jonas Finger

In the dark, early morning Jones drank his coffee in the kitchen with Scrap.

'Take care, Scrap, when you go down to the shop. Keep a watch at the door. If you see a tall, handsome man, young with fair hair — a toff — you'll know he's wrong if you see him, a man who shouldn't be at the stationery shop, then lock up. Go in the back, take Mrs Jones and the children with you and don't leave until you are sure he's gone. Then go out the back way and come for me.'

'Yer think 'e might be arter us?'

'I doubt he'll come, Scrap, but I just want you to be careful.'

'Doncher worry, Mr Jones, I'll look arter 'em. I'll do jest as yer say. Yer can trust me.'

'I know. Take a cab to the shop.'

Jones had already warned Elizabeth to be careful, and he would put a policeman on patrol in Crown Street. There was, he thought, no real danger, but he wanted Scrap to be on the alert. He knew, too, that Scrap's intelligence would pick out Crewe — Scrap would know he was a wrong 'un.

He walked down to Bow Street. It was just becoming light and the densest fog had lifted, leaving ragged remnants of mist which gave the streets a kind of weary greyness as if they had not slept well. Jones had slept well even on his sofa after Elizabeth had gone to bed. Their conversation about Edith had dissolved the hard lump of grief that had seemed so solidly a part of him after Edith's death. He had believed Elizabeth when she had said that Edith had been happy. Elizabeth was not a woman who would try to console him with a lie. She was too honest for that and Edith had been too innocent to know what Stephen Wilton had, in any case, so carefully concealed from her.

He heard the clocks strike the hour. Unconsciously, he quickened his pace. Time, he thought. We're running out of time. The inquest on Blackledge would have to take place early next week. He could not ask for more time on that, and there would be the inquest on the little nameless girl whose death had already been reported to the coroner. And there was no concrete evidence at all to prove that Crewe had murdered Blackledge or Patience. They needed to find Louisa Mapp and Jenny who could give evidence of abduction, and only then could they bring Crewe in.

But at Bow Street there was no news of Crewe. He had not returned to the Albany or he had not been seen to do so. There was no news of Louisa Mapp or Jenny. Dickens came in, looking weary. He told Jones of his experience in the fog, of his hearing the song and the empty carriage in the street, and his fears for his daughters.

'I still do not know if I imagined it all,' he said. 'Reflecting on it now, it seems too dreamlike to be true. It might just have been the fog. You vanished completely and so did everything else yet — even that carriage might have been a ghost thing, the horse enveloped in mist. When I looked back it had vanished as completely as you had.'

'It's odd though. When I got home, I found Scrap crouched at the kitchen door and the dog with its ears cocked. Scrap said he had heard something. I went out, but there was no one. I did hear a carriage — I thought it might be a late cab — unlikely in that fog, now I think about it.'

'So it might have been him?'

'It might. Did you tell your servants to be careful? I told Elizabeth and Scrap to be vigilant.'

'I did — I told Georgina that I had heard that thieves were about, and I told the servants to be careful.'

'So, where is he now? That's what I want to know. He could have gone back to the Albany. Will you go to the Home and question Lizzie Dagg? I want a description of the man she met. We have to have some evidence. Then we will question him again — if he is there. I have a horrible feeling that he is going to escape us; that we will never be able to prove anything against him.'

'And, worse, that he will kill again and we cannot stop him.'

'The men are out looking for Louisa and Jenny. Now the fog's clearing, we might find something.'

An urgent knock at the door interrupted them. Rogers was there, grinning. 'They're here, sir. Louisa Mapp and the little girl.' He ushered them in.

Louisa and Jenny as Scrap had reported them, ragged and dishevelled, but very much alive. Without her velvet dress and black feathered hat and with her black hair knotted and tangled, Louisa was transformed into the girl who had come from that squalid room in Lavender Lane. Yet, there was still a spark in the dark blue eyes. Seeing Dickens, Jenny burst into tears.

'Miss Mapp, tell us,' said Jones, motioning them to sit.

'Teddy found me. I left Mrs Cutler's arter you told me abaht Alfie. I woz scared 'e might come fer me. I went ter Liddy Flowerday's — she's — well yer know —' She looked at Jenny. 'She 'as a room off Eagle Street. Told 'er someone woz arter me, but 'e found 'er at the Turk's 'Ead — give 'er as much gin as she wanted an' she told 'im where I woz. 'E come an' took me to 'is lodgins an' there woz Jenny.'

'He had lodgings? Where?' Jones asked.

'Off Wild Street — Chapel Yard. Old 'ouse — landlord's a crook an' all. Jonas Finger, 'e's called. 'E'd say nothin' if a girl woz took there. Teddy told me to stay wiv Jenny an' 'e'd come back. Give me money — thort 'e could buy me an' I'd let 'im do wot 'e wanted wiv 'er. 'E went off an' locked us in. Sed Finger'd look arter us. Well, I knew wot that meant so I 'ad ter get us out. Waited a bit. Shouted for Finger. Sed I'd be good to 'im if 'e give us some food — yer know wot I mean. I sez ter Jenny to pretend to be asleep an' be quiet. Well 'e come up an' sed 'e'd bring us somethin' so I sez wot abaht a drink? 'E came up wiv some bread an' gin. I makes sure Finger 'ad plenty o' gin an' I 'ad a bit. I sits on 'is knee, let 'im — yer know — 'e's drunk as a fish — drops on ter the floor wiv me on top pretendin' to like him an' 'e falls asleep. I waits an' then we scarper.'

'Where?'

'I takes 'er ter Liddy's — I 'ave ter get us some different clothes. Liddy's there, but too drunk ter care so I 'elps us ter some old rags. I 'id our clothes in the yard and we went off up by Eagle Street. I got a friend up there, Maggie. She took us in an' we laid low. Didn't dare move. An' this morning when 'e 'adn't found us, I decided to risk it an' 'ere we are.'

'We'll keep you safe. Don't worry. We'll be going to Finger directly and we'll bring him in, and he will tell us all about Teddy. He saw you both?'

'Yer, 'e saw us when we went in. Teddy sez we woz friends of 'is — Finger laughed — 'e knew wot woz goin' on — Teddy musta took girls there before.'

'With Jonas Finger's evidence, yours and Jenny's, we'll have enough to arrest him.' Jones looked at Jenny's white, tear-streaked face. He had to find out what had happened to her. He looked at Dickens, indicating that he should ask her.

'Jenny, my dear, can you tell us what happened to you? You are safe now and soon you will be back with Mrs Morson to look after you.'

Jenny wept and they waited.

Louisa understood what they wanted to know. 'I don't think 'e touched 'er, Mr Jones. I asked 'er that an' she sed 'e 'adn't. She knew wot I meant.'

'Jenny, try to tell us. We need to know so that we can find him and stop him doing this again.'

'Lizzie Dagg an' me, we met 'im in the village when we woz shoppin'. 'E talked ter Lizzie, sed 'e thort she woz pretty. Lizzie liked 'im an' then 'e sed 'e'd give me a present cos 'e could tell I woz a good girl.'

She wept again, and they waited.

Jenny wiped her eyes. ''E sed 'e'd come an' find us. An' that 'e wanted to give Lizzie a present as well. I knew we shouldn't 'ave spoke to 'im but 'e woz nice an' 'andsome an' Lizzie sed no one would know an' why shouldn't we 'ave a present. An' she sed that would show Isabella Gordon wot's wot. Isabella's always teasin' 'er, yer see, Mr Dickens.'

Dickens thought about the broken mug they had seen, and the dead girl with her bruises, and what Teddy Crewe might have done to Jenny Ding if Louisa had not been as resourceful and brave as she was.

'And he came to the Home?'

'They woz all busy in the kitchen. I 'eard the knock at the door an' it woz 'im. I sed did 'e want Lizzie, but 'e sed 'e'd got my present like 'e'd promised. It woz in 'is carriage an' I could get it if I wanted. I went out an' 'e sed I could 'ave a ride in the carriage so I did an' 'e sed 'e'd take me to London for a treat an' bring me back. So I got in —' she cried again — 'an''e took me to them rooms an' I woz scared cos 'e said I couldn't go back till next day. 'E sed 'e'd bring a friend an' 'e locked me in an' then Louisa came.'

Dickens turned to Louisa. 'Miss Mapp, you need to get away. I would like you to go with Jenny to the Home in Shepherd's Bush. You will both be safe there until we need you to give evidence.'

''Ome?'

'I can't explain it all now, but the matron, Mrs Morson, will take care of you both. There are other girls there. You must not say what has been happening — they will accept that you are just a new girl who wants a new start, and that is all that is needed now. Jenny, I will write a note to Mrs Morson. The girls will simply be told that you ran away because you wanted to see your sister. No one need know what really happened. ' He turned to Jones. 'I'll write to Mrs Morson now.'

'Yes. Rogers, you take them and then come back. Take a fly — it'll be quicker than a cab or a bus. Will you arrange that now?'

Rogers went out. Dickens wrote a note to Mrs Morson, telling her that things were moving quickly, that the girls should be told that Jenny had gone to see her sister, that Louisa was a new girl, and that he would come as soon as he could. He knew that she would understand it all. Rogers took the two girls away. He would come back within the hour.

'We need to get Jonas Finger here immediately. Crewe will know that Louisa and Jenny have escaped, and that they could give evidence against him — at least we'll have evidence of abduction, and of Crewe's relationship with Blackledge. And, there may be something in the room he rented which might give evidence. We need some men. I'll organise that now.'

253

The superintendent sent four of his constables to Chapel Yard. Finger was known to them as a receiver of stolen goods, a pimp, a thief, a coiner — in short, a man who would do anything for money. Two were to arrest Finger, and to use whatever force was necessary, and the other two were to make sure that no one left the house.

By the time Dickens and Jones reached Chapel Yard, Jonas Finger was shouting the odds, demanding his rights, and swearing ferociously at the two constables. He was a big, coarse brute of a man with black hair and eyes to match, strong as a bull, fighting with the constables who were struggling to restrain him.

Jones stepped forward. 'You can stop that, my lad.'

Dickens heard the steel in his voice and saw the steel in his eyes, and so did Finger who stopped struggling suddenly, though his mouth still snarled. 'Wotcher want? Yer ain't got nuffink on me. I'm a respectable 'ouseholder, I am. Yer can get these brutes off me.'

Jones laughed. The two constables were hanging grimly on to Jonas Finger. One of them was a young man only just tall enough for the regulation height. Finger could have made two of him. The other was Stemp who had found the body of the little girl. His anger was palpable — he was not going to let go. Jones continued, 'So you say, Jonas Finger, and you can tell it all to the magistrate. I'm arresting you as an accomplice in the abduction of two girls. And you can tell me where Teddy is — I want him as well.'

Jonas Finger looked sick suddenly, but he blustered on, 'I dunno no Teddy, an' I dunno nuffink abaht any girls.'

'I have witnesses, Finger. They've told me all about it, and I have a dead girl you might want to tell me about.' Jones was brisk, his voice cutting through the bluster. 'Accomplice to murder, you might be — unless I can find your friend, Teddy.'

'Dunno where 'e is. An' I dunno abaht any dead girl. 'Oo 'e brings 'ere's 'is own business — nuffink ter do wiv me. Yer can't pin no murder on me.'

'I shan't be pinning anything on you — Teddy lodges here. You knew about those girls and you know about him so I've cause to suspect you. So, you'll be coming down to Bow Street to tell me all about it. You'll be on remand for some time, Finger, and you'll have plenty of time to think about what you want to say to me. Which room is Teddy's?'

The fight went out of Finger. He was sweating now and frightened, his rat's eyes darting. Whether he knew about murder, Jones did not care. It was enough that he could give evidence about Crewe, and he would talk, Jones had no doubt. He was a bully and a rogue, and loyalty was no part of whatever code he lived by. He wouldn't swing for Teddy and he wouldn't care if Teddy went to the gallows on his evidence.

'Upstairs, on the right,' Finger told them sullenly.

One of the constables was sent back to Bow Street for the police wagon while the other two guarded the subdued Jonas Finger. Dickens and Jones went into the house and up the rickety stairs. It was a shabby place smelling of rot, bad food, smoke and sweat, and something that Dickens felt was evil, a sense of a place where terrible things had happened. *Is there any cause in nature that makes these hard hearts?* Shakespeare's question in *King Lear*, and there was still no answer. What had made Edmund Crewe into the monster he was? What had made him relish these vile places, he who had enjoyed the splendour of Crewe Hall and the marbled elegance of Cavendish Square and their like?

The room was not as vile as the outside stairs and hall. There had been some attempt to make it fit for habitation. The bed was draped with a velvet cover and the linen looked clean. There were a couple of velvet chairs and a round mahogany table. There were thick velvet curtains, presumably obscuring the window. There was the gin bottle of which Louisa had spoken, tipped over with the lees of the gin spilled onto the bare boards. They could smell it and something else — the sweet, cloying smell of opium. There was a gold-framed mirror over the fireplace very like the one at the Albany. What had Crewe seen, thought Dickens, when he had looked at himself in the two mirrors? Was the self that he had watched in this tarnished glass a different self from the one in the polished surface of the Albany mirror? *Look here upon this picture and on this.* The divided self, he thought, two men in one, the self in this mirror like *a mildew'd ear, blasting the wholesome brother.*

They looked at the bed where Jenny Ding had lain terrified, listening to Louisa tempting Finger to drink more and more gin. Underneath it was hidden a locked box chased with silver, made of walnut. It was fastened with a little padlock. Jones wasted no time, but flung it to the floor where its lid split creating a gash which Jones prised apart with his knife, breaking the shining wood. Inside, there were notes, a velvet pouch in which there was a string of pearls which shone palely in the half darkness of the room, and there were papers. A letter in an envelope addressed to Mr Edmund Crewe at the Albany. Dickens wrenched open the velvet curtain to let in some light.

'Pray,' said Jones. 'Pray that this is evidence.' He opened the envelope, scanned the letter inside and handed it to Dickens. The letter was to Crewe from Blackledge written from Ducat's:

My Lord,

I am glad to have been of service to you in the matter of your financial needs. Be assured that any alteration to the Crewe papers will not be found out. I have been careful and Mr Ducat has expressed his trust in me. I thank you for the recompense you made me for my work.

You mentioned that you would be glad to find a discreet lodging in the area of Lincoln's Inn and that you wish this to be a private matter. I have found what you need at the house of Jonas Finger in Chapel Yard off Eagle Street. He is somewhat of a rough man but he will understand your needs. The house is, I am afraid, not what you are used to but the room he has to let may be made comfortable enough for a gentleman and any visitors he might care to entertain. Should you wish to take the rooms I can make all the arrangements necessary.

I hope I may be of service in the future.

Your humble servant,

Alfred Blackledge.

'He thought Crewe was a lord. He must have been impressed by that. Little did he know that his lord would be the agent of his death,' Dickens sighed.

'It ties them together, and there is some suggestion of fraud here which we will ask Mr Ducat to look into. He won't like it if the Crewe family takes its business elsewhere, but that's too bad. The rest, however, is all euphemism. Finger will understand his needs, will he? I bet he did. And Blackledge — visitors, indeed. Still, we've got something, and Finger will talk. It's time we got hold of Mr Crewe. Let's have a look to see if there is anything else.'

Jones investigated under the bed and pulled out a suitcase which was not locked. Inside were the clothes they had seen at Lantern Yard, the rough workman's trousers, the coarse shirt and waistcoat. There was a velvet smoking jacket and a soft shirt with ruffles, the one he had worn last night and the dark trousers and waistcoat — his dress for the Cavendish Square Ball. Placed side by side on the bed, the two outfits were a simulacrum of the two men in one. There were ropes, too, and their purpose was easy to guess. There was the paraphernalia of the opium addict, the pipe, the opium, too, and crumpled up in the corner, a girl's flimsy shift stained with flecks of blood.

'It's enough. Let's go and get him — if we are not too late.'

The suitcase and the broken box with their contents were given to the constable outside to take back to Bow Street. Just as they were leaving for the Albany, Rogers arrived to tell them that Louisa and Jenny were safely stowed away.

Of course, as they had half expected, he was gone. They stood again in the narrow hall with its gilded mirror. The servant was nervous; he knew there was something wrong. His master had gone out to supper after the visit of Dickens and Jones. Since Mr Crewe was to attend a ball in Cavendish Square, the servant was not surprised that he did not come back before midnight. His instructions were always to wait up, all night if need be, and so he did, dozing intermittently until morning. At six he had thought he might come, but it was not unusual for Mr Crewe to stay out all night, for several nights, in fact. Then he came at about eight o'clock.

'How was he dressed?' asked Jones sharply.

'In a suit — just a day suit.'

'Not in evening dress? Not the clothes he had gone out in?'

'No — he had changed — somewhere.'

'Where?'

The boy did not know — his master had another lodging, he was sure, but he did not know where. He was frightened by the superintendent's brusqueness, torn between his fear of his master and the authority of this intimidating policeman.

'When did he go out?'

'About an hour ago — I'm not sure.'

'Did he take anything with him?'

'Yes, just a small case — I don't know what was in it. He was angry, impatient. Told me to mind my own business when I asked if he was coming back.'

Jones asked him if Crewe might have gone to the family house, but the young man did not think so — not if he had been out all night. He could not tell them anything more. His face with its anxious frown suggested he might know or suspect something about his master, but they had not time to question him further. They could come back. The boy might run away. However, they had to risk that.

'He had changed his clothes,' Dickens said when they were on the street again, 'so it would not appear he had been out all night. Suppose he has gone to the town house? If he is intending to fly then he might hope for money, or there might be something he wishes to collect or to take. It is worth our trying.'

'You're right — Sir Hungerford may know something.'

Rogers had waited outside. There was no need for him to come to Grosvenor Street, no need for Mollie Spoon to see him again and start talk in the kitchen. He went back to Bow Street, and would send to them if there were any developments.

26: Who is He?

A cab took them to the town house in Grosvenor Street. Dickens stood on the steps, wondering whether his grandmother had been here. Would his grandfather have answered the door if they had come sixty years ago when he was butler to the Crewe family? Would Sir Hungerford Crewe refer to the Dickens servants as the sneering Edmund had? God, he thought, how all occasions do inform against me. He shook off these unwelcome thoughts, standing straight, and rang the bell. He introduced himself and asked to see Sir Hungerford Crewe on a confidential matter. A powdered replica of the footman at Hanover Square admitted them to a spacious hall from where a marble staircase rose as large and cold as an iceberg to the floors above. The hall was circular, and in the niches in the walls were marble busts of Greek and Roman philosophers or senators whose blind eyes stared at them with lofty indifference. The footman disappeared to enquire if Sir Hungerford would see them.

'Same scene, several hours later,' whispered Dickens, making the joke to steady his nerves.

The footman returned to take them to the library where Sir Hungerford came from behind his magnificent desk to greet them courteously. He was tall and elegant, with thick, dark, straight hair, a handsome, scholarly looking man, unlike his relative, though Dickens discerned a resemblance in the long fine nose and high cheekbones. He was thirty-seven, the same age as Dickens, born in 1812 when old Mrs Dickens worked as housekeeper at Crewe Hall and the town house.

'Mr Dickens, I am very glad to meet you, but I cannot imagine of what matter of confidentiality you wish to speak to me. I know your work well. Your books are here and read, of course.' He smiled but then looked pointedly at Jones. No reference to any other Dickens, just to the famous writer. Dickens relaxed. The solitary, hungry boy from the blacking factory disappeared.

'May I introduce Superintendent Jones of Bow Street? He is concerned in this matter,' he said smoothly, confidence restored.

'You are here on a police matter then?' Sir Hungerford's eyes registered alarm.

'We are,' said Jones who had seen the alarm and guessed its cause. There was no time for polite expressions of regret for intruding, nor time for delicacy. 'We are keen to find your relative, Mr Edmund Crewe, in connection with a series of crimes in which we suspect he is involved.'

'You had better sit down and explain precisely what has happened.'

Jones told him. He left out nothing. Sir Hungerford listened intently, his face betraying horror as every detail, including the murders of Patience Rivers, and Blackledge, the suspicions of fraud at Ducat's, the abduction of Jenny Ding, was related to him.

At the end of it all, he asked only, 'Have you proof of all this?'

'Enough,' said Jones tersely, 'enough to make it imperative that we find him. Is he here?'

'No, he is not. I have not seen him. His way of life is one of which I cannot approve. He is heedless, a spendthrift, a gambler, but I had not thought him capable of this.'

Dickens asked, 'Was he married to Patience Rivers? He told us he was not, that she was his mistress, and that she left him because he would not marry her. They had a child, too.'

'It was my belief that he had married her. She came here with her father to teach music to my sisters. That is how he met her. He told me that they were married. I did not mind — she was an educated girl, quiet and with all the qualities of a lady. It did not matter that she was of relatively humble stock. Her father, though not rich, was a gentleman in all his ways. What did it matter? Edmund was not going to be the heir. I was prepared to settle money on them, give them a house in Cheshire. I hoped he would settle down, live the life of a gentleman farmer, but he wished to stay in London for the time being, he said. They lived in a small town house we owned. The child came and I thought it time they moved to the country. I told him so. Then came the news that Patience had left him. He said she was unhappy, that she no longer loved him, and that the marriage was a mistake. He told us that he had accepted a separation, that he was supporting her, but he wanted the child to live in Cheshire. He said he hoped she would come back. Time went on and his story was that she was living with another man, and that he had cut her off entirely.'

'You believed all this?' said Dickens. 'You believed his version of Patience Rivers?'

'What reason had he to lie to us? I accepted what he told me — they were young. I thought a mistake had been made.'

'And when he wanted to marry another, what then?' Jones was sharp.

'I heard that he was pursuing Laetitia Topham, and I told him he could not put in hazard the girl's reputation. He was married, and until he could divorce Patience his name could not, must not, be linked with another woman's. I was firm and I told him, too, that his way of life was not fitting, and then he told me that he and Patience had never been married, that she had been his mistress and when she tired of him, she had left him for another man. I thought —'

'That since she had consented to be his mistress, she was not the woman you thought she was, and that what she was explained why she would leave him. That is what he wanted you to think. I knew Patience and she was not the girl to become a man's mistress. I think he married her, and that he tired of her. She was too good for him.' Dickens was angry at the lies and deceit, the tarnishing of Patience's reputation. 'He killed her because she left him, she would not be what he wanted her to be — he could not drag her down to his level.'

The angry words hovered in the silence that followed. Sir Hungerford looked appalled at what the words implied.

Jones had a thought. 'Who is he, Sir Hungerford, this young man whose viciousness you had not known?'

'He is the illegitimate son of my father's cousin. He is not a Crewe at all. He was left orphaned at his mother's death. The father died earlier before there could be any marriage. His father was a man called Frederick Lee. That is the name on his birth certificate.'

'*Bereft of my parents, bereft of my home,*' murmured Dickens.

'What?' asked Sir Hungerford, his tone sharp.

'It was the song he sang — a boy heard him when we think he killed his wife.' Dickens was determined. Patience was his wife.

'I know it. His nurse sang it — insensitive, really. Servants can be — we had a housekeeper once who —'

Dickens froze. Here it was. The boy from the blacking factory, the little ghost stood with him.

Jones interrupted, 'You were telling us about Edmund Crewe.'

'I am sorry. Yes. My father took him in, gave him our name, educated him, and he paid us back with resentment. He hated his subordinate position — he could not bear that he was not a Crewe, that he could not be the heir. He did not want to be an obscure gentleman farmer with a good wife and children. It was not enough. I knew that but I thought, in time, that Patience might — and then came the story of her leaving. He is always very persuasive, charming, remorseful. I believed him.'

Yes, thought Dickens, we have seen him play that part. 'Where will he have gone? Could he have gone north?'

'He might. He might want to see his child. I do not know now after what you have told me.'

The footman came in. He looked flustered. 'I beg your pardon, Sir Hungerford. There is a young man who insists that he must see Mr Dickens.'

To their astonishment, a dishevelled Oliver Wilde came in.

'Forgive my rudeness, Sir Hungerford, but this is most urgent. Mr Dickens, I know where he is.'

'Edmund Crewe? This is Superintendent Jones, by the way. He will want to know all.'

'Yes, Crewe. After you had been to see me, Mr Dickens, I thought about what you had said, and how I had told you that I would be an armed guard if necessary. I was worried about Miss Topham. I was invited to the ball at Cavendish Square. I wondered if he might do something — I don't know what really. But she was not there. I saw him, but he did not stay long. I wanted to know if he was going to try to see Miss Topham so I thought I would follow. However, he got into a carriage. It was impossible in the fog so I went to the Albany — I asked for him but the servant said he was not there. I didn't know whether to believe him — just a young man — he would have said anything Crewe wanted. I waited in a doorway opposite — in the fog. It was freezing, but I didn't care. I saw him come back about eight o'clock. I was going to go home, but I thought I would wait — I couldn't get any colder or more uncomfortable, and he did come out — after an nearly an hour — I followed his cab in another to Euston Station. I went after him — he was waiting for the nine o'clock express — then, I thought about your advice — you told me to be careful so I went to your house — to see what you thought, and they said you were at the police station. It made me think something was wrong. I went there, said it was urgent that I should see you, and Constable Rogers sent me here. He seemed to think it very important — he told me to hurry so I did.'

'You did well,' said Dickens. 'It *is* important that we find him. We cannot tell you why just now.'

'We are grateful, Mr Wilde, but you must leave it with us now. We need to question Mr Crewe on some matters which are of concern to Sir Hungerford here.'

'You must find him, Superintendent, and you must do whatever is right. I shall not protect him for the sake of our name.'

Sir Hungerford was pale, but composed. It was clear to Dickens that he was deeply shocked by all that he had heard. Dickens felt sorry for him — he could not quite forgive him for his easy belief that Patience had been promiscuous, but he was not responsible for Edmund Crewe's actions, and he was not prepared to cover up what had been done to prevent disgrace.

'The nine o'clock express from Euston goes north — he must be going to Crewe Hall,' said Jones.

'Liverpool,' said Dickens. 'We took a ship from there to America. Perhaps he intends to leave the country.'

'Would he take the child?' asked Jones.

'I do not know,' replied Sir Hungerford. 'He might. He might go to Crewe Hall for money — there are many valuable objects, jewels which he could sell. He has little ready money, I know — to my cost. You must go to Crewe. I will write a note to my aunt, Lady Amelia. If you present it to my steward, he will let you in.'

Oliver Wilde stood silent and amazed by what he was hearing. Dickens saw his discomfort. It was time to release him from this awkward situation. 'Mr Wilde, I think you might leave us now. Miss Topham is safe, and you have done your part for her. Her father knows all so you need say nothing to her or him. We can, I know, rely on your discretion about this matter. I'll come out with you while Sir Hungerford writes his letter.' It was a gentle dismissal.

'I am glad to have been of service. Sir Hungerford, I am sorry for intruding here, and you may, of course, rely on my discretion. Good morning to you all.'

Sir Hungerford bowed but said nothing.

Dickens turned to Sir Hungerford. 'Sir, I am sorry to have brought such bad news to you.' Then he walked out with Oliver Wilde, leaving Jones to wait for the letter.

In the hall, Oliver Wilde looked at Dickens, a worried frown creasing his amiable, open face. 'Something dreadful has happened. Sir Hungerford looked so weary and crushed.'

'It has, but I cannot tell you any more, only that the superintendent and I must find him — and soon. Goodbye, Mr Wilde. I am sure we will meet again.'

'I hope so. Goodbye, Mr Dickens.' Oliver Wilde went out, his face still puzzled and anxious. Jones came out, tucking the letter into his pocket.

'We must go back to Bow Street immediately,' he said, 'and then we must go to Euston and follow him north. Let's assume that he will go to Crewe Hall for money and valuable objects. He'll leave the train at Crewe and go to the Hall where we may apprehend him. We need to discover when the next ship sails from Liverpool so that we may know how much time we have.'

'If we can't find him at Crewe then we go to Liverpool?'

'We must and we must board whichever ship he is on.'

'I hope we shall not have to go a-sailing, Sam. One day I will tell you of our voyage to America aboard *The Britannia* steam ship — suffice to tell now, apart from the sea sickness, there was a raging storm, so ferocious that I never expected to see the day again. Truly, Sam, I gave it up as a lost thing. So, let us devoutly hope that we do not have to sail to find him. I wish to catch him as you do, but I am fain to lose our lives in the chase.'

'Then, we must hurry to Bow Street and then the train, and pray we find him at Crewe.'

At Bow Street they consulted the shipping announcements which told that the SS *Europa* of the Cunard Line would sail for New York on Tuesday, 23rd February, giving them time to find Edmund Crewe, assuming that he was on his way to Crewe Hall.

According to Oliver Wilde, Crewe had taken the nine o'clock express which would arrive in Crewe at about two o'clock in the afternoon. There was an express at noon which, if they were quick, Dickens and Jones could catch — it would get them to Crewe at about five o'clock if there were no delays. There was not time to lose if they wanted to catch him at Crewe Hall.

27: Pursuit

Euston Square terminus: porters, clad in green with white letters on their collars, manoeuvred their luggage trucks between the crowds of passengers. Top-hatted businessmen made for the first-class carriages, as did the well-dressed matrons in their wide, flounced skirts, men in patched, worn-out suits and shawled women laden with baskets and oddly shaped bundles hurried to find a place in third class, some still crowded at the ticket booth, and there were children swarming about. Who they belonged to it was difficult to tell — most seemed to attach themselves to any available adult. No doubt the mothers knew their own despite the similarity of these wrapped-up heaps of rags and shawls with their misshapen caps and bonnets and identical screams and shrieks, almost loud enough to rival the bells and whistles and great snortings of the steam engine which waited, clouds of vapour billowing from the brass chimney. It was impatient to go, and so were Dickens and Jones who had got their tickets for a first-class carriage. They pushed through the groups of labourers, soldiers, sailors, navvies, servants, milling guards and porters to settle themselves at last in their comfortable carriage with its upholstered seats, with a pie each in their pockets and Seltzer water, refreshment for the four hours or so of the journey.

There were two other passengers, one rather bad-tempered mottle-faced businessman whose skin was stretched over his face like that of a sausage. He hid behind his newspaper. There was a pious-looking lady in black who hid behind a thick veil, so thick it was that Dickens wondered whether she might be Crewe in disguise. Unlikely, he concluded, glancing at the neat

269

little feet encased in little black boots which peeped briefly from under the black skirts. One black-gloved hand held tightly on to her hamper and in the other she grasped a wicked-looking hatpin — to ward off a potential attacker, perhaps, who might launch himself upon her in a conveniently dark tunnel.

A monstrous heave and a piercing whistle signalled their departure. An anguished face appeared briefly at the window and was left behind, the door being locked. Whoever it was had missed the train. But for them the chase was on. Dickens saw that Jones's face was alight. In five hours or a little more, they would be on their way to Crewe Hall, and this time he would not escape them, even if they had to pursue him to the sea itself. The train gathered speed, the rich and varied landscape began to rush by, flashing unrolling pictures of heath and orchard, graveyard and factory, rivers and green hills, spires and towers, cottages and castles, through stations, stopping but for a moment then dashing on, roaring and rattling through vistas of red brick houses, railway arches and black chimneys crowding the skyline.

It was impossible to talk while they had neighbours to listen in, though judging by the explosive snores coming from mottle-face, it was unlikely that he would hear what they might say. As for the woman in black, she might have been some spectre, so motionless was she, still clutching her hatpin. Dickens felt that she might stab him with it. Every time they entered a tunnel, he thought he heard the faintest rustle of her skirts. Was she moving nearer with her weapon poised to strike? They hardly liked to whisper, either. They might give the impression that their business was nefarious, and then, indeed, she might strike.

After an hour, they ate their pies for want of anything better to do. The pies seemed composed of unknown animals within, the meat, glutinous and gristly — perhaps it was bear? Dickens felt the crust settle in him like cardboard. He drank some Seltzer water; it was unpleasantly gaseous and the cardboard seemed to swell inside him. Jones read the book he had scooped from his desk as they left Bow Street. It was *Dombey and Son* — Jones's second reading.

'Any good?' Dickens asked in his cockney voice. Sam Weller come to life. 'Yer book, I mean.'

He detected a faint rustle. He did not dare look, but imagined the bony hand gripping the pin even more tightly.

'Very good,' said Jones, his lips twitching.

''Oo wrote it?'

'Charles Dickens.'

'Oh, 'im.'

'Do you know him?' asked Jones.

'Met 'im wonce — a rum'n to look at, all eyes and nose. Flash sort o' cove, though. Don't go in much for readin' meself. Prefer cards. Got a pack 'ere — fancy a game of whist — low stakes o' course.'

The rustling was louder now, though, fortunately, the snoring went on.

'No thank you — I do not approve of card playing of any kind — especially on trains.' Jones's voice shook slightly but the rustling ceased. 'Have you read this book?'

'Nah, but I tell yer wot I do know — if yer ain't got to the end — there's a man killed on the railway — mortal lot o' blood.'

There was another rustling. Jones hid behind his handkerchief, being taken by a sudden attack of coughing.

'It woz them pies we 'ad — like eatin' cardboard. Lodged with a pieman once — a werry nice man — make pies out o' anythin', 'e could. Werry fond o' cats 'e woz.'

The coughing seemed more acute now so Dickens kindly supplied the remains of his bottle of Seltzer, saying as he did so in the manner of Mr Weller, 'Out wiv it, as the father said to the child, wen 'e swallowed a farden.'

There was a strangled splutter then the coughing subsided into an asthmatic wheeze. If you had not known better, you might have thought it sounded suspiciously like laughter.

Dickens dozed from time to time, conscious only of the sound of wheels on iron, sometimes jerked awake by the sound of the whistle signalling its warning that the express was coming. It stopped at Birmingham, Coventry, Stafford, and mottle-face snored on — so loudly that Dickens was afraid the sausage skin would burst. And still the veiled one sat like a waxwork — perhaps she was. Perhaps at journey's end, mottle-face would lift her out of the carriage and carry her under his arm away to some mouldy exhibition — she was small enough.

They entered his fitful dreams, the woman in black lifting her veil so that he saw the face of a ruined angel. Mottle-face opened his mouth and became Carker, Mr Dombey's mortal enemy, with his rows of glistening teeth. Dickens saw him again stepping off the platform into the path of the rushing train to be torn into fragments. He heard the shriek of iron and then woke suddenly as the train stopped. Stafford — not long now. Jones woke, too. The veiled lady got out and walked away on her own legs, vanishing into the crush of alighting passengers and porters. The mottle-faced man woke, realised that he was about to be whirled away to unknown regions, grasped his carpet bag, and hurried away without a backward glance.

Dickens and Jones got out into the press of boarding and alighting passengers. They had ten minutes. A cold wind whistled down the platform, blowing rain into their faces. They peered into the refreshment room and looked at the card showing what was on offer.

'No thanks,' said Dickens. 'That pie was bad enough. The soup will be brown hot water stiffened with flour, and if you want a mouthful of sand, try one of the cakes!'

'That pie is my constant companion,' said Jones. 'I feel as if I've swallowed a rock. Another hour, I should think, after Stafford. We will take a fly to the Hall and get there as quickly as we can. He has three hours' start on us — time for him to get to the Hall and away again. We must hope that he is still there, delayed by the child, perhaps, or family obligations. He won't want to seem in too much of a hurry.'

The whistle blew again, and they climbed back into the carriage where a new passenger was ensconced. He was a thin, lugubrious individual who gazed at them mournfully as they entered. Perhaps he wanted to be alone. He took out a book. Dickens tried to see what it was, lowering and twisting his head round, and squinting his eyes in a manner that might have suggested lunacy had the melancholy man looked up.

'Neck troubling you again, my boy?' Jones asked with a gleam in his eye.

'Yes, Father,' said Dickens, his handkerchief out.

'Well, sit still then.'

With that admonition to his restless son, Jones returned to his book. Dickens looked at the slanting rain. He watched the raindrops blown diagonally across the window, and was aware of the darkening skies. He cast a rueful glance at Jones who was thinking, too, that a rain-soaked dash to Crewe Hall was not an inviting prospect.

At last the train slowed, the brakes made their grinding sound and the great engine wheezed and belched out a great cloud of smoke. It rolled into the station with its glass roof and iron pillars, and they climbed out, glad to stretch their legs.

Outside the station there were vehicles for hire. A fly would take them to Crewe Hall. How strange, thought Dickens; that I should be coming here on such an errand. Through the darkening country lanes they drove. In what direction, they did not know. It was a pretty, flat country with low hedges lining the lanes where the occasional gap revealed low buildings humped in the falling darkness. The trees were winter bare, black against the fading sky.

Dickens did not want to announce himself. Someone there, a servant, perhaps, might know the name, might wonder at his coming. The name Dickens here would not immediately be associated with the writer, but with William and, especially, Elizabeth Dickens who had worked here so long. It was impossible to imagine. He had known little of her; he recalled a grim old lady who lived not far away when they were in Norfolk Street, and whose legacy had released them from the Marshalsea. What she had thought of the son who had got his wife and children in there, he did not know, and his father had not spoken at all of the days when he had lived in this vast mansion. Had John Dickens spent all he had trying to live something like the life he had seen at Crewe Hall?

Jones interrupted his gloomy reflections. 'No need to explain anything to the servant or whoever answers the door, we need only say that we wish to see Lady Amelia and we simply present the letter.'

At length they came to the handsome gateway of the house with its red brick lodge built in the Jacobean style. The park was vast, stretching away to the shining levels of a lake, and there was enough light to see how enormous the house was with its great windows, diapered brickwork, balustrade parapets and Jacobean chimneys.

Jones instructed the driver to wait for them. They stood on the massive steps and rang the bell. An imposing figure answered the door — the steward or butler, William Dickens's successor, perhaps. Dickens regarded him curiously as Jones stated their business. He was certainly an impressively dignified and grave figure, more so than Sir Hungerford himself. Jones wasted no time, merely offering the letter addressed to Lady Amelia Crewe, and giving his own name as Superintendent Jones from Bow Street, London.

They stepped into the Jacobean panelled entrance hall with its marble chimneypiece supported by Tuscan columns. A heavily carved Jacobean staircase was decorated with gilded, heraldic animals. Dickens gazed at it all while the imposing man looked at the letter. His face betrayed nothing. And then he went away up the staircase with the letter on a silver salver taken up from a massively carved chest in the hall. They watched him come down, impassive, imperturbable, the ideal, discreet servant. Dickens found it very hard to imagine careless, convivial John Dickens here. They were taken upstairs at the same measured tread and announced or, rather, the superintendent was.

They entered a panelled oak room. Dickens noted the large Jacobean overmantel with its intricate carvings. Lady Amelia rose to meet them, the letter in her hand. She wasted no time, either. She was tall and thin with pale parchment skin, the Crewe nose and intelligent hazel eyes. Dickens guessed her age at about sixty.

'Superintendent Jones, and?' Her voice was crisp and authoritative. She wanted to know with whom she was dealing.

The superintendent introduced himself and told her that his companion was Mr Charles Dickens. The boy from the blacking factory appeared again — the little ghost who had come with Dickens to Crewe Hall.

'Mr Dickens? The writer?'

'Yes, ma'm,' Dickens answered. The little ghost vanished.

'I am very glad to meet you. Your books are well known to us here. Mr Pickwick has given us many hours of enjoyment. But how is it that you are here with the superintendent?'

'I have an interest in Mr Crewe and the superintendent wishes to find him.'

'I have read the letter, Superintendent. However, I am afraid that Edmund Crewe is not here. He arrived a few hours ago to collect some luggage and papers and then he departed in some haste, saying that he was to catch a train to Liverpool. You have missed him, I fear. The Liverpool train will have gone by now. The letter from my nephew says that this inquiry of yours concerns Patience. Has she been found?'

'She is dead, Lady Amelia,' said Jones.

Lady Amelia looked back at the letter and again at them. Her sharp eyes told them that she had worked it out. After all, she must have known Edmund Crewe all his life, and she must have known something of what he was.

'You think that Edmund is linked to her death? And you have told my nephew all of this?'

'We have — he knows it all, and he does not wish to protect Mr Crewe for the sake of the family name,' said Jones.

'No, he would not. Hungerford is an honourable man. He will be much distressed by all this. Where is Patience now?'

'Her body lies at the infirmary until the inquest can be held.'

'When it is over, she must be brought here to be buried in the churchyard. She was Edmund's wife and there is her child to think of.'

'They were married then?' asked Dickens.

'I am certain of it. Of course, Edmund tried to deny it when it suited him to be rid of her. Superintendent, Mr Dickens, I have no illusions about Edmund Crewe. My brother, Sir John, was generous. The boy was an orphan. He was brought up here, educated with tutors and allowed the Crewe name, but, I think it was a mistake. He is ungrateful — and worse, if what you suspect is true. His own father, Francis Lee, was a wastrel who seduced our cousin and left her. He died in penury, a drunkard and a gambler, as his son came to be. But I liked Patience. I found it very hard to credit that she had left him for another man or, indeed, that she had lived with Edmund as his mistress. Bring her home, Mr Dickens, for her child's sake.'

'The child is brought up here?'

'Yes, a little girl. You may see her, if you wish. I will ask nurse to bring her.' She went out with a firm step, a tall, stately old woman, whose carriage was as upright as her nature. If she believed that Patience had married Edmund Crewe then it had to be true.

She came back with the nursemaid who carried the little girl, about two years old with Patience's grey eyes and pale skin. Dickens saw, too, the Crewe nose which would give her older face distinction. He was glad for Patience's sake that she was well cared for and had a home. If she took after her mother and this clear-sighted, intelligent old lady, then the strength of the two would drive out the weakness of the father, he was sure. One little girl he did not have to worry about.

'Have you daughters, Mr Dickens?'

'Yes, two.'

'Good. I am sure that they will be intelligent and strong-minded — you will make sure of that. It is not easy for girls in our time — so easy for them to be used and abused like poor Patience. Her daughter will have a very different fate as long as I am here to ensure it. However, I am keeping you from your task, Superintendent. I am sure that you wish to be after your quarry. There will be another train to Liverpool in an hour's time.'

They bade farewell to that formidable and surprising woman and the child who waved her little hand. They descended the magnificent staircase to the hall where the butler showed them out into the cold twilight. The fly was waiting to take them back to the station. And then to Liverpool and the vast, lonely stretches of the sea, perhaps. Dickens looked back at the great house outlined against the darkening sky. The huge door shut against them. I shall not come here again, he thought. I have seen enough.

28: The Fall

There were a few disconsolate travellers shivering in the cold on the platform for the Liverpool train. Porters lounged against the walls, there were mailbags heaped on the platform, trunks and portmanteaus stacked next to them. On enquiry, they discovered that the next train would be late because the earlier train had not yet arrived which meant that Edmund Crewe could not yet have gone on to Liverpool, so where was he? Had he changed his mind and taken a fly or hired a coach to take him the thirty or so miles to the port? They scanned the faces of the waiting passengers. A tall man in a tweed greatcoat and hat over his eyes glared at them as they threaded their way through — he wasn't Crewe nor, obviously was an elderly man with spectacles. They looked down the empty platform to where it ended and the line went on into the empty distance. They retraced their steps. In the waiting room, a few coals flickered reluctantly in the black grate, but he was not among the shivering group gathered there. They went back from the platform to where there was a refreshment room and peered in through the misty window.

'There,' breathed Jones. 'It is he, I'm sure.'

Dickens looked at the figure hunched over the marble table top, the coat collar turned up and the hat pulled down. But there was something about the head and the broad shoulders. The stranger looked up and at the window. Dickens eyes met his and Crewe knew him. He was up in a flash, pushing his way to the door where a woman was just going in. He shoved her aside and ran onto the first platform, leaping over the boxes, pushing a porter with his trolley out of the way. Jones darted after him, leaving Dickens to assist the toppled lady whom he thrust without ceremony into the arms of an astonished porter. He flew after Jones who was extricating himself from an encounter with a porter's trolley. They ran onto the platform where knots of travellers were alighting from the train that had just come in. They could see Crewe, his hat fallen off, his blonde hair streaming as he ran along the platform pushing through indignant crowds, leaping with athletic grace over tumbled boxes and trunks. Would he board the train?

No, they saw him enveloped for a moment in vapour, careering down the platform towards the emptiness beyond. Where was he going? Did he think he could escape along the line? A whistle sounded in the distance. There was the sound of a train slowing as it was coming into the station on the other line. Surely he would not risk it? They ran on, their progress impeded by the passengers alighting and boarding. They could hardly push through as he did, heedless of anyone else. Jones sidestepped a woman with a large basket and found himself in an embrace with a corpulent man who would not let him go. Dickens ran on, zig-zagging through the crowd, losing his hat, barking his shins on a porter's trolley, reaching almost the end of the platform. But, impossibly, Crewe had disappeared. Where?

Dickens looked round, baffled. Was Crewe on the track, running for his life? The other train was coming in, belching its steam into the air. He looked beyond the platform and looked up. He was there, climbing up a precarious iron ladder which led onto a narrow gantry. The train's whistle sounded as it approached the gantry upon which Crewe was now balanced. He looked down at his pursuer. Dickens saw the ruined face in the clouds of smoke, and Crewe looked at him. He seemed to smile, and raised his hand as if in farewell. Involuntarily

Dickens raised his hand as if in acknowledgement. Of what? Of Crewe's choice? In that moment they were connected. He understood the man and pitied him. Then, as if in slow motion, Dickens saw him fall into the steam and sparks and vanish. *Hurled headlong, flaming from the ethereal sky*, thought Dickens, remembering Satan's fall from heaven. There was a moment of silence, then someone screamed, and the people on the platforms turned to see what had happened. Dickens turned away, sick suddenly.

Jones caught up with him. He had seen for himself that dreadful fall. 'Accident?'

'I do not think so. He knew it was all over. I saw his face and that terrible smile.' He shuddered. 'I do not want to see. I wrote about it. I described Carker's death and I can imagine what he looks like now. The train must have gone over him.'

'I think it did. Well, I shall have to deal with the authorities. We were seen chasing him. The police will come soon. I must speak to them, and send messages to London and Crewe Hall.'

''Tis better as it is,' said Dickens.

'I think so, too.'

They went back along the platform and Jones went to speak to the stationmaster. Four porters took away the body on a board; a sheet of rough canvas had been thrown over the mangled thing to cover it from the stares of frightened passengers who crowded on both platforms, peering at the line where the bloodied body had lain, crushed beyond recognition. They were curious, too, but had trains to catch, and so they reluctantly dragged themselves away when the whistles sounded. The Liverpool train left at last, leaving the platform empty but for a few loiterers, hoping to see something more, and the London train departed, too. The station was quiet now, and Dickens saw the wooden board carried away into the stationmaster's office, out of sight. He felt relief and pity, wondering again what had made that young man into what he was. He had been generously and kindly treated, educated expensively, and loved by a beautiful girl and he had gone wrong. Yet Scrap who had nothing and no one, as far as he could tell, would certainly go right.

The authorities dealt with, and satisfied that the superintendent from London had hunted his quarry to Crewe Station, and that the criminal had fallen in his attempt to escape, and that the superintendent and Mr Dickens would return for the inquest, Dickens and Jones were free to return to London on the last express which they caught just in time, which saved them a night in the station hotel. The stationmaster's wife had given them hot tea and good sandwiches, so there was no need for bear pie or sand cakes.

They stared out at the dark which enveloped the speeding train. Somewhere across the black fields Lady Amelia Crewe would be getting the news that Edmund Crewe was dead and would trouble them no more.

'Justice?' asked Jones. 'Did we get justice for Patience as we promised?'

'I think we did, and for the living, which is just as important. It is better for Patience's daughter that he is dead. And for Mrs Blackledge and little Rose. There will be no sensational murder trial to wound any of them. Better for the Home, too, and for the girls, and for Jenny and Louisa. Better for Sir Hungerford who is, I think, as his aunt said, an honourable man. And Patience will be buried where her daughter can visit her grave and know her in a way. Lady Amelia will see to that.'

'And Edmund Crewe?'

'Doomed, I think. And he destroyed himself when he murdered Patience, if he had not done so before.'

'What made him, I wonder?' asked Jones. 'He had so much to make him envied: good looks, wealthy benefactors, the Crewe name, a woman who loved him, at first, at any rate, a lovely child, yet he threw it all away. What a waste. When I think —' Jones's lips tightened in anger. Dickens knew he was thinking of Edith, who had wanted to live.

'The song tells us — *bereft of my parents, bereft of my home* — I suppose he felt cheated. When the nurse sang it, did he feel, even then, that he was slighted, excluded?'

'But he was not, was he? They gave him everything,' Jones pointed out, reasonably.

'But it was not enough. Edmund, the bastard — perhaps that was it. Edmund in *King Lear* — *why bastard, wherefore base?* he asks, *and why brand they us with base?* Perhaps, the bitterness corroded his soul so that whatever was done for him was never sufficient to erase that early sense of dispossession. Perhaps the nurse who sang the song to him meant to be cruel. Childhood leaves its indelible mark. I know that. And, I think sometimes, Sam, that there is in us all an impulse of self-destruction, but it is held in check by our responsibilities, our sense of duty to others and ourselves. Even Edmund in *King Lear* says he means to do some good at the end. You know, Crewe raised his hand to me at the last moment — perhaps his last act was the only good he has ever done — to die and release us all as well as himself.'

Jones thought a while in silence. 'You may be right, I don't know. I find it hard to believe in any good in him after what we have seen. Little girls — there's no excuse for that.'

'No, you are right.' Dickens thought about the little, forgotten girl in that rank garden.

'But the worst is over, as you have said, and it is better for all those left behind. And though I said I would see him hang, I never do want it really.'

Dickens looked at what remained of his hat. Sam Weller came into the carriage. 'Ta'nt a werry good 'un to look at, an' afore the brim went, it was a werry handsome tile. Hows'ever it's lighter without it, and every hole lets in some air.'

Jones laughed. 'At least you got it back. I don't know where mine went — I was fond of that hat. I like Sam Weller, he makes me laugh.'

'I like him, too, though I have a fancy that David Copperfield will be my favourite child.'

They were quiet then, thinking of Edmund Crewe and Patience, and where it all began when they had driven through the night to Urania Cottage just over a week ago. Jones did not know, he thought, whether Crewe meant to do some good by his last act. He was a policeman, not a writer like his dear friend, and he could not help feeling somehow dissatisfied. Perhaps when the inquests were over and the dead buried, he would feel that the case could be closed. He closed his eyes.

Dickens saw his frown. He did not know, he thought. Perhaps he had imagined the meaning of that last smile; perhaps Crewe was bad through and through — he had abused children, as Jones had reminded him. That was unforgiveable. His last act did not redeem his crimes. Still, Crewe was dead, whatever meaning there was in his fall. And the dead would be buried and the living could get on with their lives, and make the best of them, he hoped, including himself and Jones in that company.

The train thundered on, the night rolling by. They could see a starlit sky, and the empty vastness above and beyond them. They thought of the mystery of it all, and, finding a kind of peace in each other's presence, slept.

Epilogue

The inquests were over; the law had given its verdicts on the deaths of Patience, Blackledge and Edmund Crewe, and the unknown little girl they had found. The documents were sealed with red wax and stored away in black boxes, and the newspapers finished their speculations. Mrs Blackledge and Rose started a new life, Patience's daughter learned to walk, and Francis Fidge, as Dickens had foretold, lay at peace in the quiet churchyard of St Mark's. Jenny Ding went back to her lessons, but Louisa Mapp did not stay at Urania Cottage. Who would support her mother and sister? she had asked angrily. Dickens had no answer. Superintendent Jones felt better and turned his mind to other cases, though Patience somehow stayed in that part of his mind where Edith was.

And Charles Dickens went on with *David Copperfield*. Some days he waited for him to come, staring at the blank piece of paper on his desk, but most days David was there, and, later there would be Dora and Jip who would turn out to be an irritant to David, always in the way when he wanted to kiss Dora, though Dickens would not tell Eleanor and Tom Brim that — he would only say that Jip could never be Poll's equal. And, yet, poor Jip. Dickens would relent and show him faithful to the end, dying with Dora. The Brims would like that.

On a spring day when the early sun promised warmth, four people took the express train to Crewe and a fly was hired to take them to a quiet country churchyard not far from the great house. Dickens and Jones, Mrs Morson and Davey came to turn the last page of the story of Patience Brooke.

The gravestone was simple, just of grey stone, with a short inscription:

To the memory of
Patience Lee
Wife and Mother

There were fresh spring flowers on the green mound. Superintendent Jones and Charles Dickens looked at the words — justice, they thought, had been done.

HISTORICAL NOTE

In February 1849, Charles Dickens began *David Copperfield*. The first number was published by Bradbury and Evans on 1st May 1849.

Dickens married Catherine Hogarth in 1836; by 1849 they had eight children, the baby, Henry Fielding Dickens, was born on 16th January. Henry Fielding was the most successful of Dickens's children — he became a judge. Alfred D'Orsay Tennyson Dickens was born in 1845 and Francis Jeffrey Dickens in 1844. Charley, the eldest son (b.1837) went to Eton in 1850; Katey (b.1839) married Charles, the younger brother of Wilkie Collins, and Mamie (b.1838) stayed with her father until his death in 1870.

Dickens established the Home for Fallen Women with Angela Burdett-Coutts in 1847. He said that Georgiana Morson was the best matron he ever employed. Isabella Gordon and Anna-Maria Sesini were dismissed from the Home in November 1849 for misconduct.

John Forster, Dickens's close friend, wrote the first biography of Dickens, and Mark Lemon, another close friend, was editor of *Punch* magazine.

Elizabeth Dickens, Dickens's paternal grandmother, and her husband, William Dickens, worked as housekeeper and steward for the Crewe family at Crewe Hall in Cheshire. Sir Hungerford Crewe inherited Crewe Hall and the Crewe family estates in 1837. The characters of Lady Amelia and Edmund Crewe, and the story of his mother are inventions.

Charles Barrow, Dickens's maternal grandfather, was Chief Conductor of Moneys in Town, for the Navy Pay Office. In

1810 he was found guilty of embezzlement and absconded to the Isle of Man.

The actor, William Macready, was a close friend of Dickens. He was godfather to Kate Macready Dickens, the second daughter of Charles Dickens. Dickens was godfather to Macready's son, Henry. Dickens admired Macready's acting, particularly the Shakespearean roles for which Macready was acclaimed.

The periodical *Household Words* came out in March 1850. It was in this magazine that Dickens wrote his articles on the London Police, including the anecdote *On Duty with Inspector Field*. The character of Superintendent Sam Jones of Bow Street is fictional, though his character does owe a little to Inspector Field, particularly his authority over the criminals he and Dickens encounter. A police constable named Rogers appears in the anecdote *On Duty with Inspector Field*. There is no evidence that Dickens was ever involved in a murder case, but he was interested in crime, and a recent biographer observed that he had a secret desire to be a detective. In this novel, the first of the cases investigated by Dickens and Jones, I have imagined what might have happened if Dickens had been given the opportunity to investigate a murder.

A NOTE TO THE READER

Dear Reader,

Thank you for taking the time to read this first Charles Dickens mystery. I hope you enjoyed reading it as much as I enjoyed writing it and want to read more of Dickens's adventures in detecting. I think Dickens makes a good detective. He was fascinated by crime and murder; there are plenty of murderers in his novels. One thing he always asked about his characters was 'What's his motive?' The detective wants to know why as well as how and when. Dickens analyses the murderer's motives in an article on capital punishment. If a murder was not committed in hot blood, Dickens speculates that the murderer wants to rid himself or herself of someone dangerous to his or her peace of mind, someone who is, Dickens writes, 'a dreaded or detested object', and he goes on to say that at the root of this dread is a 'corroding hatred' – that was pretty powerful and I thought about it when I created my first murderer. Dickens is observant – it was said of him that he never forgot a face or a place. And he cared about justice for the victim. He went out with the police doing his own research into crime and police methods of investigation and I enjoyed researching his accounts of the criminal underworld in his magazine *Household Words*.

Dickens couldn't go about London on his own trailing murderers so I gave him a professional policeman as his partner, Superintendent Sam Jones, who is inspired by Inspector Charley Field, a real life policeman whom Dickens knew, though Superintendent Jones is a very different character. You can find out more about the real life characters in the historical note below.

Reviews are really important to authors, and if you enjoyed the novel, it would be great if you could spare a little time to post a review on **Amazon** and **Goodreads.** Readers can connect with me online, on **Facebook (JCBriggsBooks)**, **Twitter (@JeanCBriggs)**, and you can find out more about the books and Charles Dickens via my website: **jcbriggsbooks.com**

Thank you!

Jean Briggs

Sapere Books is an exciting new publisher of brilliant fiction and popular history.

To find out more about our latest releases and our monthly bargain books visit our website:
saperebooks.com